THE ANATOMY OF WINGS

THE ANATOMY OF WINGS

karen foxlee

ALFRED A. KNOPF   new york

THIS IS A BORZOI BOOK PUBLISHED BY ALFRED A. KNOPF

Visit us on the Web!
www.randomhouse.com/teens

Educators and librarians, for a variety of teaching tools, visit us at
www.randomhouse.com/teachers

Library of Congress Cataloging-in-Publication Data
Foxlee, Karen.
The anatomy of wings / Karen Foxlee. — 1st American ed.
        p.   cm.
Summary: After the suicide of her troubled teenage sister, eleven-year-old Jenny struggles to understand what actually happened.
ISBN 978-0-375-85643-3 (trade) — ISBN 978-0-375-95643-0 (lib. bdg.)
[1. Suicide—Fiction. 2. Grief—Fiction. 3. Sisters—Fiction. 4. Family problems—Fiction.
5. Australia—Fiction.] I. Title.
PZ7.F841223 An 2009
[Fic]—dc22
2008019373

The text of this book is set in 12-point Sabon.

Printed in the United States of America
February 2009
10 9 8 7 6 5 4 3 2 1
First American Edition

Random House Children's Books supports the First Amendment and celebrates the right to read.

For Dad

Years later when I go to the dry river everything is less than in my memories. The riverbed is narrower, there are fewer ghost gum trees. I remember an entire stand behind the sand track, or this is how it seemed. They were evenly spaced, each giant with its own territory of solitude. I remember the quiet. How there was only the sound of our footsteps on the fallen leaves, our voices in the stillness.

Now many of the trees are gone, fallen or cut down. There are more paddocks instead, the beginning of a new housing estate.

I walk in circles unable to find the place at first but our tree is still there.

When at last I find it I am surprised at the smallness of the marks we left. I kneel and run my fingers over our carved letters. All this time and the tree has kept them for us. It could have easily healed itself. The cuts were not deep. They were made only with children's hands.

CERTAIN THINGS WERE PLACED IN THE BOX. We were not supposed to touch them. No one said it but we felt it. It was the way our mother held the box to her chest as she walked along the hallway, protectively, as though it was a baby. She hid it from us in clear view.

Angela and I removed it from the top shelf of the linen closet. The door creaked. In the weeping house the only sound was our breathing in the silence that followed. Already, in the few weeks, a light layer of dust had settled over its lid.

It was Angela's idea. She said we needed to look inside to find my singing voice. It would help me to remember exactly when and how it happened that the words lodged in my chest quite close to my heart.

You'll never get it back unless you know why it went away, she said. She was full of ideas.

It was a simple blue cardboard box. I thought it

would be heavy. I thought the weight of it would make my arms shake but it was light. The writing on the lid said in flowing white script CARNEGIE ELEGANT GLASSWARE. In blue ink in the right-hand corner was one more word. DARLING.

My sister Danielle was sleeping when we entered the room. She was facing us with her knees drawn up. In those weeks all anyone did was sleep. Our house was like Sleeping Beauty's palace after the enchanted spell is cast. People slept on beds and on sofas. They closed their eyes in chairs with cups of sweetened tea in their hands. Mum slept with pills that Aunty Cheryl counted out into her hand and guided to her mouth. Dad slept on the floor between us with one arm slung across his eyes.

Angela and I sat on my bed with the box between us. She looked at Danielle sleeping and then at me, asking me with her eyes if it was all right. I shrugged. I didn't know what my mother would do if she found us with the box. I didn't know if she would sense it had been opened and leap from her bed and come running to find us. I didn't know what it would contain.

When I opened the lid the smell of fifty-cent-sized raindrops hitting dry earth escaped.

Angela opened her mouth into an O.

Up rose the scent of green-apple shampoo. Of river stones once the flood has gone. The taste of winter sky laced with sulfur fumes. A kiss beneath a white-hearted tree. A hot still day holding its breath.

We removed the contents one by one.

There were two blue plastic hair combs. A tough girl's black rubber-band bracelet. A newspaper advertisement for a secretarial school folded in half. A blond braid wrapped in gladwrap. A silver necklace with a half-a-broken-heart pendant. An address, written in a leftward-slanting hand, on a scrap of paper. Ballet shoes wrapped in laces.

From the box came the sound of bicycle tires humming on hot pavement. Of bare feet running through crackling grass. Of frantic fingers unstitching an embroidered flower. Of paper wings rising on a sudden wind. Of the lake breathing against the shore.

I didn't say anything. I kept very still. Danielle turned on her bed but kept sleeping.

"Somewhere in here," whispered Angela, "is the answer."

On the day of the funeral my nanna let the cat out of the bag about an angel and caused a great ruckus and then left squealing the tires on her beige Datsun Sunny. Even before that Kylie went ballistic and punched one of the Townsville twins on the nose. My singing voice disappeared long before then though the words to songs still ached inside my chest. I could feel them in my stomach and taste them in my mouth but they wouldn't come.

After the funeral the house was full of the rustling of black chiffon and the smell of Cedel hair spray holding up stiff French rolls and already wilting roses dropping petals onto the shag rug. The visitors pressed themselves against the living room walls and tried to drink their tea without clinking their cups and saucers. They used up all the air-conditioner coolness and sweated around their necks. Men undid their ties. Women pressed handkerchiefs to their foreheads. They used up all the oxygen. I could feel my lips turning blue.

Our mother was laid out on the sofa as still as a statue and surrounded by aunts. Her only movement was to occasionally blink her see-through blue eyes. Her long eyelashes hit her tearstained cheeks and caused a faint and momentary breeze.

In the middle of the room the nest of tables had been spread apart from smallest to largest like a set of stairs. On the lowest were jam drops with smooth skin and jelly eyes. The middle held a round unsliced tea cake. On the top step there was a host of fairy cakes, still-winged, standing on each other's shoulders.

Nanna sat in Dad's recliner. She didn't have her legs up. She sat on the edge of the vinyl, knees together, legs sweating in her stockings. Dad didn't have a seat. He stayed in the kitchen with the other men. They tried to remove beers quietly from the cooler but every noise they made was magnified in the house, the hushed rumble followed by an avalanche of ice, the exhausted sigh of the pulled ring top.

Nanna made a quiet moaning noise in her throat. Everybody tried to look the other way. She was building up to something and it wasn't a good idea to encourage her. Uncle Paavo, her brother, sat next to her. His funeral suit was two times too big for him because he only ate when he came to our house for weekend lunches and that was how he became a millionaire. Every now and then he blew his nose very loudly and interrupted the silence.

The Townsville twins were the first cousins to move. Patrick in his powder-blue suit reached out, removed a jam drop, and sauntered toward the front door. His mother, Aunty Margaret, made a deflating noise. Jonathan followed in his tan suit, running his fingers back through his hair. Outside they rounded the house and found a piece of shade on the back steps and lit up their Peter Stuyvesant cigarettes, which were the Passport to International Smoking Pleasure. They were identical apart from the color of their suits and the fact that Patrick had slightly more sensational hair flips. They both had small smiles, which they executed without opening their mouths and exposing their teeth. Nanna said they had superior attitudes.

Jamie and Samantha were the Brisbane cousins. Sometimes the Townsville twins showed their teeth to them. The Brisbane cousins wore real Sportsgirl espadrilles and jeans. They had long shiny blond hair and Jamie said she was already a model and one day she'd be in *Dolly* and that perms were yesterday's news, which made Danielle feel bad because she'd waited her whole life for the one she had on her head.

The Brisbane cousins sat down beside the Townsville twins and took drags on their cigarettes. They waved their hands in front of their faces to keep away the flies. Patrick called our town Nowheresville, which made the Brisbane cousins laugh, and Jonathan tipped back his head and looked down his nose at us with one of his smallest smiles.

Kylie was our cousin who lived in Nowheresville with us. She lived two streets away in a house right beside the park and she spent hours lying in her backyard on her trampoline staring into the sky. No matter how much you tried to sneak past she always saw you and asked to come too even if you were just going nowhere in particular. Kylie had brittle bones and buckteeth and a bad temper. She'd been born prematurely. Kylie got angry or sad very easily.

"Don't call it Nowheresville," she said to Patrick.

We stood at the bottom of the back steps in front of the city cousins like strangers in our own backyard despite being the Most Bereaved.

"No-wheres-ville," said Patrick.

He enunciated the word slowly.

"Don't say that," Kylie said.

She made two fists with her hands by her side. She was fourteen, only two years younger than them but half their size. Her arms and legs were stick thin but the twins didn't know how strong she was. They didn't know Kylie could perform headlocks and give terrible Chinese burns and horse slaps. She could tear herself away from the restraints of two grown-ups by thrashing her legs in the air. She could spit across whole rooms.

"Calm down, you pip-squeak," said Jonathan.

"Leave her alone," said Danielle.

Our mother said we had to look after Kylie on account of her having very breakable bones and a very small amount of retardedness. Kylie's teeth hung over her bottom lip. She breathed loudly through her nose. She stared at Patrick, willing him to say it again with her eyes. Danielle's tight curls bobbed on her head. Jamie and Samantha regarded them with disdain.

"Bush turkey," said Patrick, and covered it up with a cough into his hand.

"What did you say?" said Kylie.

"Gobble-gobble-gobble," said Jonathan, hardly moving his lips, like a ventriloquist.

"What did he say?" Kylie asked Danielle.

"Leave her alone," said Samantha.

"Why?" said her sister, genuinely surprised.

"Because," Samantha whispered, "she's slow."

Our mother said we should never call Kylie slow. I wished if I put my hands over my face everything would disappear: all the cousins, all the rustling sweet-smelling aunts, and Nanna banging her head with the Bible. The whole town too, all the pink and green and lemon-colored houses, the red hills that crouched around them, the whole bright blue day.

Afterward Dad peeled Kylie off Patrick. She was still kicking her legs and spraying saliva. The damage was assessed. Patrick's powder-blue suit pocket had been torn clear off and lay on our dead lawn. Aunty Margaret held a Kleenex to his nose and tilted his head back. She screamed at the Brisbane cousins to find ice. It made them cry because they were not used to being screamed at. Especially not in a strange town called Memorial. In the middle of nowhere. On a high summer's day that burned their faces and hurt their lungs. After the funeral of a cousin they did not know.

Nanna waited until all the visitors had gone and the cousins were reassembled along the floor before she let the cat out of the bag. She was back in the recliner. She put her cup of tea down on the occasional table and folded her hands in her lap. Dad raised his eyes. He'd been begrudgingly given a seat beside Mum on the sofa. He held one of her limp hands in his.

"You must all listen to me," Nanna said.

"Don't start, Anna," said Dad.

It was strange to hear her real name like that. It sounded like he was talking to a little girl.

"Don't say don't start to me," said Nanna.

"Be quiet," said Mum.

Aunty Margaret, Aunty Louise, and Aunty Cheryl gathered around Mum murmuring as they squeezed Dad off the sofa. There was something in the air.

"Beth spoke with angels," said Nanna, and everyone shut up.

She looked around the room daring anyone to disagree.

"Holy shit," whispered Patrick, who was dabbing at his nose with a tissue and examining the blood.

I'd been placed as a buffer between the away cousins and Kylie. Patrick's powder-blue suit scratched against my arm. His Peter Stuyvesant packet poked into my thigh.

Nanna put her hands across her heart. She looked straight at me. I felt a hot flush on my cheeks. I looked at the shag rug. I pulled at some strands. I imagined what it would be like to be so small that I could get lost in the jungle of white and brown loops.

The away cousins didn't know Nanna like I did.

"Beth told me," said Nanna.

Her straight gray hair hung in two curtains to her jaw. She stared at me. I refused to meet her eyes.

"When did she tell you?" shouted Mum.

Mum rose up from the sofa like a vampire from a coffin. She was wringing her hands.

"After it happened," said Nanna, "in the beginning, after the lake."

"I don't believe you," shouted Mum. "You witch."

The clutch of aunts moved closer. They stroked her hair and her shoulders and tried to lay her back down. They stared down Nanna from across the room. They tried to look angry but a ripple passed over them. They shivered. They exchanged glances beneath their hair-sprayed bangs. Hands went up to pale pearl-ringed throats.

"Stop it," hissed Aunty Margaret.

She was the eldest daughter. Her voice quivered with excitement.

"You don't tell me to stop it," said Nanna.

"Right," said Dad, "that's it."

I thought he was going to make her leave the room but he didn't. He walked toward her but then veered off at the last minute and staggered down the hallway. He slammed the door to our bedroom. The living room was silent. The door slam toppled the host of fairy cakes from each other's shoulders. Kylie reached out for one but Aunty Cheryl slapped her hand away.

After Nanna's words people wilted where they sat. They closed their eyes. They held their heads in their hands. The Brisbane cousins bit their bottom lips and exchanged hidden glances with the Townsville twins. Kylie scratched at a scab on her leg. Uncle Paavo removed the hankie from his pocket and blew his nose. He coughed and then sobbed.

Our water was poisoned. Our air was poisoned.

"Get out," shouted Mum, "get out, get out. Don't ever come back."

Nanna wouldn't go at first. My cheeks burned to look at her.

"You've really done your dash this time," said Aunty Margaret through a cloud of cigarette smoke.

The cousins stood up and moved slowly from the room. Nanna picked up her teacup and tried to have a drink. Her hand shook. She picked up her glasses case and fumbled with her glasses until they were on her nose. She opened her Bible. Her dentures clicked inside her mouth as she tried to swallow. She closed her Bible. She stood up.

She left a Nanna-shaped bottom imprint on Dad's recliner.

It slowly vanished.

The bottom imprint reminded me of plaster of Paris. It reminded me of Mrs. Bridges-Lamb, my grade 5 teacher, who let us make casts of our own footprints. She said now our ten-year-old footprints were immortalized. Nanna took her Bible and a plate of biscuits and let the screen door bang behind her.

She would not come back to our house for a very long time.

She started her Sunny with too much pedal and squealed her tires. On the mattress between our beds Dad's closed eyes flickered at the sound of her leaving. He lay on his side with his flip-flops still on. Danielle lay behind him on her bed. They grieved in formation, breathing softly.

After the words the aunts removed our mother to her bedroom. They unzipped her from her dress. It whispered a sigh as it fell to the floor. Aunty Margaret directed her to lift her feet over the puddle of material. Mum stood in her petticoat facing the wall. They turned her toward the bed.

After she was laid down the aunties removed their own dresses and placed them on coat hangers in front of Dad's side of the cupboard. The black dresses moved in the breeze from the air conditioner. The aunties unzipped suitcases and found suitable after-funeral wear. Aunty Margaret examined herself side-on in the scallop-edged duchess mirror. The glass was distorted in the middle and I could see she didn't like it. She frowned and pulled her belly in. When she saw me at the door she laughed, a little nervous laugh, and it was a very strange sound among all of the misery. Aunty Louise put her finger to her lips.

After the words Aunty Cheryl turned her teaspoon slowly in her teacup at the dining room table. The sun hammered at the closed curtains. There was a whole cloudless bright day outside. Kylie sat near her nursing her punching hand.

The house filled up slowly with the sound of nothing. The stillness dripped in, second by second, minute by minute, measured by the Bessemer clock on the kitchen wall. No one spoke. The aunties' hands murmured between teacups and pot and bowl. Sugar rained into tea. Napkins were unfolded and folded again. Crumbs drifted slowly from chins.

Nanna believed in miracles. The day of the funeral they were burning very brightly inside her mind. After she left our house she was driving fast and crying hard. She didn't see the cousins moving slowly through the heat. She didn't recognize them, her own flesh and blood. They went up through the long grass of the park.

The *Merit Students Encyclopedia* says a miracle is an event that cannot be explained scientifically and is probably caused by a supernatural power. Miracles are things like the sea parting and walking on water and statues crying blood or milk and the appearances of people like Mary surrounded by heavenly light in unexpected places on ordinary days.

It was Nanna who started everything.

The "miracle" entry is in volume 12. Our mother bought the set from a one-armed salesman. We couldn't afford an Australian set even though the salesman said it would be much better for us in the long term.

Volume 12 also contained the map of the moon. "Maria" is the plural of "mare," which is what the moon's dark seas are called. And once Beth and I divided up the whole moon between ourselves. I was ruler of the Sea of Rains, where there is a Bay of Rainbows, and also I was queen of the Sea of Storms. Beth owned the Sea of Serenity and the Sea of Tranquillity and the Sea of Clouds. Then Danielle came late to the game and wanted her own territory and we gave her a small section, which was the Sea of Moisture, and she complained. She told Mum and we had to give her more and it ruined everything.

Volume 12 contained everything you could ever want to know about Minnesota, Mississippi, and Missouri but nothing at all about Memorial.

When Jamie and Samantha came back from their walk they were pale-faced and exhausted by the sun. They'd been to the park; it was written all over their faces. They were folded up into the arms of their mother, Aunty Louise. Patrick and Jonathan looked at the floor.

"It's too terrible, I know," whispered Aunty Louise into Jamie's and Samantha's ears. "Try not to think about it."

It would have been easy for them because there was so much they didn't know. For instance they didn't know that:

1. The wilder Beth grew, the bluer her eyes became, and the bluer her eyes became, the wilder she grew.
2. She chewed her nails. She chewed them down to the skin until they bled.
3. When she laughed she closed her eyes and tilted her head backward. She put one arm across her stomach.
4. She could melt Nanna's stony heart with one smile. After her heart was melted Nanna always said, "What on earth will we do with you?"
5. She ran away often and when she returned we all tried to act as though she had never gone.
6. She felt keenly the pain of insects and then the pain of people.
7. She gave up dancing at thirteen.

8. Parts of her kept disappearing. Small pieces that she gave away.
9. Sometimes she drank methylated spirits with her wine, just a dash.
10. She wanted to save everything but couldn't even save herself.

We put the box away before Danielle woke up. Angela stayed sitting on my bed memorizing the contents while I went through the bottom of the cupboard looking for a blue-lined exercise book. I found an old grade 5 book that was only partly used. It contained mostly information about Greek and Roman history, which was Mrs. Bridges-Lamb's favorite topic, especially the Spartans, who made her glasses fog up. Mostly the pages were filled with towering roman numerals. Angela ripped them out to make a clue book into how I lost my voice.

The ripping woke Danielle and she scowled at us when she opened her eyes. Mum said Danielle was an expert at scowling and she could win a medal for it. I held my breath. Angela held the exercise book in her hand. Danielle sat up ramrod straight in her Milwaukee back brace. I thought she knew about the box from the way she looked at us. She scowled more and looked suspicious. But then she took the sketchbook from the desk so she could draw a picture of the end of the world and went away. Her Milwaukee back brace clunked as she left the room. The quietness in the house settled again like dust, it rained from the roof onto our faces, it clung to our eyelashes.

Angela took the exercise book and a pencil. I took the cricket bat and tennis ball from under my bed. We went out through the still house. The washing was piled up in the laundry. Ashtrays had filled and overflowed. All the roses and lilies had thrown back their heads over the edges of vases and died. They had cast their petals on the floor. The living room smelled of dead water-logged greenery. Even though Christmas had been and gone the calendar stayed on November 1982.

We passed my mother sleeping on the sofa. We moved quietly so she wouldn't wake. When she was awake she moved from room to room like she was lost. She opened doors and peered inside with one eye. She wept suddenly and wildly when we least expected it. At night great storms of tears came and went and woke me from my sleep and made me rise up in bed.

"Lie back down, chickadee," Dad said each time.

And he got up slowly from the mattress between our beds to go to her.

But none of this was visible from the outside. From the road I was surprised to find our house

looked no different from the others in Dardanelles
Court. It stood brave-faced. It stared with its front
sliding glass windows straight ahead. It kept its
screen door mouth shut tight. Its little porch chin up-
right. I looked at our house from the footpath and
Angela, chewing on the end of one of her golden
braids, waited for me.

The five houses in Dardanelles Court faced each
other across the cul-de-sac, which is French for dead
end. They were all identical: rectangular, metal-clad,
and mint green. They were exactly the same as every
other company house in Memorial South. The poinciana trees reached out to each other across the pavement and dropped their red flowers. It was very quiet
except for the droning of the outdoor air-conditioner
units.

There was no Mr. O'Malley singing about the sea.
No Mrs. O'Malley nodding from her patio to me. No
Miss Schmidt peeping through her venetian blinds.
No Irwin girls sitting on their front steps dreaming of
escape. There was no Marshall Murray standing beneath the fountain of his yellow cassia tree. The five
houses faced each other as though nothing remark-
able had ever happened.

We walked out of Dardanelles Court onto
Memorial Drive. We passed the entrances to all the
other courts, which had the same houses huddled in
circles. We didn't talk.

In Memorial Park I had to squint my eyes after spending weeks in the weeping house. I was unsteady on my feet. The park tilted toward the sky. The calf-high yellow grass shone. The sunlight rested its hands on my shoulders and burned a crown on my head. Angela bowled to me and I cracked the tennis ball into the sky. It was only when we had exhausted ourselves that we lay down in the grass and Angela opened up the book.

"Let's begin at the beginning," she said. "What do you remember?"

She had her pencil ready to write down what I said.

"What do you mean?"

"About what was in the box."

"The braid," I said.

Angela wrote

the braid.

"The hair combs. The piece of newspaper."

"How do you spell 'combs'?"

"C-o-m-b-s."

the piece of newspaper.

"The black band," said Angela, writing slowly, "the ballet shoes."

"Why are you asking me if you remember already?"

"Because," said Angela when she had finished writing.

"This is stupid," I said.

"No it isn't."

She showed me the cover, where she had printed in her messy handwriting *The Book of Clues*.

"All we have to do is go backward," she said.

Angela Popovitch was my best friend. She'd been my best friend since grade 1. She had two sisters like me but none of hers had died. She had never lied to me.

She watched me, her brown eyes and freckled nose screwed up against the sun.

"Trust me. We can find your singing voice," she said. "It's simple."

The unstitching of an embroidered flower.

The unraveling of moments.

The unspooling thread of things.

THIS IS THE STORY OF ELIZABETH DAY. I have pieced it together with my own two hands. I have made it from things I saw and things I did not see but later knew. It is made from the tatters of terrible things and the remnants of wonderful things. I have sewn it together before it fades.

My nanna said everything began at the lake. The day Beth fainted and afterward saw the whole world with a golden glow.

"You can take it or leave it," she said, "but I know it, something happened that day and nothing was ever the same again."

We had begged for that day. Dad hadn't wanted to go. He didn't want to take the car out on a dirt road. It was Saturday. The races were on. He was feeling lucky and the radio wouldn't work out there. The corrugations would wreck his wheels. We'd all get duck lice. The place was full of weeds.

"You promised us," said Beth. "First you said after I turned thirteen, then you said when school finished."

"School finished a week ago," said Danielle. "Beth's been thirteen forever."

"Bloody hell," said Dad. "All right then."

I cheered and clapped my hands.

"What are you so happy about?" he asked.

"You always say you're going to do things but then you don't and this time you are," I said.

Mum told me not to be rude. She smiled her I-told-you-so smile at him from the bathroom door.

Dad combed his hair back slowly so it met in a ducktail at the back. He had sea-green eyes and a teardrop-shaped birthmark on his cheek that made him look sad. He shaved his face slowly with the razor. He shaved close to where the teardrop birthmark sat beneath his left eye. Sometimes when Dad held Mum around the waist and kissed her in the kitchen and they thought we weren't watching, Mum put her finger up to the teardrop birthmark as though she was going to wipe it away. After he finished shaving he coughed into the sink. He always coughed into the sink in the morning and the night. It was a perfectly ordinary day.

Dad packed his beers along the bottom of the cooler in the ice. Mum made us sandwiches. She asked Dad would the ice melt? Would the sandwiches get wet?

"Of course it'll bloody melt," he said. "It's a hundred frigging degrees outside."

Mum wrapped the sandwiches in gladwrap. Twice. She got out the tape and taped the gladwrap edges down when Dad left the room. I could tell she was panicking. She put some of the sandwiches in my lunch box and some in Danielle's and then because the lids wouldn't shut properly she sticky-taped them down.

When we left we each took our turn to hug her. When she hugged me some of her worry about the sandwiches rubbed off onto me. When it was Danielle's turn she got tears in her eyes.

"Give me strength," Dad said.

The station wagon had no air-conditioning. We drove with the windows down. The road was long and dusty and dead straight. No bends. It headed straight for the horizon. Long flat-bottomed boat clouds sailed low across the sky. My job was to open the cooler and pass the beer to Dad. When I took the beer out I looked down at our lunch boxes. They were entombed in the ice. I tried to rearrange things a bit by bringing them to the surface but Dad heard me rummaging.

"Shut the lid, Jenny," he said. "Everything will melt before we get there."

I tried not to worry about the sandwiches swimming in the melting ice. I sang some Slim Dusty songs and everyone joined in, even Danielle, who usually told me to shut up when I sang.

It usually takes a long time to get to somewhere you really want to go. For instance it takes a whole day to travel through the desert to the sea. A long day. The parched plains with their bleached grass and white bones try to exhaust you with their emptiness. The flattop hills in the distance call out we are all there is. They want you to wander off toward them. The land pretends to contain nothing. You have to concentrate on where you are going. That makes it take a long time to get there.

Beth, sitting in the front, moved the blue plastic combs through her long blond hair.

When I asked her how long till we got there she said soon.

And then the landscape started to change.

The long straight road to nowhere started to bend. Hills sprang up with mangy coats of spinifex and yellow grass. They were speckled by trees with wild lady hair. Sheer rock faces, almost pink, almost orange. We hit a cattle grid and the road became pavement. A little unmanned ticket box stood beside an open boom gate. We rounded the last corner and there the blue water lay, the white dam wall shining in the sun.

The last time we'd been to the lake our mother had been with us. We had been smaller; she hadn't let us wander around by ourselves. She said stay where I can see you, so many children have drowned in this lake, the weeds hold on to their legs and drag them down. They are never seen again. This is what happens to little children, she said.

But Dad gave Beth a five-dollar note.

"Go and buy yourselves some ice cream or something," he said.

It was very hot, even beside the water, which was too bright after the desert. Stars danced on its surface. We had to walk with our eyes half closed. There were canoes out on the water and people everywhere cooking barbecues and there were pelicans wandering between the tables. The sunlight flared around their open wings. The hot grass crackled beneath our feet.

"I'm going to swim for hours," said Beth.

Then we had a normal conversation about lollies: candy cigarettes, cobbers, musk sticks, Milkos, and Redskins.

If we had known everything would change we would have turned back. But we didn't know. That's how things happen. Especially sunny days hide dark moments in their pockets.

At the kiosk counter Beth had the five-dollar note in her outstretched hand. I thought it was weird the way she was holding it, as though it was a golden cup or a flame.

"Come on, love," said the kiosk lady, "we haven't got all day."

Beth was going to speak; her mouth opened. Her pupils expanded inside her blue eyes. She fell backward, gracefully, perfectly straight, the way a tree falls. Her head hit the ground with a thud. Her mouth made a clunking noise like Nanna's false teeth. She expelled a small noise. It could have been a no. Her eyes rolled back into her head.

The kiosk lady didn't open the kiosk door but jumped straight over the counter. She bent down beside Beth and then called out for help so loudly that I had to cover my ears. People looked up from their picnic tables and came running from the shore. Danielle shook Beth's shoulder but she wouldn't wake up.

"Find Dad," she shouted at me.

While I ran I mostly thought about what would happen if Beth died, for instance that Mum would get a shock, especially since her main concern was the state of our sandwiches. And at the back of my mind was Beth's face as it looked after she hit the grass and her eyes had closed: luminous.

"Beth's fallen down and she won't wake up," I said when I finally found Dad untangling a fishing line beside the wall. I wiped the snot from my nose with the back of my hand.

A large crowd had gathered. We had to push our way through the damp bodies that smelled of the lake and suntan lotion. Beth had opened her eyes but she seemed dazed; she kept looking past all the faces bent over her toward the sky. Her lips moved. A very faint smile crossed her mouth. The crowd was very quiet. Other than for the craning of necks, no one moved. Someone brought lemonade. Dad lifted Beth's head and Danielle put the tin against her lips. Some of the sparkling liquid rolled down her chin.

"What is she saying?" said the kiosk lady.

"Shush," said Dad.

He bent his head closer, bringing his ear to her lips, but she stopped her whispering then and woke up. Her eyes found Dad's face and recognized him. When she saw she was on the ground she started to cry.

The crowd shivered and moved backward in a single motion. Dad picked Beth up. He lifted his arm to move the crowd aside but it had already parted in two waves. A corridor was opened up. Dad carried her through it. Danielle and I followed in the strange parade.

"You'd want to get her checked out," said the kiosk lady, who walked beside us.

On the way home Beth lay on the backseat with the blanket rolled up for a pillow. Danielle and I sat in the luggage compartment behind her. The kiosk lady had given us bags of lollies and we ate them while we watched her. I lit a candy cigarette with my imaginary lighter and passed it down to her and she held it between her pale lips.

"I'm sorry" was all she had to say.

Mum sat Danielle and me down at the kitchen table and grilled us over what had happened. What had we seen? What were the series of events? When did it start? When did it finish? Nanna screeched into the driveway with her smelling salts. She yelled at Dad. She said we should have eaten our sandwiches as soon as we got there. She took the wet sandwiches out of the cooler and waved them in front of him as evidence. Dad told her to keep her big nose out of it. Beth, on the sofa, called out for them to be quiet.

"What happened?" Mum pleaded in a soft voice.

"She fainted," Dad pleaded back.

Nanna made a clicking noise with her tongue.

"Her face was shining," I said.

"What?" shouted Mum.

"Ping off," said Dad.

"What's she talking about?" asked Nanna.

"She wouldn't bloody know," said Dad.

But I did know. I knew a lot more things than him. He didn't know, for instance, that sparrows were passerines, which meant they could sing, and that some swifts built their nests out of saliva and that Sirius was the next closest star to the sun. That was just for starters.

I knew a butterfly wing couldn't repair itself once it was torn.

This was a very important fact. A butterfly wing is built of veins and covered in scales made from a substance like dust.

All through their sleeping stages butterflies dream of flying but when they first open their wings they need to wait. They must be patient. The wings are wet and they need time to dry. Butterfly wings are easily broken.

There is no hope for a butterfly once this has happened.

If you find a butterfly in a spiderweb with a broken wing there is no point in removing it however sad it might seem. If you remove it, it will only struggle on the ground and die some other kind of death. It will be carried away on the backs of bull ants to a bull ant feast and eaten alive.

Beth was always rescuing winged insects from spiderwebs. She stood on chairs and rescued moths and climbed trees to save cicadas.

"Here," she said to them, "let me help you."

She used pencils and scissors and her own fingers to release the trapped things. She held them in her hand or on her fingertip until they flew away. If they couldn't, because they had stopped struggling and given up or the spider had already started wrapping them up for later, it made her very sad. Even if you said to her don't worry, it probably didn't feel a thing.

It couldn't be explained to her that at the very same moment a butterfly is struggling in a web, all over the world there are insects eating insects, hundreds of millions of spiders eating butterflies, lions eating gazelles, crocodiles eating cows, and countless worms turning inside of perfectly normal-looking fruit.

Dad shooed me away with his hand.

"Go play outside," said Mum. "We're discussing something important."

After the lake everywhere Beth looked there was light. Dad, face bent over her, wore a halo. A tree was on fire with white cockatoos. The dam wall shone like a bride's skirt. The star-covered lake moved inside her. In the car our faces glowed. The sky pressed its bright face to the window.

At home our mother noticed the stain on her shorts, and in the toilet even the blood on her underpants shone.

"Do not be afraid," whispered Nanna at the toilet door.

She said the prayer for young girls who are menstruating.

"I'm not afraid," said Beth.

The door lock shone like new silver. Light beams rained from the toilet doll's upraised arms.

"It is a normal thing," whispered Nanna. "All girls must have it happen."

"Leave her alone, for God's sake," said Mum from the hallway. "Give her some space."

"I'm all right," said Beth.

On our bedroom floor I sang "Speed Bonny Boat" because it was a song about having to leave everything behind and saying goodbye to everything you know and because I was definitely going to run away as soon as possible. I had never wanted to break anything before, but when Dad told me to ping off because I didn't know what I was talking about, I felt like breaking something for the first time. I took out the box of Barbie dolls and the first thing I broke was Ken's legs. They weren't easy to break. I broke one off where the joint was. It took a long time. First I did it with my bare hands and then I used scissors. I felt better but only for about ten minutes. Then I felt bad and I went out to the Drawer of Everything in the kitchen and found some sticky tape and Mum saw me and said I thought I told you to go outside.

"I'm busy," I said.

Nanna clicked her tongue and followed me down the hallway and I only had time to throw Ken back in the box and push him under the bed and didn't get to tape up his legs till later, after she had gone.

"What did you mean she was shining?" she asked when she came into my room.

"You shouldn't say 'she,'" I said. "'She' is the cat's mother."

"Be quiet," she said. "Tell me what you meant."

Nanna told me to get off the floor and sit beside her on the bed; she could be very nasty if she didn't get her own way. Nanna had blue-gray eyes that bulged slightly and she leaned in close with them and I could see the very old blackheads on her crooked nose.

Nanna grabbed my hands and held them between her own. This was called the Hand Press. It was very important to keep our hands in our pockets if we did not want to tell her the truth. When Nanna held our hands between her own there wasn't enough air. All we could do was answer the questions.

"She was just shining," I said.

"What do you mean shining? I don't understand this talk. Was the sun shining on her face?"

"Yes, the sun was there but she was shining too. She was looking past us at the sky."

Nanna took a long deep breath in.

"Holy Virgin of virgins, Virgin most wise, pray for us," she said.

She released my hands for a moment, crossed herself, and then placed them in the press again.

"I couldn't see what she was looking at," I said.

"Shush, shush," said Nanna.

"Dad shouldn't say I don't know anything," I said. It was the thing that hurt me the most.

"I know, I know," she said, and she released my hands before I could say anything else. "Don't think about it now. Everything will be all right. I know these things."

Before everything happened, that year Angela and I were ten, my second-greatest love was collecting facts. Danielle said it was an unusual love and why couldn't I just collect cereal packet Crater Critters like everyone else or ceramic dogs and Virgin Mary statuettes like Nanna or have a hobby like Hobbytex crafts, which was our mother's number one passion.

Some of my fact collecting rubbed off on Angela but sometimes she didn't understand that you can't just say something is a fact because you believe in it strongly. Facts are found in fact books or in encyclopedias and if they aren't there you have to do research, for example, by asking someone who knows a lot about stuff. For example, Mr. Willow would be the man to ask about the history of macramé because he taught it in grade 7.

My mother liked to use the word "fact" a lot. Her favorite saying was "It's a fact." Her facts included our faces being frozen into a frown when the wind changed direction or how lots of children are killed by chewing on their pencils and getting lead poisoning or by accidentally slipping and having the scissors they had in their mouths enter their brains. I didn't know any children who had died that way. She said there were lots of them. Whole cemeteries. Children buried on top of children. She said it was the most common cause of death apart from drowning but I could tell she was making it up.

"It's a fact," she said.

"It's not a fact actually," I said.

"I think you're getting a little bit too big for your boots lately," she said.

"I'm not wearing boots actually," I said.

"You wait until your father comes home."

Because my number one passion was birds my favorite facts were facts about birds. A good fact about birds is that despite having wing bones very similar to human arm bones, birds are more closely related to reptiles. The *Merit Students Encyclopedia* said birds were only glorified reptiles, which is weird, and I think it was written by a man who was probably a herpetologist.

The *Merit Students Encyclopedia* didn't mention the wedge-tailed eagle of Australia, which is my favorite bird, because it was written in America and they don't live there. Another fact is that I could sing. I could sing beautifully. My mother said it was a gift from heaven even though when she fought with

Nanna she said there was no heaven or no hell. Also when my singing voice went away she didn't notice for quite some time. It would be Nanna who first pointed her bony finger into my chest and asked me where it had gone.

I learned all my facts about Dardanelles Court from Mrs. O'Malley, who lived opposite our house in number 3. She lived with Mr. O'Malley, who never said much but usually sang songs about the sea. He usually sang them when the sun was going down and some of the heat had gone out of his cement yard. His voice drifted through the streets. Usually I went to Mrs. O'Malley when no one would listen to me at home. For instance I may have told Danielle that a starfish broken in half can become two new starfish and she may have said do I look like I care. Mrs. O'Malley always said go on, or you wouldn't read about it, or you're pulling my leg, aren't you.

Mrs. O'Malley was short and round and she owned one hundred colorful dresses made out of nylon that billowed outward from a puckered circle at her neck. She rocked from side to side as she walked because her hips were very bad. Her gray hair was often stuck down to her sweaty red forehead. She collected facts about people like I collected facts about birds and North American capital cities and the great disasters of the world.

When I went to tell Mrs. O'Malley a fact she usually said come round the back with me. This was so we could get away from Mr. O'Malley's singing because he usually wanted me to join in all the choruses with him. Their whole yard was cemented in except for one small square with an orange tree. There were a lot of cracks to break your father's back; you had to be careful to not accidentally step on them.

Mrs. O'Malley knew who was married to who and who their children were and if they had any problems, for instance, a harelip or a clubfoot. She knew when they had first arrived in town and how and from which state or foreign country. She knew who was born in the new maternity wing and who was born in the old hospital and who was buried in the cemetery. But mostly she was an expert on our street.

"The stories in this street," she said. "The things I could tell you."

Mum said she was nothing but an old stickybeak but I didn't agree. We traded facts like collectors.

"A nighthawk flies with its mouth open swallowing insects," I said.

"Marshall Murray in number one is dying from regret," she replied.

"The New York Public Library has over four million books," I said.

"A secret. Those Irwin girls in number two are plotting a great escape."

"Sunflowers turn their heads to face the sun."

"That Miss Schmidt lost her touchable skin when she was just a child."

My mother warned me: she said take everything Mrs. O'Malley says with a grain of salt. And some afternoons at Mrs. O'Malley's house it did feel like she was stuffing me full of strange, ripe stories.

Only she never once told me her own.

And she never once told me ours.

Instead, on that very last day, when Dad collected us from school long before any bell had rung, we turned into Dardanelles Court. From the car window I saw her standing on her patio.

That very last day, stumbling from the car we could hear our mother screaming in circles. When we climbed the front stairs it was like walking a gangplank onto a ship in high raging seas. I looked back once at Mrs. O'Malley from across the street before going inside. She didn't say anything. She only nodded at me.

The cicadas were singing a song.

It was one-noted, one-worded; the word sounded like "please."

They were singing and singing and singing and the whole world was falling down.

Once Angela had decided to find my voice there was no stopping her. It was all she talked about. She carried the exercise book with her everywhere.

Just after school started she got six new under-arm hairs and a training bra even though she didn't have any breasts. She counted the hairs every morning and also at night. She showed them to me. I didn't have any underarm hairs at all. Angela said her mother told her it was probably because of shock that my puberty had been retarded, and I said shut up.

We were in Angela's house, which was a house with no doors. There were only bead curtains and bits of tie-dyed material swaying in doorways and Angela's mother had made Angela's bedspread out of leftover red velvet from their redback panel van, which had won the Panel Van Club Van of the Year twice in a row. The panel van had red velvet benches in the back and mirrors on the ceiling. It had two red stripes painted down either side even though a red-back only has one stripe and any arachnologist would know that.

"So you still had your voice at the lake?" asked Angela.

"Yes."

She wrote:

still singing at the lake.

"Did you lose it after you got home?"

"No."

"What happened next?" Angela asked.

"How would I know?" I said.

"God," she said. "Don't you want to sing again? I bet you don't even care if Anthea Long wins the Memorial Talent Quest. I bet you don't even care if you never get pubic hair."

"Don't say pubic," I said.

"Pew-bic," said Angela loud and slow.

I covered my ears.

I said what if instead of underarm hair at puberty girls got two little wings budding on their backs and all their friends and sisters and mothers and aunts and grandmothers praised the day they appeared.

And steadily year by year instead of girls getting more hair under their arms and down below and instead of larger breasts their wings would grow.

They would start off downy and colorless but end up the velvet green of a peacock's tail or budgerigar blue or the crimson of a king parrot. Every girl would be different. And in the afternoon, after school, they would practice flying in their backyards.

"I think my wings would be very pink," said Angela.

My wings would be brown. I knew it in my bones. They would be earth brown. Mountain brown. Riverbed brown. They would be the magnificent wings of a wedge-tailed eagle. When they unfolded, the golden tips would be revealed.

"I would never have brown wings," said Angela.

The *Merit Students Encyclopedia* says that like other animals birds face many hazards in their lifetime and many chicks do not get a chance to grow up. For example, it says, two robins might have eight chicks but only two will survive until springtime. They might get blown away by the wind or drowned in their nests by rain or eaten by a snake or a lizard.

I used to think that maybe it was the same for humans, that one out of three young in a family might be always going to die. Then I realized that the only other family I knew where one of the children died was the Martins and that child was Ben and he got run over by a truck and sometimes kids went to look for the stain of him on the road.

"Let's start again," said Angela. "I don't think the blue hair combs were a real clue."

"Der," I said.

"I wish you'd take this seriously."

Mrs. Popovitch came to the bedroom door. She was very pretty with long amber hair. She wore see-through caftan tops, which Aunty Cheryl said was an absolute disgrace. She smoked roll-your-owns instead of tailor-mades like my mother. She gave Angela a look from the door and then gave me a look too. The look she gave me was one I was getting used to. Angela's sisters, Rolanda and Natasha, looked at me the same way. It was with sadness and interest and pity all rolled up into a neat face with a smile. No one ever mentioned Beth's name.

Now I knew what it must have felt like to be the brother or sister of Ben Martin when they saw children whispering and planning excursions to see the stain of their brother on the highway.

On the first day back at school Mrs. Bridges-Lamb was on lunch duty and she came up to Angela and me where we were practicing Classic Catches on the parade ground. She told us it would be better to do it on the oval rather than on the cement. I hadn't talked to her since the year before. The last thing she had ever said to me was "And what does three-sixths equal?"

This time she asked me how I was traveling as though I was on some kind of holiday. I said not too bad and I might have said more—for example, that my mother mostly just sat in the recliner and watched television and didn't brush her hair—but some kids thought we were getting into trouble so a crowd had gathered to watch.

When it was my turn to collect the cafeteria basket I heard the cafeteria ladies inside talking about Beth. When I rang the bell the lady who came looked very ashamed but tried to cover it up by patting me on the head and I felt like growling and biting her hand.

Our new teacher, Mr. Barnes, was not very strict and didn't watch us the way Mrs. Bridges-Lamb had watched us, which was very carefully. When Mrs. Bridges-Lamb watched us she wore her glasses and she did not move her head. Her eyes moved, though. They were a flat gray-green and impenetrable as a crocodile's. They slid slowly from side to side.

When Mrs. Bridges-Lamb took off her glasses and began to wipe them with her handkerchief it meant someone was in trouble but first she had to think about it. Without her glasses her eyes were smaller. She peered into the classroom as though we were all in the distance. She forgot about not moving her head. She moved it from side to side, slightly, like a snake listening.

Aunty Cheryl had heard Mr. Barnes was very laissez-faire and thought we might all go wild after being so strictly schooled the year before. It made me think of the whole class suddenly going crazy and hanging out windows. I wished I could have told Nanna because it was the sort of thing that would have made her laugh but we were banned from visiting her because she was a religious maniac. I hadn't seen her since the day of the funeral.

The *Merit Students Encyclopedia* didn't have an entry on famous maniacs, which I had hoped for, but the dictionary said a maniac was an obsessive enthusiast. That made me think of when Nanna made me help her take out all her Virgin Mary statuettes and put them in the bathtub full of soapy water and they bobbed there like a boatload of ladies lost at sea. And after we had tea-towel-dried them she kissed each one and they all went back into the glass cabinets beside the ceramic dogs, which would get bathed another day.

After Mrs. Popovitch was gone Angela lay back on her red velvet bedspread and opened up *The Book of Clues*. She took the pencil from behind her ear.

"What happened after the lake?" she asked a little quieter.

"Nothing," I said.

Angela raised her eyebrows.

And everything.

When Beth met Miranda Bell it was two weeks to Christmas and the whole world still shone. At first she told us it openly.

"Can't you see it?" she said.

"See what?"

"The way that tree is shining, or look, look at Mum's hair, it's on fire. Don't you see it?"

But then, after a while, she stopped asking.

Mum took her to Dr. Cavanaugh, who ran his soft white fingers, which radiated a soft glow like candlelight, slowly over her skull. When he sat down he folded his arms and leaned back in his chair. His wood-paneled office sat in the shadow of a mountain of black slag. It was near the first gate, where a thousand miners entered each day to go down the hole. The train tracks ran behind the walls. Dr. Cavanaugh shut his eyes while the bell signaling the boom gates closing rang out. All the plaques and certificates rattled on his wall as an ore train passed.

"Simple hysteria," he said once things had quieted down. "Quite common in relation to the onset of menstruation and quite common for young girls to faint too. Perhaps this light, these halos she sees, are the tail end of a moderate concussion."

"Keep up the fluids," he said. "Very important."

Beth was in her blue leotard embroidered with gold flowers when she met Miranda. We didn't know she was Miranda then. She was just an angry-faced girl with long brown hair going backward and forward slowly on the swing. The swing was in Memorial Park, the slice of knee-high yellow grass laid down like a blanket between the houses of Memorial South.

Beth had her tutu in her bag. She had her shorts over her leotard and her ballet shoes strung around her neck. We were wearing new happy shoes, which had tags that said MADE IN JAPAN. We'd been at the dress rehearsal for the end-of-year breakup concert for Miss Elise Slater's Jazz Ballet Dance Academy.

"Hey, why've you got that stuff on?" the girl on the swing asked.

The swing was beneath a small crowd of Moreton Bay figs, which bowed their dark heads over her. The girl came in and out of the shadow as she swung.

"For the end-of-year concert," Beth said. "These are called happy shoes."

The girl's skin shone like fine bone china when Beth looked at her. The yellow grass of the park waved like flame. The dome of the sky was incandescent.

"You look stupid," said the girl.

"You should look in a mirror for a change," Beth said.

"How long is your hair?" ordered the girl.

Beth took out all of her bobby pins and undid her bun and shook out her hair. She put her hand behind her back and pointed to where her hair stopped beneath her shoulder blades.

"You're tipping your head back," said the girl.

"She is not," I said.

"Who asked you?" said the girl.

She turned her back to show us how long her own hair was.

"Mine's much longer," she said, "and, anyway, all blondes go brown in the end and then they have to get it out of a bottle."

Beth asked her where she got her information from. The girl said her stepmother knew for a fact and she didn't lie. Beth asked her what happened to her real mother.

"I don't know and I don't care," said the girl.

"I'm going to be dancing in the National Ballet by the time I'm seventeen," said Beth.

"You are not," said the girl.

"So I suppose you can see into the future, can you?"

"Maybe."

She got off the swing. She said she was going down to the river to look for wild horses. She was going to ride one bareback. Did Beth want to come? Beth said no, she couldn't go in her leotard because it had taken Nanna three weeks to embroider. The girl shrugged and turned away, easily, as though she didn't care either way. Beth shrugged too as if it didn't matter as well.

But at home that night Beth had a faraway look in her eyes.

"Penny for your thoughts?" asked Mum, not knowing Beth was already taking her first small steps away from her and us and everything.

"No thoughts," Beth said.

She was seeing the girl in her mind. They were riding wild horses. They thundered across the dry riverbed. Up and down dirt tracks. They rode them bareback. They were flying like the wind.

Mr. O'Malley sang a sea chantey even though we were a thousand miles from any sea. I leaned on the outside of the metal fence and Mrs. O'Malley leaned on the inside.

"In 1919 a great disaster occurred," I said.

"Oh dear," said Mrs. O'Malley.

"A tank with millions of liters of molasses burst and flooded Boston."

"Go on then," said Mrs. O'Malley. "You're having a go at me."

"It's true," I said. "Lots of people died. And in 1966 another great man-made disaster happened in Wales."

"Oh dear," she said.

"A slag heap collapsed and fell on top of a school."

"I remember it, you know, a terrible thing."

"I'm glad there's no slag heap near my school."

"They wouldn't put them near schools anymore."

Mrs. O'Malley pulled a hankie from her bra strap and wiped her face. She looked annoyed as Mr. O'Malley swept around her.

"Don't sing so loud, Mr. O'Malley," she ordered. That's what she always called him. "Me and young Jennifer can't hear ourselves think."

"And how is the young Miss Day?" asked Mr. O'Malley.

"Pretty good," I said.

When he was gone Mrs. O'Malley leaned closer over the fence to me.

"Here," she said, "tell me who this new girl is with the long dark hair."

She nodded her head toward the patio of our house, where Miranda Bell was sitting with Beth. Mrs. O'Malley wanted to know who her parents were and where they'd come from and how and why and what part of town they lived in now.

"Just blew into town, hey?" said Mrs. O'Malley when I couldn't answer any of her questions. "I thought as much."

Miranda had an aristocratic face but she lived in a caravan with a broken door. Sometimes she used the window beside her narrow bed to come and go. She was named after a wine and she lived with her stepmother and her stepmother's boyfriend, who had David Essex eyes. She was porcelain-skinned. Sometimes her cheeks flushed red like an English girl's in a storybook. Like Snow White's.

She said she had red cheeks because she was from down south. She had lived everywhere. She had lived beside beaches, beside rivers, real rivers, rivers that ran, in small towns and in big cities with ten thousand streets. Her whole life had been spent heading up north. She had been to at least fifty schools. She couldn't remember the real number. She didn't count them anymore. She was going to start grade 9 with Beth.

"Who cares?" she said. "It's only school. My stepmother says one school is the same as any other."

"But where's your real mother?" Beth asked.

It was the first time we went to the creek together. Miranda thought for a while. She looked through her mental catalog of towns and cities and rivers and bridges and seaside roads while biting on her bottom lip.

"I think she is somewhere near the Big Pineapple," Miranda said. She'd seen most of the Big Things in Australia. "Or maybe she's gone back to Sydney. Dad left her on the side of the road. I don't know. She could be anywhere. But we were near the Big Pineapple."

"Has she ever written you a letter?" asked Beth.

"How long ago did it happen?" asked Danielle, appalled.

"Do you know the address of the Big Pineapple?" I asked.

"Don't be stupid," said Miranda. "As if the Big Pineapple has an address."

We were sitting on the bank of the dry river in a long strip of shade cast by a white gum. The pale river stones reflected the sun. We had to cover our eyes. The hot blue sky weighed down on us.

"It might," said Danielle quietly before Miranda cast her a glare from beneath her heavy bangs. Even Danielle, who was the Queen of Mean Stares from Beneath Bangs, couldn't equal her.

"I was seven," said Miranda. "I got my stepmother a little bit after that."

"You should try writing to her," said Beth.

"Why?" asked Miranda. She seemed interested.

"I don't know. Because she's your real mum. She might be looking for you."

Miranda laughed at that.

"Don't you get it?" she said. "She asked to be dropped off. She didn't want to stay in the caravan anymore."

"Did you say goodbye?" asked Danielle.

"I was asleep," said Miranda.

That made it even worse.

"Stop talking about it," said Beth suddenly.

She looked at Danielle and me as though we were the cause of all the trouble.

"Let's look for the horses," said Miranda.

We stood up to go, dusting the pale dirt from our bums.

"Not you two," said Beth.

It was like a slap. I don't remember her being mean before that. It made Miranda smile. The smile unlocked something in Beth like a key.

Miranda slept at our house night after night. Mum asked her if she was sure her stepmother approved and Miranda assured her everything was fine. Miranda's stepmother worked late at the Imperial Hotel in the Blue Tongue Lounge Bar. Lounge bars have comfortable chairs instead of bar stools and Aunty Cheryl said certain types drank in them. Miranda didn't like staying at home with Kevin. She said he was annoying after a little while.

Miranda was good at sounding certain about things. Mum liked Miranda then. She liked her in a Christmas holidays type of way. She thought it would all be over once grade 9 began and Beth would be back to her normal self.

Beth's old grade 8 friends knocked on our front door. She received them sullenly. She stood with her arms folded without inviting them in. She answered in single words: yes, no, dunno, sure, maybe. Miranda waited in the living room with the pleased look on her face.

"I don't think I like the way you're behaving," Mum said when Beth came back inside. "Why didn't you ask Tiffany in?"

"She didn't ask to come in," said Beth. "She just wanted to say hello."

"Well you should have offered."

"I will next time."

"That's not good enough."

Miranda and Beth went to the bedroom and closed the door. When I knocked they told me to go away. If I told Mum and they were forced to let me in they made me sit at the bottom end of the bed.

"If you say a word I'll kill you," said Beth.

Sometimes they sat on the floor and made friendship bands. The bands were made out of colored cotton and woven like the macramé that Mr. Willow taught in grade 7. They made lots of them. They sat cross-legged, heads bowed, blond hair and brown hair nearly touching, as they weaved. They didn't talk but sometimes looked at each other and laughed. Beth wore six and so did Miranda. They made them for each other to remind themselves that they were best friends. They wrote FRIENDS FOREVER in black pen on their arms.

Sometimes they braided each other's hair into hundreds of tiny braids. They used up whole packets of rubber bands. Sometimes they played records on the record player Beth had gotten for her thirteenth birthday. Sometimes they put black kohl on their eyes and rouge on their cheeks and practiced making their lips red by biting them. They pouted in front of the mirror. They compared their breasts. Beth's breasts still only fit into a training bra but Miranda wore real bras. If I giggled Beth put her finger to her lips.

Christmas came and went. The silver tinsel Christmas tree dropped its tinsel on the ground. Christmas beetles the festive colors of anodized baubles flew into the patio light and banged against the walls. No matter how much Beth put them back on their feet they rolled over onto their backs. It is a well-known fact that Christmas beetles cannot be saved.

Mum had a worried face. She put the tree away and vacuumed up all the tinsel.

"I'm not sure about this Miranda girl," she said.

In the evenings the sun didn't set until nine o'clock. Beth and Miranda walked out of town along the riverbed. They took whatever food they could steal: bread, sugar in a jar, arrowroot biscuits. Miranda assured her she had seen the wild horses before, it was just a matter of finding them. Miranda talked about her stepmother's boyfriend, Kevin, with the David Essex eyes. He was going to buy her a horse. He'd promised it. A horse trailer too.

"What happened to your father?" Beth asked.

"He took the car," Miranda said. "He went to the pub one afternoon and never came back and that's how we got stuck here with just a caravan and no way to tow it in this stupid town."

"But aren't you sad he's gone?" Beth asked.

Miranda laughed at that.

"A bit, at first," she said. "Kevin's nice, but don't you love his eyes?"

They followed the river out to where it snaked

through the new half-built suburbs. Where the bush had been bulldozed and the trees piled up into pyramids and the air rang with the sound of hammering and the clatter of aluminum sheeting hitting the earth.

Miranda had cigarettes. They were Winfield Greens because menthol cigarettes were good training cigarettes. They sat inside the burned-out shell of a ghost gum tree and practiced smoking them. Miranda was an expert. She rested her back against the blackened wood and sent plumes of smoke up through the empty innards of the tree into the sky.

After the builders went home the half-built suburbs became very still. They walked among the houses. Some had no roofs. Others had no walls. They went inside and imagined the rooms. Miranda knew exactly how she wanted her house to look. She walked and pointed: sunken lounge, shag rug, queen-size water bed.

When Beth tried to describe her dream house the words got stuck on her tongue. She felt strange. She tried hard to picture it but couldn't and instead she found herself imitating Miranda's descriptions. She preferred to look up through the framework as dusk came and the sky changed to a deeper blue. The bushland at the edges of the bulldozer scars changed too.

Everything that she saw glowing during the day

seemed tarnished beside the light that was at the heart of evening. The bleached color of things was replaced by a beauty that stole into everything. The pale yellow leaves grew golden. The white gums opened up their hearts and shone.

I DARDANELLES COURT

SOMETIMES AT NIGHT, WHEN HIS BROTHER FINISHED YARNING AND TELLING JOKES AND STAGGERED OFF TO BED, MARSHALL REMEMBERED HER. His memories were curiously silent, even though in those days the earth still talked to him. The background of dirt streets, tin huts, the hospital tree full of brawling cockatoos were all soundless but her face, her perfect round face, it spoke to him. He heard her eyelashes closing over her black eyes, her breath against his cheek. He liked to remember her late at night; he hoped she would appear in his dreams.

They had always lived together, Arthur and him. They'd never left the town since they arrived except once to go to war and after that they vowed never to leave again. Or at least Arthur vowed (in the same way he'd vowed that they should never love another woman) and Marshall listened. They'd lived in the town since before the pavement roads or bridge across the river and since the mine was just a head-frame on the tallest hill.

In the beginning Marshall tried to describe it to his mother in letters, the sheer size of the sky, the sound of the bush at night, rustling and clicking and shivering in its own skin, the sight of the stars, the smallness of their canvas tent. In each letter he enclosed a bob, king faceup, between the pages.

It was Arthur who fell in love first. Arthur, who preferred the public bar, tobacco smoke and sweat, the slow unwinding of stories, the uncomplicated company of men. It was an unexpected event. The girl was Mary Price, the daughter of the publican of the Imperial Hotel. He tried very hard to ignore her but she was nearly a woman; she had red hair and wore trousers and swore. She'd been kicked out of three boarding schools and didn't care. She was forbidden by law and by her father to come into the public bar but she slouched around the door to the kitchen making eyes at Arthur.

They heard the publican telling his daughter to steer clear of him, Arthur Murray, a scalawag and a drunk who would amount to nothing but would break her heart. Marshall sat and drank his beer and watched his brother grow quieter. He watched the exchange of glances from kitchen door to bar stool and back again.

Mary Price and Arthur Murray began their love affair behind the Imperial in an alleyway lined with kegs. She smoked his cigarettes and stuck out her chest like in the movies. They kissed beneath the hotel rooms. He told her he would marry her, he'd build a house, he'd treat her like a queen before he went back inside for last drinks.

God knows Marshall could remember trying as well back then. He smiled shyly at the girls returning home from boarding school and at the ladies in their sun-faded whites lining up beside the picture theater. But he felt too large beside them, grotesque, with his chipped front tooth from a split rock and his faded hat-flattened hair. Instead he picked Arthur up from the ground more nights than he could count and lurched home with him along the dusty streets. He cooked dinner and cleaned the plates. He put Arthur to bed and woke him in the morning. He explained away his brother's absences from work. He washed away the vomit stains from the front canvas wall.

Arthur took the wild Mary Price for drives in the desert, first parking his borrowed truck down the road so her old man wouldn't see. She smoked cigarettes beside him as he drove. On the way he didn't say a word but by the brown water, beneath the noon sun winking and scribbling messages in light on the rock walls, he promised her everything. They undid their clothes and hung them from the trees.

When the war came they trained for a year beside the sea. Arthur could've returned twice but didn't.

"I should've gone home," he said each night when he'd finished staggering the length of Flinders Street after drinking in every pub. He wrote to Mary Price telling her he'd be home soon.

"You should have married her," said Marshall quietly. "You should have married her before you left."

Marshall wrote to his mother. He explained what the jungle sounded like at night, so close, like someone constantly whispering in your ear, then the sudden deafening roar of rain. He described the intricacies of drinking raindrops from palm leaves, in dripping groves, above the millpond sea. He wrote when Arthur lost his right arm.

In the hospital, where the sea sighed loudly through the windows, Arthur waited daily for Mary Price's letter. He waited hourly for her letter.

When the war was over they headed west again. For a while, after the closeness of the jungle, Marshall found he was terrified by the open space. It was the flat faded land, the straight road, the towering sky. It was too full of air. He felt buoyant himself, that if he stepped from the truck his feet might not even touch the earth and he might instead drift upward and slowly away.

Mary had married another man and run away to Sydney. Her father told them at the pub door. Arthur was still in his uniform. He held his arm out to shake the publican's hand before he realized what was missing.

"I can't fathom it," said the publican, "why she'd give up on a fine man like you?"

Arthur and Marshall took up their stools at the bar and began to drink again. They bought a block of land alongside the empty river and began to build a house.

"We are better off this way," said Arthur. "I'm going to keep away from them from this day on. You'd do well to do the same, my brother. I don't want a woman to set foot in this house again."

Marshall didn't disobey. That life was not for him. Women were a puzzle that could not be solved. He listened to his brother as he always had. But he fell in love. Without warning. By accident.

The woman's name was May, a nurse, five years older than him. She had long brown hair that she wore pinned back with fifty bobby pins. She had a curious squashed-in face and fierce black eyes. Arthur had fought a man on the main street and busted his nose and May had dressed it. Each week Marshall needed to find a new excuse to be near her.

He had a cough that would not go away.

"Your temperature is normal," she said.

He had fallen and hurt his back, oh, how his back ached.

"Bend over, see if you can touch your toes, there, you see, it can't be that bad."

He had injured his arm in a drunken football match.

"Show me, bend the wrist, can you feel me touching your fingers? It seems fine to me."

They met first on the hospital grounds beneath the cockatoo-laden hospital tree. Then later, in the evenings, after he had taken his brother home from the pub and cooked him dinner, he walked back into town and talked to her over the nurses' quarters fence.

They promised to meet each other in their dreams.

The matron reprimanded her for kissing in public, waving her hand at the white wards and the shining linoleum and the pale faces with the sun streaming in through the windows.

"How can you risk losing all this?" she asked.

Arthur was angry with his brother.

"You'll be left with nothing," he said. "Trust me."

Marshall drove May for a picnic by the water hole. When he held her he was still filled with the miracle of it. When she leaned into him. When she looked up at him. But she ruined everything when she hinted at marriage and children.

"It's not so easy as all that," he said.

"Why not?"

"Well I have Arthur to consider. I can't just up and leave him."

He remembered the sunlight there. How the trees had hung their heads in shame. Later they had walked a short way up the hill to the painted rock but she had been tense beside him, fighting back tears, silent.

Soon he forgot to walk by the hospital in the morning to kiss her good day. He stopped coming in the evening to kiss her sweet dreams.

"Where have you been?" she asked. "I waited all yesterday."

"Do you think I've nothing to do with my time? I'm building a house with my own bare hands. My brother has one arm."

"Don't you love me anymore?"

"Don't."

"Don't what?"

"Don't try to trick me with all your questions."

In the afternoons when she went to buy stamps or an apple or the *Women's Weekly* she looked into the dim interior of the public bars and saw Marshall's back beside his brother's. She cried into her hands at home. She cried into her starched dress, onto her brown stockings, into her small room, into her small life. She handed in her notice. She packed her brown suitcase. She was heading farther inland, deeper inland; there seemed no other road to take.

Before she left she walked to the house the brothers had built. When she stepped onto the land Arthur sensed it. He stood up from his seat and walked to the door. Marshall came from the back, where he had been washing in a bucket.

"I came to tell you I'm leaving," she said.

He wore a blank face.

"I'm sorry to hear it," he said.

"And that I love you."

He looked confused, ashamed; she saw it. He was embarrassed.

"It was nice to meet you," he said after a long time.

Arthur stood at the door. He didn't move. He watched them both carefully. The bush waited. It was still and quiet and emptied out of everything.

"Good luck then," Marshall said.

He did not come any closer.

When she turned she couldn't see for her tears and she stumbled and almost fell but corrected herself. She never knew a grief like it again.

All those years, there was nothing confusing about it, yet still it confused him. Each night, after Arthur had gone to bed, he remembered her. He put his head in his hands. He remembered her as she was then, a young lady, only twenty-five, turning away from him, leaving Memorial. But now they were old, both of them, and all those years and all that land grown between them.

Each night it was the same.

That day after she had gone Marshall turned back to the house. He was made of stone. His heart did not beat. Blood did not move through his veins. The river inside of him dried up. The bush began talking again but he did not hear it. He did not hear it again after that.

In the beginning Beth didn't try to save anything but insects: a black bug from a redback spiderweb, a three-legged grasshopper staggering away from an army of ants, a lacewing stuck behind a sliding glass window.

"Oh God," she said when she saw something struggling. "Poor thing."

"But it's only a moth," Mum said. "If only you were so interested in schoolwork."

School had begun. Beth's brown-paper-covered notebooks rarely emerged from her canvas bag.

"Give her time," said Nanna. "You are too hard with her."

"Kylie does hours of homework each night," said Mum. "Cheryl told me. I haven't seen any homework here."

"Cheryl," said Nanna, "she exaggerates, you know this."

Kylie had started grade 9 too. Beth complained about her.

"She won't leave me alone at school," she said. "If I smile at her she thinks she can spend the whole day with me."

"That's the meanest thing I've ever heard you say," said Mum. "Did I raise you up to be so mean? She's your cousin."

"I know."

Kylie and Beth were born only a month apart and were nearly the same height.

"Look at them, will you, like two peas in a pod," Aunty Cheryl always said.

But Kylie was a much paler copy. Her hair was thin and lank. Her pink scalp showed through it. She was sallow-skinned. Her large front teeth were stained from too many antibiotics.

"You're supposed to look after her," said Mum. "Here, you'll rescue a moth but you won't look after your own cousin. Your cousin hasn't had it as easy as you lot."

By that she meant that Kylie didn't have a father. It didn't matter that she had the Barbie campervan and the Barbie town house, a fashion stencil set, and a real rocking horse, not a hobbyhorse, which is only just a horse's head on a stick, and even though she had grown out of all these toys they were never handed down. She had a wardrobe full of brand-new clothes, her own record player decorated with love-heart stickers, and an orange bike with pristine white handlebars. Mum put her finger to her lips when I started to remind her of all this.

"She had to grow up under difficult circumstances. I want you to always be good to her."

"I am being good to her," said Beth.

"Otherwise I'll worry all day," said Mum.

Dad said Mum was a champion at worrying.

Nobody bothered about Beth's saving of insects. She had always done it. Being smaller I could not remember a time when she hadn't. But she seemed sadder now when she found things that were beyond hope. She cried over a troop of ants stuck in a pool of spilled honey on Nanna's kitchen bench. They were struggling, tiny legs swimming through the thick tide.

"Stop it," said Mum. "Why are you crying like that?"

"I just can't bear it," she cried.

"Bear what?"

"Just the thought of it."

"Stop it," said Mum. "It's nonsense."

"It's their own fault," I said. "They wanted the honey."

"They paid the ultimate price," said Danielle.

"Be quiet," said Mum, wiping the honey and the ants up with a rag in one movement.

Nanna, who was at the little kitchen table, didn't

say a thing. She reached her hand out and held Beth's arm as she passed. She tried to get Beth to look at her but Beth kept her eyes turned away and shrugged herself free.

Beth was only just beginning to change but we still didn't know it. None of us could sense it yet. It would have seemed impossible if we'd been told that Beth, ballet dancer, prettiest girl in school, would change so much. That rushing toward us, unseen, were all of the angry words and turned-away faces. All the slammed doors and keys turned in locks and all the rivers of tears. We didn't know that she would ride down the long straight streets away from us.

Beth went and sat in the backyard of Nanna's council flat. The flat was in Memorial West, where all the houses were lemon-colored, in the last street, where the backyards faced into the desert. It was a good place for thinking. The backyard didn't finish in a straight line with a fence. There was no fence at all. The dry lawn was trying to grow out into the desert, which was patched with spinifex and pale hummock grasses that shimmered in the heat. And the desert was reaching back into the yard, spreading its red fingers and erecting small anthills and sucking the color from Nanna's garden beds.

Nanna's flat was like a long thin caravan put up on blocks. It had three front steps and a sliding front door. We sometimes slept there for the weekends and Nanna told me secretly about the nine choirs of angels and the saints and taught me songs even though Mum said she wasn't allowed to be religious with us.

Mum packed me, Beth, and Danielle up with sleeping bags and pillows and inflatable mattresses with a bicycle pump to blow them up. I hated getting out of the car at Nanna's because there could be, for example, a nuclear war and then we would be separated from Mum and Dad forever.

"Don't worry, possum," Mum said, reading my thoughts. "You worry too much."

She held my face between her hands and kissed me. Her lips were painted in Frostiest Mauve and the purple kiss was left behind on my cheek.

Nanna always had her hands on her hips when we arrived. She shook her head when she saw all our bedding.

"You don't think I have beds?" she asked.

Nanna had two rickety camp stretchers with thin mattresses. Before the inflatable mattresses Beth and Danielle slept on the stretchers and, because I was the third, I got to sleep beside Nanna. She had a hard bed. Every time I moved it creaked. After each creak Nanna sighed and moved and the bed creaked again. All night we creaked backward and forward at each other without saying a word. During the day Nanna usually smelled like Yardley's lavender perfume but at night she smelled different. Up close to her in the bed in her threadbare rose-covered nightie she smelled like dust.

"Don't go on about the saints," said Mum as she handed us over. "It scares Jenny."

Nanna liked to tell me how the saints died, which was most often horribly and included being roasted on stakes, flayed alive, fed to the lions, or marched out into winter forests and shot once in the head.

Nanna only kept small traces of her old life before the ship that brought her fifteen thousand kilometers to here. The small traces included the way she stirred her giant stews and baked on Saturdays as though the world was about to end. She also sometimes said words back to front like "arse-tight" instead of "tight-arse" when she described her brother Uncle Paavo. When she said it she covered up her mouth and even though she was old her eyes shone like a young girl's.

She only had a little trace of her accent, where Uncle Paavo had kept nearly all of his. She said it was because she was only thirteen when she came to Australia and Uncle Paavo was nearly seventeen. Nanna had scrubbed herself clean of it.

Nanna sang songs with me at the kitchen table. She sang me old songs that her mother had sung to her in Finland and on the boat trip. The words in these songs felt old and well worn; they belonged to each other like threads in a patterned blanket.

We sang at her little kitchen table while we peeled potatoes. Beth and Danielle got up and went into the tiny living room and braided each other's hair.

"Don't worry about them," said Nanna. "They do not have good voices."

Sometimes after Nanna had taught me something she started to cry, which was perfectly ordinary. She put her head in her hands.

"God be merciful to us," she said.

Beth, who was sitting in front of the television, rolled her eyes as she braided Danielle's hair.

"Mum said you're not allowed to talk like that," said Danielle.

"I'll talk how I like," said Nanna.

"Suit yourself," said Beth.

"Don't be smart," said Nanna, and then she started talking in biblical phrases.

"I know thy pride and the naughtiness of thine hearts."

"O-K," said Beth, pronouncing it slowly and widening her eyes at Danielle.

"You are all from the basket of bad figs. So bad, so evil, they cannot be eaten."

Danielle started laughing.

"Out, out," said Nanna, and she would send us out into the backyard.

Usually we sat beneath the rain tree and if it was in bloom let the nectar rain on us and plucked the sickly sweet pom-pom flowers and held them like powder puffs to our noses. Or if it wasn't we picked the yellow rattlepods and opened them carefully and examined the small brown seeds sleeping in their little beds.

And sometimes Beth stood up and cleared a patch of earth with her bare foot and did pirouettes one after another until she was dizzy. Or sometimes handstands. Or sometimes cartwheels. Nanna would open the kitchen window and yell at her to stop it before she broke her neck. Beth would roll her eyes when Nanna had shut the window again.

Sometimes we'd step over the blurred edge of the yard into the desert, just one foot, the way some people test the temperature of the sea.

Angela was impatient with *The Book of Clues*. She thought all the answers should come at once. She carried the book with her on weekends when we walked along the dry creek bed through the sunbaked suburbs. She carried it in the back elastic of her shorts. She twirled the pencil in her fingers.

All she had written inside was:

> *still singing at the lake.*
> *everything glowing.*
> *beth meets miranda.*

She had crossed out hair combs in the list of things in the box as a clue to anything.

On the cover she had drawn a girl in a love-heart dress. She had long yellow hair rolling over her scrawny shoulders. Her eyes had eyelashes straight as toothpicks.

"Who's that supposed to be?" I asked.

"No one," she said. "It's just a picture."

"It's pretty dumb," I said. "It better not be Beth."

"Don't get your knickers in a knot."

I was still breaking things. Small things: Danielle's bluebird necklace, the handle off Aunty Cheryl's special teacup that she used when she came to visit us, Kylie's left-behind wristwatch. I hadn't stopped since the day when I broke Barbie Ken's legs.

I thought if I could get hold of *The Book of Clues* it could accidentally go missing. But Angela guarded it carefully. I thought she was stupid for thinking she would ever find my voice, that it was all a simple puzzle that could be solved. But I didn't say anything. If I told her it was way more difficult than that, then she would ask me to explain. And I couldn't, not properly; not Beth locked up in her room like Rapunzel, the running and falling with scissors, cicadas screaming and a storm, the lake breathing slowly against the shore.

Angela thought if we could find where I lost my singing voice it would be given back but I knew that wasn't true. I knew I was never going to sing again.

We walked up the slope of Memorial Park to the

swing, to the place where Beth first met Miranda. The swing was empty. There was only the groaning of road trains on the highway. A cloud of red dust had blown into town and settled over everything. It sat at the bottom of the sky. It covered the swing seat and the splinter-filled seesaw.

There were hawks twisting in the sky.

I wanted to see a letter-winged kite. The letter-winged kite's Latin name is *Elanus scriptus* and it is my third-favorite bird. It has a body white as snow and black wings. When its wings are closed it looks just like the black-shouldered kite but when it soars it has two *M*s written beneath like black lightning strikes. Once when I did a talk on the letter-winged kite Mrs. Bridges-Lamb asked if the class had any questions and Massimo Gentili put up his hand.

"How come if they live around here nobody ever sees them?" he said.

I wanted to say you have to be patient to see a letter-winged kite. I wanted to say you have to spend a long time looking upward. You have to look up for so long that you might even get a sore neck and sometimes you can only see them at night when they shine by moonlight.

But I couldn't get the words out.

I just shrugged and it was like I had made the whole thing up and *Elanus scriptus* wasn't even a real bird.

We stood near the swing for a long time thinking of what might be a clue and what mightn't be a clue. Behind the swings and the Moreton Bay figs the park changed into pale scrub, white grass, and ashen trees peeling bark. We climbed up to where the fence had been erected around the water tower. We walked around the perimeter. The February sun burned our faces.

"Everyone blames Miranda," I said so we could think of something else.

Angela's hand went to *The Book of Clues* in her waistband and hovered.

My mother blamed Miranda. In the end she'd hated her. She thought Miranda Bell was the problem, not Beth. My mother had hissed the name Miranda when she said it but mostly she didn't say her name at all. She said she and her and that girl. Miranda had led Beth astray.

"Astray" sounded almost like a country. It would be populated by Astraynians. There would be a queen but probably not a king because it seemed to be mostly girls who went to live there. When Beth was led astray she took hardly anything with her, just her little canvas bag. When she came home she never brought anything except something in her eyes. A secret she kept from us. When she came home she sat on the sofa and looked exactly the way that she always had only the hidden thing made her seem very different.

"We'll need to talk to Miranda," said Angela.

"God," I said, "as if that'll help."

We walked back through the park. We had to be careful near Kylie's house because if she saw us she'd want to come. We went past the opening of Dardanelles Court, where Mrs. Irwin in number 2 was unloading her groceries from her car. Mrs. Irwin had thick black eyebrows and impossibly green eyes. She had dark hairs growing on her top lip almost like a mustache although if we mentioned it Mum put her hand up and made us stop.

Mrs. O'Malley said she didn't know why Mrs. Irwin was so high-and-mighty now as she knew for a fact she was brought up in a tin shed and would've had to wipe her bum with gum leaves when the newspaper ran out. "And now she's gone and homeschooled those poor girls," said Mrs. O'Malley, "so they'd never get to make a proper friend. Ruined them," she said.

Mrs. Irwin called me over and asked me did my mother need anything. She said nothing was too big or too small. She sent her three daughters to our house every week to ask exactly the same thing.

Each week they stood at the front screen door and peered past me with their wild green eyes into our house. They wore long-sleeved dresses that reached the floor and I'd seen the same dresses among Nanna's Butterick patterns from 1974. I would have asked them in but I couldn't, not with Mum lying on the sofa in her yellow Japanese happy coat smoking cigarette after cigarette until a slow whirling cloud hung from the ceiling. Not with Dad swearing in the kitchen because he couldn't find a single clean plate. Or Danielle refusing to hear the simplest of questions while writing sad poems or drawing pages full of girls with melancholy eyes.

"I don't think we need anything," I said to Mrs. Irwin.

"Are you sure?" she asked, and made a sad clown face and a sighing noise. Later that afternoon I threw some rocks near the opening of Dardanelles Court with the hope that I would accidentally break her car window.

But first Angela and I crossed the creek. We crossed where the silt had been baked dry by the sun and cracked into scales like a snakeskin. Our feet crumbled the scales. We left our footprints on the snake river's back. The snappy gums still lay where they had fallen when the river last ran. Yellow grass grew up through the broken fences.

"This is it," I said.

We walked beside the crumbling bank where the giant ghost gums arched their backs and stretched their smooth white arms toward the river. We dipped our heads beneath the branches and ran our hands over the satin skin.

"What?" said Angela.

A sand track ran behind the bank. Beyond that the gums straightened themselves up and stood tall. They were perfectly spaced, as though they had been planted in an orchard. It was a quiet place. We walked between them, stepping over fallen branches, not speaking.

"What?" whispered Angela again.

There was no wind. It was almost as still as the day it happened. I could feel it, almost, hanging in the air.

We had arrived at the place of the kiss.

We stood where Beth had kissed the boy with crow-colored hair on a hot still February day. She kissed him beneath the trees beside the sand track and the empty river.

By then the light had started to fade from within everything. Nanna had stopped asking if she had a halo around her head.

"Is there any light at all left?" she asked Beth instead, hopefully.

"No," Beth said.

"What, none?"

"None. Everything is ugly again."

"Ugly?"

"Earth-colored."

Nanna looked at me and back to Beth.

"Tell me again, what did you see that day at the lake?" she asked.

"Nothing," said Beth.

Beth kissed the boy for a dare but straightaway recognized something terrible in him. I saw the way she looked at him. It was just the way she looked at a bird with a broken wing.

Marco rode a trail bike and was seventeen. His hair was thick, lustrous, worn long like Chachi's hair in *Happy Days*. He had a little mustache. It was just a few wispy hairs at the corners of his mouth.

He didn't speak. Another friend, Tony, did all the talking. Tony wasn't Italian. He had sandy hair and a face full of freckles, even on his lips. He had watery blue eyes and he stank of sweat.

"What are you doing down here?" asked Tony. "Don't you know this trail is only for motorbikes? I could call the fuzz on you for trespassing."

Tony spoke to Beth and Miranda. I was left out because of my age and size. Miranda put her hands on her denim-clad hips. Beth pushed her hair behind her shoulders and tilted her head to one side.

Marco stood silently beside Tony. He looked at Beth from underneath his long black eyelashes but only once. Then he looked everywhere but at her. He ran his eyes over the satin-skinned trees, the long grass in the paddocks, the sand road that bent away into the bush. Beth ignored him back while Tony dared Miranda to a ride.

"No," Beth said. "We're going home."

Marco's eyes came back to her from a close examination of the sky and then fell quickly to the ground. He jumped to start his bike. It roared to life. It drowned out the sound of Tony's daring. It exploded the silence between the two of them. Her mouth was open, as though she had something else to say, and then closed.

She looked angry all the way home but Miranda was excited.

"He loves you," she said. "I know he loves you."

"Don't be stupid," said Beth, but her voice came out breathless, as though she had run a mile.

Whenever they walked along the creek Marco and Tony followed them. The two parties ignored each other but watched each other out of the corners of their eyes. The first kiss was for a dare. The boys were doing wheelies and burnouts and great clouds of dust rose and hovered in the air. We were at a place where the river bent and widened, dangling our feet in a small pocket of brownish water that had remained long after the rains had gone.

"I can just tell he wants to kiss you," said Miranda.

"Don't be stupid," said Beth.

She kissed him at noon when the sun beat down on the rocks and stones and the creek bed burned white. The trees were motionless. It was so hot that nothing stirred. All of the birds rested, hidden. The only noise was the sound of cicadas humming. A mirage wobbled over the pink pavement of the crossing.

Freckled Tony had picked his way across the rocks toward us; his whole shape rippled in the heat. Both sides knew what was to happen next. They knew it without words. It was written, already, into the hot still day.

"Go on," Tony said to Beth. "We know you won't."

"She won't," said Miranda. "I know her."

"Come with me," said Beth.

I got up off the bank. I started to put my flip-flops on.

"Hurry up," she said.

Tony laughed. Miranda looked at him with half-closed black eyes.

"Do you want me to come?" she asked.

"No," said Beth.

Marco was waiting off the sand track. His trail bike was on its side. The scent of eucalyptus rose with each of our footsteps.

"Wait here," said Beth.

She took me by the shoulders and placed me against a tree.

She walked across the trail, not looking left or right, walked right up to the crow-haired boy and kissed him on the lips. He was taller than her by a head. She had to stand on her toes.

When she stopped kissing him his hand went to her waist to pull her back. The sun beat down on us. The day quivered. The sky was as deep as an ocean. We breathed underwater. I lifted my hand to brush my hair from my eyes and it ached. The cicadas dropped a note. Beth moved backward, away from his hand. She turned toward where I was standing.

"Wait," he said.

He said it loud, his first word.

Beth kept walking.

"Come on," she said, taking me by the shoulder.

She held on to my shoulder the whole way down the bank. It was only once we were across the creek and into the shade that the day took a deep breath again.

After the kiss some of it still sparkled in the air around her.

I thought I was the only person who could see it but then Mr. Murray, who was watering his lawn, called out. He was standing in the shade of his yellow cassia tree.

It wasn't the scary Mr. Murray, who sometimes had pee stains down his trouser leg and sat all day on his patio drinking from brown bottles. Mum said we should never go near him. It was the nicer Mr. Murray, with the broken front tooth and the purple nose, who Mum said we could talk to from a distance.

The nicer Mr. Murray always asked questions that had no real answer: Tell me what you know? How long is a piece of string? What's a girl like you doing in a place like this?

"Breaking hearts yet?" he asked Beth from among the yellow bells when we were on his footpath. His face was spotted with light and shade.

Beth stopped and put her hand up to shield her eyes from the sun.

She smiled, one of her best saved-up smiles.

"No," she said.

She had less than one year to live.

I didn't go to Nanna's flat until after school started. I rode to all four corners of the town but avoided her street. I entered each court in Memorial South, looping round each dead end like a small boat into a bay and out again. Up and down the long straight streets of Memorial East, where the rows of baby-blue houses faced the highway in regimental lines. Into Memorial North, stained, kneeling at the foot of the mine beneath the smelter stacks, the workshops, the slag heaps, where the hills rose higher than anywhere else in the town, blackened, birdless, stripped of every tree.

I was looking for something but I didn't know what. I rode up and down the street before Nanna's. I rode past the end of Nanna's street. I saw her Datsun Sunny, which smelled of Craven "A"s and Yardley's lavender. Everywhere on its floor and seats were Butterick patterns and bags of rags for cleaning. Saint Christopher was Blu-Tacked to the dashboard. In her garden all the roses had turned brown. The air conditioner whirred beside the flat.

One half of me didn't want to see her. The day of the wake still burned my cheeks. One half of me longed for her.

I thought if I could be any bird I would be a wedge-tailed eagle. If I was a wedge-tailed eagle I would live only for the joy of flight. I would soar at great heights, on top of the wind. I would be above everything, over the desert and scrub, over the long empty rivers, over the little towns clinging to the highway. I would be apart from everything.

If I could have sung then it would have been a very sad song. I would have sung *If you miss the train I'm on, you will know that I have gone, a hundred miles, a hundred miles, a hundred miles.*

A long time before then Mum said I was born

with my singing voice already inside me like a gift. She said everyone was born with a talent waiting to be discovered. When she said it she was putting on her Grape Freeze lipstick in front of the mirror and I was sitting on the edge of the bathtub making up songs.

There are many different types of singing. There is singing to keep yourself company, which is like talking to yourself only with a tune. There is singing onstage to make other people happy, which requires practice and sweaty palms. And there is sudden singing, which happens when songs rise up, without warning, inside you and there is nothing that you can do but open your mouth and sing them.

Sudden singing was the only type I really missed. When sudden singing happened it came out of the blue and made me feel so good that my toes curled up and I got goose bumps all over my body and tears in my eyes.

Sometimes it was a simple unannounced *Somewhere over the rainbow* at the kitchen table. I would feel the tune coming. It unwound inside me. The words followed quickly and I couldn't stop them. They came out of my toes and my stomach and my skin. They flew out of my mouth like they had wings.

It didn't matter at home because everyone was used to it. Danielle would tell me to shut up. Occasionally a wild and unexpected *Hey sister, go sister, soul sister* would startle someone or Dad would shake his head and say Jesus Christ after a surprising *Hallelujah*.

After my singing voice got stuck I could still feel the sudden songs inside me piling up. I didn't know which songs they were, just that they were there. I could feel the outlines of them. It felt wrong. I held my stomach while they struggled. I couldn't even sing the anthem at school. I just had to hum quietly and the humming sounded strange in my ears. It had no tune.

When I knocked on the door Nanna didn't answer straightaway but I heard her moving slowly toward the door.

Finally her old crinkled hands came out of the dark cool inside and held my sun-warmed face between them.

"Jennifer," she said. "I knew you would come."

Inside everything was the same but she had changed. She was thinner. Her back hump stuck out more. The lines on her face had grown deeper. She hadn't brushed her two curtains of hair. When she opened the fridge to give me water there was only a packet of biscuits and nothing else. The kitchen window was shut and a fly buzzed madly against it. When she came close to me her breath smelled of sweet tea and sadness.

"Tell me," she said, pulling out a kitchen chair for me and dragging hers closer. "Tell me."

I told her about when the aunties and the cousins left. I told her about the beginning of school and Mr. Barnes. I told her about Angela but not the underarm hairs bit. I told her that Dad had gone back to work and how he made his own lunches. I told her that Danielle's perm had dropped quite a bit. I told her I was not allowed to visit her.

Nanna looked very tired and when she spoke it was as though finding the words made her feel weary.

"It is our secret," she said.

She poked her bony finger into my chest.

"And what of this?" she said. "Is your voice still here?"

"Yes," I said.

"Still stuck?"

"Yes."

"Here, I have been thinking, I would like you to try this."

She took my cup and demonstrated for me. Instead of drinking from the side closest to her mouth she put her lips over the farthest side. She leaned her head forward. Her chin was in the cup and she let the water enter her mouth from the wrong side.

"It is like drinking backward," she said, and wiped her chin and neck, where a lot of the water had dripped.

She gave the cup to me and I had to do the same.

She made me drink the whole cup that way. She said drink it faster and it may dislodge something. I coughed and burped.

"Ah," she said. "You see."

But my songs didn't seem any closer to the surface.

"Some days I cannot breathe," she said, "for all this sorrow."

I didn't know what to say so I just let her hold my hands the way she liked and I kicked my leg backward and forward softly against the chair and I wondered if she could read my thoughts.

"Well I better go," I said after a while.

"Yes," she said.

"Do you want me to bring you some food?" I asked.

"No, do not worry for me."

"I don't want you to starve," I said.

"I have starved before," she said. "After the War of Brothers everyone starved. Paavo, he was as thin as a skeleton. Men and women, they would do anything, anything, Jennifer, even for some flour. Things you cannot imagine."

She had told this story one million times before. Especially at the dining room table if we didn't eat every last centimeter of our meal.

"This is not starving," she said, pointing to herself.

"OK," I said.

At the front door she held my hands. I was in the sunlight again and she was in the shade.

"Let us be honest with each other," she said before I went.

IT WAS HARD TO BE HONEST WHEN THERE WERE SO
MANY LIES. Everyone had their own explanation for
why things turned out the way they did. Everyone
grabbed for a scrap of the story and held it. Now,
when I am older, I hold on to pieces so shiny that they
must surely be untrue.

And other parts much darker.

If I am to be honest.

The party was at a house on Amiens Road. Before
they went they made sure their center parts were
dead straight. They put eye shadow on. Beth wore
Miranda's red pedal pushers and black corduroy
vest. Miranda applied rouge to Beth's cheeks and
then wet her fingertips in her mouth and rubbed it in.

Danielle and I sat on the living room floor.
Danielle had to kneel because of her brand-new
Milwaukee back brace for her curvature of the spine,

which Dad was paying her by the hour to wear. She put the money in a jar marked with pen PERM.

She had come back from Brisbane with it, as well as a sketchbook and new watercolors and two new dresses. She wanted to have radical back surgery rather than wear the brace. She was going to research one hundred science books to find a cure. She fought with Mum every night, she said she did not want to be a cripple.

The brace was a hard plastic shell that encased her torso and three steel rods, one at the front and two at the back, that joined a metal ring that circled her neck. She wore it under her clothes. It was fastened by various metal screws and leather belts.

We were marrying Malibu Barbie to a Luke Skywalker action figure when Miranda and Beth walked past. The radio was on. Mum was ironing.

"You're both very dressed up," Mum said. "Where are you two off to?"

"We're just riding to show Tiffany," said Beth. "We'll be back soon."

"Can I come?" I asked.

"No," said Beth, but she said it too fast and too loud and Mum heard her.

"I'll just ride with you for a little way," I pleaded.

"Oh, let her ride with you," said Mum. "Just to Tiffany's and then she can ride back. Hasn't Tiffany got a little sister she could play with?"

When we got outside Miranda and Beth rode very fast down Dardanelles Court and I had to pedal standing to keep up with them.

"Why aren't you going to Tiffany's house?" I shouted.

"Be quiet," said Beth.

Amiens Road, where Marco lived, was only three streets away. There were cars parked on the footpath and a tangle of bikes near the gate. There was music coming from inside.

"You have to wait outside over there," said Beth, pointing to the gutter on the opposite side of the road.

"Why?" I said.

"If you go home you'll tell Mum, won't you?"

"No," I said, but I mustn't have sounded certain enough.

Miranda rolled her eyes.

"Why did you have to come?" she said slowly.

"Up your arse with a can of sars," I said slowly back.

They left their bikes and went up onto the patio and knocked. I sat on the gutter on the other side of the road and watched them. A boy came to the door and took them inside.

I waited. I left my bike on the footpath and walked up and down the gutter of Amiens Road. I looked for interesting things. I found a box of Redheads matches with three left inside, which was interesting because three was my lucky number. If Dad ever asked me to pick a horse for him when he wasn't sure who was going to win I always said three.

Inside the house a group of girls banged their hips into Beth as she passed. They were big girls, grade 10 girls, with black bands on their arms and blue ink tattoos. She tried to ignore them. They stared at her from where they sat in a circle on the living room floor. She drank the beer Marco gave her. A John Cougar tape played in the tape recorder in the kitchen. Miranda and Beth lit their cigarettes and they were glad they had practiced.

Outside I found three burning beans, which was a good find. If you rubbed burning beans very hard on your clothes they heated up and you could put them on someone else's skin to burn them and they were a good weapon to have in case you ever met a stranger who was trying to kidnap you.

"What would you do if a stranger pulled up in a car and asked you to get inside and said your mother wants me to bring you home?" Mum often asked us.

"No thank you," we said.

"And?"

"Keep walking," I said.

And burn him with a burning bean.

"And what if he said he had lost his kitten and could you help him find it?"

"No way, Jose," I said.

"Good girl," said Mum.

"What if he really had lost his kitten?" said Danielle.

"Don't start," said Mum.

Inside the house the beer wasn't cold. Beth forced each mouthful down. It tasted warm and rich, like drinking earth. Marco stood beside her. His little mustache twitched every time he smiled at her. She flicked her cigarette on top of a full ashtray and some of the ash fell on the floor.

"Sorry," she said.

"Don't be stupid," said Marco.

She put her fingers up to her lips, which were tingling.

Her cheeks flushed.

She felt like part of her was vanishing.

Inside the house long shafts of afternoon light fell through half-open venetian blinds. She passed her hand through them, through the slow-turning dust motes. She watched her cigarette smoke scroll its way to the ceiling. The tough girls watched her from the floor.

Marco gave her another beer.

"Yum," she said, and he laughed.

He had skin like marble. It gleamed in the kitchen. His black hair fell across his eyes. He pushed it back with his hand. He stood in the slab of sunlight and was illuminated.

Miranda sat on top of the kitchen bench. Tony was telling her again about his car: the upholstery, the wheels, the wings, the side detailing. How fast it would go. From zero to one hundred. The tape player.

"No, I'm not kidding," he said. "A tape player."

Beth listened to his voice. She watched Miranda. Miranda kept pushing her long dark hair over her shoulders and looking up at Tony. She was telling him about the horse her stepmother's boyfriend had promised her. She was excited. She described in detail what colors the horse trailer would be. But Tony didn't look that interested. He told her to come outside and look at the car.

"You better come with me," Marco said, motioning with his eyes to the girls in the circle on the living room floor, "or they'll beat the shit out of you."

Outside I found a feather that could have been from the wing of a whistling kite. I needed to take the feather to the town library because Mum wouldn't buy me *A Field Guide to Australian Birds,* volume 1 or volume 2. It was a long feather that was honey brown. I immediately looked in the sky to see if the bird was still around but instead there were just two very plain sparrows.

The whistling kite has a very distinctive call. It sounds like it is asking the question "Where you?" It even sings the question in a proper tune. It sings Where you? Where? Where? Where? Where? It sings it higher as it goes. It is my sixth-favorite bird in the world.

There was a mirage at the end of Amiens Road hovering glass blue above the pavement but the closer I walked to it the farther it moved away. I went back to my bike and sat down.

Inside Marco closed his bedroom door and put the chair in front of it. His teeth were very white. They shone inside his mouth. Everything was over-flowing in the bedroom. Clothes spewed out of open-mouthed drawers. The sheets tumbled onto the floor. Newspaper stuffing erupted from half-unpacked boxes. He lay on the bed beside her.

A lady came out of the house behind me. She was about my mother's age but brown-haired and very plain. She had no lipstick on. She had dark-rimmed glasses like Nana Mouskouri's.

"Are you all right?" she asked.

"Yes, thanks," I said, and I picked my bike off her footpath because I thought maybe she was angry at me because she had nice grass almost like on a bowl-ing green. My mother would have liked her lawn be-cause, after Hobbytex and dancing, watering the lawn was her third-favorite passion.

"Are you waiting for someone?" she asked.

She didn't sound angry.

"My sister," I said, and pointed to the house across the road.

"Oh," she said. "Do you want to wait inside? It's very hot out here."

I fingered the burning beans in my pocket and tried to imagine burning her but it didn't seem right.

"No, thanks."

"Well come onto the porch and I'll bring you a drink," she said, and I followed her.

On the front porch there was a tile on the wall that said HOME SWEET HOME. The lady went inside and I stood outside and waited and she came back with orange soda in an old Vegemite glass, which was comforting because that is exactly what our mother did with old Vegemite jars. We sat on the steps together.

"How many sisters have you got?" said the lady with Nana Mouskouri glasses.

"Two. And five cousins but only one that lives here. She is only a little bit retarded."

"Oh," said the lady.

"She's pretty normal really. Only sometimes she has rages."

"Oh."

"And my other sister just got curvature of the spine and has to wear a Milwaukee back brace twenty-three hours a day even though she is trying to find a cure."

"I see," said the lady. "This sister here?"

"No," I said. "That's Beth. She's normal. Only last year she fainted at the lake and my nanna said she may have seen an angel."

Inside Beth felt scared. She was scared by his glowing kisses, which were small. It was like being nibbled by a fish. He kissed her all along her jaw and lightly on the mouth. His whiskers tickled her face like a feather. Whenever he stopped he drew his head back and looked at her with a half-puzzled smile. The sun shone through the blinds. His face was crossed with lines of light and shadow. Sometimes the shadow fell upon his eyes. Sometimes across his mouth.

He was shaking hard. She tried to push him off but he held one arm across her chest. His breath burned her skin. He pulled down the red corduroy pedal pushers. She watched the white ceiling. A dirt-colored cloud moved slowly between two slats of the blinds.

When he had finished he lay beside her.

"You're not supposed to cry," he said. "You're supposed to enjoy it."

In the backyard Miranda waited beside Tony's car, which had no wheels. After a while Beth came down the back steps and waded through the long grass toward her.

When she came out of the house on Amiens Road that day Beth's eyes were bluer than I had ever seen them. She smelled like Winfield Greens and Dad's beer and something else.

"I didn't think you'd still be here," she said after she called me down from the Nana Mouskouri lady's front steps.

We rode the long way to the corner shop. She bought chewing gum and a bag of lolly hearts and she gave me a packet of candy cigarettes. My first lolly heart said YOU'RE COOL. Miranda's said the same. Beth's said BE MY SWEETHEART.

"It's a sign," said Miranda.

"No it isn't," said Beth.

"You did it, didn't you?" said Miranda.

"Yes," said Beth.

I lit up a candy cigarette, which is a practicing cigarette for smaller children.

My second heart said YOU'RE BEAUTIFUL.

"And you are," said Beth. She tucked my hair behind my ear.

We left Miranda at the gate to the caravan park and then wheeled our bikes home. We crossed Campbell Road and entered into the back of Memorial Park. I kicked a rock with my foot. I counted my steps. Beth didn't say a thing. She didn't say don't tell Mum.

That side of the hill always made me feel lonely. The path was rocky and choked in parts by lantana. Campbell Road disappeared quickly even though we could still hear it. The bush closed in along the path to get a better look at us. Crooked rain trees bent over and rattled their seedpods softly above our heads. Cicadas changed their tune as we passed. The only noise was our bike tires and our feet crunching on the path.

When we turned into Dardanelles Court the sun was only just starting to set and Mr. O'Malley was singing while he swept his front yard. He sang "Botany Bay" very slowly; each word hung in the hot summer air and then dissolved. When Mr. O'Malley saw me he put out his hand and I sang a few lines with him from where I stood in the middle of the road but Beth walked ahead like she couldn't even hear us.

She went straight to her room and lay on her bed with her knees drawn up to her chest. Mum came and stood at her door.

"How was Tiffany?" she asked.

"Good," Beth said.

"I think it's really nice you're still friends with Tiffany," said Mum. "Even though you've got this new friend. You always need more than one friend."

"Yes," said Beth.

"Did you play with Tiffany's sister?" Mum asked me.

She seemed extra nosy.

"No," I said, "but I found this."

I held up the possible whistling kite feather and twirled it.

"Don't bring that inside, please," said Mum. "It could be covered in bird lice."

She tried to take it off me but I dodged her and took it into my room. I opened my cupboard and took out my box marked FEATHERS, and put the feather inside. She didn't try to chase me.

"Come and wash your hands, Jennifer," she said.

Mum came to my door and I closed the cardboard lid.

"You know small children who handle bird feathers can get terrible diseases and some of them have even died," she said.

"Show me the facts," I said.

She made an annoyed noise.

We heard Beth go into the bathroom and turn on the shower. We heard her slide the lock. Mum went away and then came back. The shower had been running for a very long time.

"What are you doing in there?" said Mum with her ear pressed to the door.

"Nothing," Beth said. "I'm coming out now."

"Are you all right?" said Mum. "You look very pale."

Beth looked at her like it was a difficult question. A dangerous question. She crossed her arms. That she hadn't been to Tiffany's house was burning in painful letters all over her skin. She looked at Mum like she thought she already knew. Mum was trying to trick her. She could read the writing.

"I just feel sick, that's all," she said.

She lay down on the bed and let Mum stroke her hair.

I sat in the hallway with a pile of magazines and started ripping out pictures.

"What are you doing?" Mum asked.

"I need pictures of animals with fur," I said. "I told you it was mammal week."

"Well don't rip them," said Mum. "It's too noisy. Cut them with the scissors. Don't you know your sister is unwell?"

I was cutting out a picture of a wombat when Beth sat up and vomited over the side of the bed. The vomiting caused a wild commotion. Mum went running for a bucket. She wanted to call Dr. Cavanaugh. She wanted to take her to the hospital.

"It's so colorful," said Danielle, looking at the spew. The pastel shades of intermingled lolly hearts.

I looked for messages.

"I hope you don't die," I said.

After vomiting she fell asleep. We were allowed to have a look at her before we went to bed. She was sleeping on her side. The moon was gazing serene-faced through the window and illuminating her cheek, with its one mole.

It was only in the morning that I realized part of her was missing.

THE MISSING PART WAS A SECTION OF HER EASY
LAUGH, THE BIT WHERE SHE TILTED HER HEAD BACK,
HELD ONE ARM ACROSS HER STOMACH, AND CLOSED
HER EYES. That had vanished. She had the same
blond hair, the same almond-shaped eyes, the same
constellation of freckles across her nose, the same
mole on her cheek just like mine. But she was different. On the outside no one noticed it. Not Mum. Not
Nanna, who noticed everything. Beth still held me
down and tickled my ribs but sometimes when she
did it she stared right through me at something else.

Beth grew suddenly beautiful. It surprised us, the
speed at which it happened. Her eyes were a deeper
shade of blue. Her lips were rose-petal smooth. She
moved with a new grace. Everywhere people could
not tear their eyes from her or could not look at her
because of her beauty.

The grade 9 boys couldn't look at her. They

averted their eyes when she moved past them like a vision. The grade 9 girls fell at her feet. She sat with them in their tight circles at lunchtime with Miranda at her shoulder like a shadow.

She used their language, copied their wide-eyed innocence. She tried on their giggles and shrieks. She slouched her shoulders. She wore her hair in one plain braid. She tried to blend in but she was different. Everyone smelled it.

Grade 10 boys followed her like a pack of dogs wherever she went. The grade 9 girls watched her in amazement as she dealt with them. How did she know what to do? How did she know how much to give and how much to *not* give? The boys followed her down to the laneway beside the science block. She rested her back against the wall. She brought her braid over her shoulder and touched it as she talked to them. She fiddled with the rubber band like she might undo it.

They waited for her on the footpath outside the bike racks but she rode straight past them with a smile over her shoulder. They followed her and Miranda, a small flotilla, home along the straight highway.

Dardanelles Court became steadily crowded with bikes. Boys rode up and down the cul-de-sac hoping for a glimpse of Beth. Some with older brothers came in cars. They did burnouts at the entrance to Memorial Drive. Marshall Murray unwound his garden hose and threatened to wet them.

"Get," he shouted. "Leave her alone."

Mrs. Irwin called her three girls inside.

Miss Frieda Schmidt opened her venetians with two fingers and shivered.

Mr. O'Malley sang to his new audience; he sang songs about tall ships and sea spray and storms.

At first Mum was unaware. She sat at the table doing Hobbytex. She opened up the blue Hobbytex tin and took out all of her colors and arranged them in a neat line. Then she clipped a T-shirt with the iron-on transfer stencil onto the work frame.

She had made me a T-shirt that said GOING MY WAY, which had a big purple thumb beneath it, and a T-shirt that said DADDY'S LITTLEST ANGEL. She made Danielle a T-shirt that said COOL, which was big enough to go over her Milwaukee back brace, and when Danielle said she wasn't going to wear it Mum said she was extremely ungrateful.

"I don't want a T-shirt that says COOL," said Danielle.

"Well what do you want?" asked Mum.

"One that says WORLD'S BIGGEST RETARD," I said.

"Jennifer," shouted Mum. "Don't say retard."

I couldn't stop laughing.

"Shut up, arsehole," said Danielle.

"Arsehole," said Dad, and that made *him* laugh. He was reading the form guide with a pencil stuck behind his ear.

His T-shirt said WORLD'S BEST DAD.

"Put those scissors away from your mouth," Mum said to me.

"They weren't even near my mouth," I said.

"They were," said Mum. She took the scissors off me.

"That's how children die," she said. "They slip and the scissors go into their brains."

"Cool," said Danielle.

Mum leaned over and opened the blinds. She looked out at the boys on bikes going round and round in circles.

"Where are all these boys from? They don't live in this street."

"They're from the high school," said Danielle. "They're all Beth's boyfriends."

Mum put down the color she was using.

"What are you talking about?"

"They're the boys who love her, only her real boyfriend is Marco," said Danielle.

I started going through the Hobbytex catalog pretending I wasn't interested and that I knew nothing about anything.

"Is he outside?" asked Mum, her voice rising just a little.

A quiet fell over the room. In the quiet I could hear Mum's breathing and the cap of a Hobbytex tube being screwed on and the sound of bicycle wheels circling on pavement.

"I doubt it," said Danielle, casually leafing through her perm scrapbook. "He doesn't go to school anymore."

"Are you listening to this, Jim?" shouted Mum.

Dad looked up from the paper.

"Hey?"

"Where's Beth now?" demanded Mum.

She looked at Danielle and then slapped a hand on the catalog so I had to look up as well.

"Where do you think?" said Danielle.

Beth and Miranda had been riding to Marco's house in the afternoons after school. After the first time it wasn't so bad. It didn't hurt so much. She took three drags on a thin joint in his messy bedroom. She coughed violently and while she coughed he laughed and then she lay back on the bed with her long hair hanging over the edge. Marco kissed her. He didn't shake as much. His breath didn't burn her cheek. He didn't hold her down with one arm across her chest. She watched his neck and his chin moving above her. Afterward he lay on his back beside her with his eyes shut. He reminded her of a statue, he lay so still; he was like a marble saint with a carved face.

After Danielle told on Beth she was supposed to meet us each afternoon to ride home from school. We waited at the back side of Memorial Park, shielding our faces from the sun. Danielle and Kylie always got sick of waiting. Kylie said her mum knew Beth was going to be nothing but trouble. They went up through the rain trees and over the hill into the park.

I rode my bike to Amiens Road and found Beth's bike outside his house. Those afternoons when Beth came out her blue eyes shone. She wore a calm face even though when she got home Mum was going to yell at her and follow her from room to room and tell her that she wasn't going to stand for it, she was going to put an end to it if it was the last thing she ever did.

When Beth saw me waiting outside the house on Amiens Road she sometimes smiled, other times she picked up her bike and started riding like I wasn't even there. She never asked me if I was going to tell. She unwrapped some chewing gum to disguise the cigarette smoke on her breath. She gave me a piece as we rode. When she looked at me she had that same face as when she'd rescued a moth from a spiderweb.

That's how I knew she was saving him.

In March Angela received four new underarm hairs overnight and three pubic hairs. She showed them to me in her bedroom. To be even I told her I had a secret.

"What is it?" she asked, pulling up her knickers.

I told her that I had secretly been to the flat to visit my nanna and I had gone inside and drank water backward from a cup to try and find my voice.

"What if your mum finds out?" she asked.

Angela was a little scared of my nanna. She didn't like the way she always hoarded lots of fruit in her little flat and kept it until it turned. Or the way she had a lot of dead flowers wrapped in bundles from the feasts of saints. And how she always asked Angela what religion she was and then clicked her tongue when Angela said she didn't know. Angela made a face.

At home when I passed Mum in the hallway I wondered if she could see in my face that I had been to Nanna's flat. If she could she didn't show it. I wondered if Angela could see in my face that I had torn up the Australian cricket team cards that had taken Angela and I weeks to collect. Tearing them made me feel better for a little while but afterward I had to worry about what I would tell her when she asked to see them, especially Rodney Marsh, who was her favorite. I decided that I was going to tell her my mother threw them out because she was Crazy with Grief, which is exactly what Aunty Cheryl said was the reason we had to go to her place each night for dinner.

Angela changed the subject from my nanna back to her.

"Don't worry about not having any hair yet," she said. "Everyone's puberty is unique."

She had read that in *The Life Cycle Library,* which Mum bought from the one-armed encyclopedia salesman when she was trying to make sense of Beth. *The Life Cycle Library* contains six thin volumes and was for Young People like Beth and Very Frightened Parents. Mum had unwrapped them and placed them in a neat pile beside her bed. When Angela and I wanted to read them we crept in softly, even though she wasn't in the room, and took one volume at a time.

Angela always wanted volume 1 because it had a large section on a boy's anatomy. She always said oh my god look at this and her cheeks went red even though it was the same diagram of a penis that we'd looked at one hundred times before. In volume 1 of *The Life Cycle Library* all the boys had side parts and all the girls wore checkered skirts and Alice bands. None smoked Winfield Greens and faintly glowed. *The Life Cycle Library* was full of underlined paragraphs and words from when Mum was trying to understand just what was going wrong with Beth.

Mrs. Popovitch came into Angela's bedroom. She asked me how my mother was doing. She said she'd seen her trying to hang out the washing and she was just skin and bones. I told her Mum couldn't eat very much. She put the food in her mouth and then it made her feel sick. Sometimes she made a vomiting noise, a bit like a cat coughing up a fur ball. I did an example of it.

"Oh, darling," said Mrs. Popovitch. "That's terrible."

"She doesn't wear lipstick anymore either," said Angela.

Mum had always worn lipstick. Lipsticks with names like Mystic Mauve, Melon Shine, and Deep-Sea Coral that lived in straight lines on her dressing table. Mrs. Popovitch didn't wear lipstick. She said she didn't believe in it. She dyed her hair red sometimes with henna but she never put makeup on her face.

"And she doesn't . . . you know," I added, and pointed to my hair and made a curling motion. I couldn't bring myself to say it. It made me sadder than everything.

Mum had always curled her hair. For a normal day she just used five or six big rollers but for a dance she used nearly twenty. She put them in after breakfast and they stayed there all day. She wore a yellow scarf around her head and practiced dance moves in the kitchen while she made our school lunches.

We were allowed to unpin them at the end of the long wait, when the sun was going down and great drifts of galahs were crossing over the house toward the creek. Even though we tried to savor the uncurling, sometimes we rushed. Somewhere on her head was the last curl and each of us wanted it to be ours.

Mrs. Popovitch prepared a tea party for Angela and me. She brought it on a tray into Angela's room with the red velvet bedspread. There was real tea in a little teapot and real sugar in a sugar bowl and real biscuits. Mum would have never let us have boiled water at a tea party. She would have said that's how hundreds of children got scalded and scarred for life and had to wear masks over their faces to hide their disfigurement.

"You need a haircut, darling," Mrs. Popovitch said, and pushed aside my bangs so she could see my eyes.

When she was gone Angela opened up *The Book of Clues.* She looked through the list of things in the box: the ballet shoes, the tough girl's black rubber-band bracelet, the half-a-broken-heart necklace, the advertisement for secretarial school, the blond braid, the hair combs, the address in leftward-slanting script.

"We've only crossed out one thing so far," said Angela.

"I know," I said.

We drank our tea.

I recited "Eye of the Tiger" like a poem.

"Try and sing it," Angela said.

"I can't."

"Try."

"I can't."

Angela sang it. She had a weak quavery voice but she tried her hardest. "We've only got four months until the Talent Quest," said Angela when she had finished.

THE GRADE 10 GIRLS FROM THE PARTY ON AMIENS
ROAD WERE CALLED THE SHELLEYS BECAUSE TWO
HAD THE FIRST NAME MICHELLE AND ONE WAS
ROCHELLE AND THE LEADER, DEIDRE, HAD THE LAST
NAME SCHELBACH.

The Shelleys didn't like the way Beth came to
school more beautiful each day. It hurt their eyes to
look at her. They gave Beth a bruise in Memorial Park
on the way to school. I was there. In return for the
bruise I saw Beth perform a small miracle. After it was
performed we all pretended that we hadn't noticed it.

Beth and I wheeled our bikes into the park
through the turnstile gate. Danielle had to walk beside us because of her Milwaukee back brace, which
glinted in the sun. Kylie was waiting for us on her
trampoline and she jumped the fence.

"I've told you not to jump the fence," shouted
Aunty Cheryl. "You'll break a bone."

Kylie ignored her mother. She showed Beth her new charm for her new charm bracelet, which was an anchor.

"Do you like it?" asked Kylie.

"It's OK," said Beth.

"Do you think I should've got the roller skate?" asked Kylie.

"Probably," said Beth. "It may've been trendier."

Beth was trying not to encourage Kylie even though Mum said she should let her hang around at school.

Already at the top of the hill we could see the group of girls beneath the trees. One girl was swinging on the swing. It was not ordinary for other girls to be in our park first thing in the morning. The only girl that was ever in our park was Angela, waiting for us. She was nowhere to be seen.

I sang the beginning of "Gypsy Rover" before Danielle told me to shut up.

"I think you should've got the dice," Danielle said.

"You're not even at high school yet," said Kylie.

"Doesn't mean she can't make a suggestion," said Beth.

"Can you get an eagle charm?" I asked.

"No," said Beth and Danielle together.

"You can get a bluebird," said Kylie.

"Maybe a blue-winged kookaburra?" I said.

"You're weird," said Kylie.

The blue-winged kookaburra was my seventh-favorite bird after (1) the wedge-tailed eagle, (2) the brahminy kite, (3) the letter-winged kite, (4) the wandering albatross, (5) the black-shouldered kite, and, (6) the whistling kite.

I hadn't ever seen a wandering albatross, although Nanna had. I had never seen a brahminy kite. I may have seen a black-shouldered kite. I had definitely seen a letter-winged kite and a whistling kite and the wedge-tailed eagle. I'd only ever seen the eagle from a great distance and once through the car window feeding on a dead kangaroo. I couldn't say why I loved them so much.

Once Mum bought me Skipper, who was Barbie's sister, so that I could be normal. She said I had to leave Mr. Edgerton, who was the president of the Outback Bird-Watching Association, which I was not allowed to join until I was at least twelve, alone.

As we got closer the girl stopped the swing by running her foot along the dirt. She stood up.

"Hey," she said.

It wasn't a hello hey.

"What?" said Beth.

"We want to talk to you."

"What about?" said Beth.

The girl was Deidre Schelbach. She was the

Queen of the Tough Girls. She had a sweet face with soft brown skin and a little nub of a nose but it was all ruined by her yellow hair with a stripe of black roots down the center and two or three teeth that were turning brown. When she started shouting her words were accompanied by a very bad smell. Deidre wore her high school uniform very short with her top two buttons undone. Her skinny legs protruded from her round body. She wore flip-flops instead of school shoes. Seven thick black rubber-band bracelets adorned her left arm.

"About the party," said Deidre.

Kylie's two buckteeth made a sucking noise on her bottom lip that she only ever made when she was nervous. Deidre reached forward and grabbed Beth's bag from her shoulder in one quick movement and threw it behind her onto the grass. The act produced a chorus of snickers from the other girls, Deidre's handmaidens, who had moved forward to watch.

"Don't you understand English?" said Deidre.

Beth didn't say anything.

"You should have kept your hands off him," said Deidre. "We bet you're sorry now."

Deidre always said we. She never said I. She said we know what you're up to. We know you think you're better than anyone else. We're going to smash your head in if you do it again. She said we know you've been going round to his place. We know you're a little prick teaser. Do you know what happens to little prick teasers?

"Go to school," Beth said to us.

We kept standing where we were. Our feet couldn't move. They had put down roots into the long unmowed grass of the park.

"Go," she said.

"Shut up," shouted Deidre, and the smell of her mouth drifted past in a cloud.

"You didn't listen to what we said, did you?" said Deidre.

She grabbed Beth by the top of her dress and looked around for something to push her against because she had obviously done it before.

"When someone says hands off, you keep your hands off," she shouted.

She pushed Beth into the trunk of one of the figs and both of them stumbled a little in among all the roots, which spread out around the tree like rays. And the tree seemed very sad to be involved in such a thing and it hung its dark head over them.

Deidre held Beth's neck with one hand, pressing her into the trunk. The free hand slapped her face from time to time. They were big, open-handed slaps.

"Don't you understand English?" asked Deidre again.

"Leave her alone," shouted Danielle.

The handmaidens turned their eyes from the slapping to Danielle.

"Shut up, cripple," said one.

Tears filled Danielle's eyes. Kylie opened and shut her fists.

Deidre stopped slapping Beth because Beth wasn't fighting back. Beth looked resigned to her fate. She was staring straight past Deidre at the slope of the park and the sky. Even if she could have got past Deidre there were the others and Danielle had the brace and Kylie wasn't a good runner.

Deidre was built like a barrel. She pressed her chest against Beth's. She was going to squeeze her to death.

"See this," said Deidre, holding up her fist. "I'll use this next time. Then you won't be so pretty."

It felt like the end of it but I wasn't sure. I kept looking at the grass hoping it was over. I had a feeling I was going to wet my pants. Also my heart was beating very fast and I thought I might die like Nanna said Grandad did, bang, right there at the kitchen table.

I heard Kylie and Danielle let out a quiet collective sigh and I looked up. Deidre was releasing her grip but then Beth smiled. She took her eyes off the sky and smiled at Deidre. It was only a small smile but it turned Deidre's face purple with rage. Beth's eyes wandered all over Deidre's face like she was looking for something. She looked very sad but she kept looking and the looking made Deidre angrier and all the angriness made Beth look even sadder. And the sadness and angriness increased.

"Don't look at me like that," said Deidre quietly.

But Beth didn't stop. The sadness came out of Beth like light.

"I said don't," said Deidre.

This time there was a whining note to her voice. She backed away one step from the tree. Beth reached her hand toward her. With her first two fingers she touched Deidre on the forehead. Deidre looked shocked. Her mouth opened up. A deep sound, a moan and a sigh, rose up from her chest. Beth removed her hand like she had been burned. Deidre's fist smacked hard into her face.

"Get out of here," Deidre shouted.

She shouted it like she was in pain. She went down onto the ground onto her knees and held her head in her hands. Her handmaidens moved toward her but she screamed at them also. Beth, holding her right cheek in her hand, didn't say anything. We followed her.

I looked back at the beginning of the dirt track that led to the back side of the park. The girls were gathering around Deidre in a circle. She was still on her knees and leaning forward with her head in her hands. From where I stood it looked like she was praying. She looked very small in a very big day. The sky stretched upward toward heaven. The grass bent over and stood up behind her in waves. The hot wind carried the sound of her tears.

At school the teachers begged Beth to tell them who had hurt her but she wouldn't tell them. She said she had fallen on the basketball court and hit her head. They rang our mother but she was with Aunty Cheryl shopping so she wasn't at home. The school nurse examined her and made her look upward and downward and follow her fingers.

Mrs. Simpson was the deputy principal who dealt with girl matters and Beth was brought before her. Mrs. Simpson began by interrogating her because she knew that there was something more to the story. She asked her quick questions to see if she could make Beth slip up. Beth kept to her story. She had been running because she was late for class. She had chosen the shortcut across the oval because it was quicker. She had tripped on the rock, it was flat and shiny, the type you can use to skip across water. She had fallen face-first.

Mrs. Simpson tried to think about more difficult questions. They began to form inside her head and then disappeared.

"I still think we must contact your mother," she stammered.

"Can I ring her at lunchtime?" asked Beth.

"Yes," said Mrs. Simpson, who could not disagree. "I suppose that will be all right."

Mrs. Simpson didn't know how good Beth was becoming at lying.

The bruise grew on Beth's cheekbone. She tried to hide it with her hair. She didn't want to go home in the afternoon and have Mum see it. We waited for her on Campbell Road in front of the caravan park for the last leg of the ride home.

"Go away," she said.

"Why?" I said.

"Because I'm not coming with you."

"Mum said you have to ride home with us every afternoon," said Danielle.

"Aren't you listening to what she said? She's not going home with you," said Miranda.

"Who asked you?" said Danielle.

"You're not even related to us," said Kylie.

"Meaning what, spaz?" asked Miranda.

"Don't call her that," said Beth.

"Take it back," I said.

"Yeah retract it," said Kylie.

"God, why can't anyone be happy?" said Danielle, who was the most miserable person in the world since she got her Milwaukee back brace and all she ever did was draw sad pictures and write sad poems.

Beth watched us all arguing and then she pushed away on her bike along Campbell Road toward the highway.

"Beth," shouted Miranda. "Do you want me to come?"

"She would have asked you if she did, wouldn't she?" Kylie said as she crossed the road into the back side of the park.

I rode behind Beth all the way to the highway but she had a good head start.

"Go home," she shouted over her shoulder.

The denim-colored highway stretched out of town in a straight line. She didn't ride on the soft red dust shoulder but right on the pavement. She only got off when a car or truck was coming. I had to wait awhile before I could cross.

"Go home," she shouted again when I crossed.

"No," I shouted back.

She sped up. She stood up on the pedals of her bike.

"Where are you going?" I shouted.

She rode past the last turnoff to Memorial South. A road train went past and the smell of cattle hung in the air after it was gone. She didn't answer me. We went past the entrances to the half-built streets of

Sunset Place. She rode straight past them on the highway heading out of town.

She turned off the highway onto a road that curved toward the train tracks. It was the road that led to the tailings dams. There were lots of signs that said MINE PROPERTY—KEEP OUT but no gates. Beth ignored the signs and kept riding.

"We're not allowed here," I shouted. "It's called trespassing."

My legs ached and my mouth was dry. She stayed ahead of me the whole way, only looking behind her every now and again and shaking her head when she saw me. The pavement ended and the road became dirt.

The few trees there were thinned out even further. The trees had leaves that were curled and brown. Some had no leaves at all. They held up their bare branches and the bark hung in long dark strips like flayed skin. Even the grass was dead. It had turned white and fallen out of the ground at its roots. There were no birds in the sky.

Finally, the chain-wire fence that surrounded the mine dam appeared and behind it, glittering, the expanse of blue. Beth dropped her bike to the ground and walked toward the fence. She rested her whole body against it, her fingers curled through the wire. When she turned to face me she had the imprint of the fence on her unbruised cheek.

"You can't swim," I said.

"I know," she said.

"It's poisonous."

"I know."

"How do the birds know not to drink it?"

"Why did you have to follow me?"

"I didn't want you to be lonely."

"I'm not lonely."

"This is a long way from home."

"It's not really that far."

She sat down in the red dirt with her back against the fence. The poisonous blue lake sparkled behind her. She folded her hands over her knees and put her head down on them. She started to cry.

A very hot wind was blowing. It felt like it came right out of the red center. It scoured the landscape. It rolled the grass that had fallen out of the ground in bundles along the dirt road. It spun the dirt in small circles for something to do. It rustled the flayed skin of the trees. It blew our hair over our faces. It made me feel scared.

"Don't cry," I said.

"I'm not," she said, lifting up her head and wiping the tears from her eyes.

She had a look on her face. It was the first time I ever saw it. Later she would always wear this face. This stillness would steal into her features. It wouldn't matter if she was hurt or happy. Her cheeks and nose and forehead were quiet. Her mouth was slightly parted. She was thinking. She was thinking and she was listening. It was like she was trying to work out a difficult puzzle.

She squatted and with a stick wrote her name in the dirt.

ELIZABETH JANE DAY.

"Everything feels wrong," she said.

"Here?"

"Everywhere."

"Why?"

"I don't know."

The sun was falling down below the hills fast. There were storm clouds building in the west. Big swollen clouds piling on top of each other but which would come to nothing. She stood up. The wind was already sweeping away her name but she kicked the dirt also so it was erased. There was nothing to say we had been there. We rode back along the road toward town.

A phoenix usually lived to be five hundred years old. It's quite easy to poison someone if you have hemlock. Some deep-sea fish have lights in their tails. Eagles are from the order Falconiformes. Anthea Long was descended from a convict. She did a morning talk on it.

"Slow down," said Mrs. O'Malley. "You're making me dizzy."

The rain clouds had come to nothing. A quick panic of wind, a sudden rush of rain.

"The earth is one hundred and forty-six million kilometers from the sun."

"Is that right?"

"I read it in a book."

"It must be true then," Mrs. O'Malley said. She took out her bra-strap hankie and wiped her forehead. "If only it would rain and rain and rain."

From across the road at our house there was still a lot of shouting going on. I could hear Mum's footsteps thumping up and down the hall.

"Trouble?" asked Mrs. O'Malley.

"Yes," I said.

"Come round the back," said Mrs. O'Malley, "and I'll tell you something new."

When the bruise was found all hell broke out. Mum found it even though Beth tried to hide it with her hair and by moving very fast past the kitchen door. Mum pounced out after her. She had her Continuous Coral lipstick on and her hair in curlers because she was going to a dance. She stalked Beth down the hall.

"God," she screamed when she saw the bruise even though she told Nanna she didn't believe in him.

"It's nothing," said Beth.

"Nothing?" screamed Mum. "Nothing?"

"I fell over on the basketball courts," Beth said.

"Why didn't you show me?" asked Mum. "If you did it on the basketball courts you would have showed me."

Everyone stayed quiet waiting for the answer. Danielle with her pencil poised about her sketchbook, me standing in the hallway tracing a toe on the gold in the linoleum.

"Who did it?" asked Mum.

"No one did it," said Beth.

"What's going on with you?" shouted Mum.

"Nothing."

It was their usual conversation.

"I'm really disappointed about how you've turned out," shouted Mum, like Beth was a slightly burned biscuit.

"Leave me alone," said Beth. She lay facedown on her bed.

"Let me help you," pleaded Mum.

But she only stood at Beth's bedroom door wringing her hands and crying because she didn't seem to know what to do.

Don't be silly, what were you doing out in the desert? Sit up. Show me this bruise. We will invoke the saints and angels who will protect us.

This is what Nanna would have said.

She knew the saints and angels who guarded against storms and strife and disasters. She knew who protected bicycle riders against animal attacks and helped find lost things. She knew which angels to call upon.

I wondered if there was an angel for confused insect-saving girls who chewed their nails and suddenly didn't feel so right inside their skin.

After my first secret visit to Nanna I told myself I probably wasn't going back. But whenever I closed my eyes I saw her all alone in the flat with the fly buzzing against the window. So I visited her most afternoons on the way home from school. I brought her food: a piece of bread that had wilted in my lunch box, a lone potato, an apple. Anything I could steal from home. I gave her the food even when Uncle Paavo had started to bring her some groceries once a week. Nanna did not leave her little flat.

Sometimes Angela came with me. She looked a little frightened when we opened up the sliding door because Nanna had all her curtains pulled and sheets put over the top of the curtains and it made the flat very shadowy. And inside it was very still. You could hear every small noise, like Angela's belly rumbling or the click of Nanna's lighter as she lit up a Craven "A." Angela also brought Nanna food because I'd told her that she was starving, usually some powdered sherbet or a white paper bag full of lolly teeth. Nanna said thank you very politely.

"I have been thinking," she said once she had kissed my head. "What if you performed the drinking from the wrong side of the cup with a fizzy drink. Lemonade perhaps or sarsaparilla."

She didn't have any lemonade or sarsaparilla in her little flat. Angela and I sat in the tiny living room side by side on the old sofa. All the dusty Madonnas held their palms up empty-handed. The ceramic dogs smiled.

"Each day I pray, Jennifer," said Nanna. "First I speak to the Archangel Michael because he has protected us this far. I pray only for today. Not for what has passed. Then I ask for the blessed saints Felicity and Matilde, who are the protectors of mothers grieving and mothers who have lost their babies, and Our Lady of Sorrows, who is the protector of those whose hearts are overflowing with sadness."

The apple I brought that day was blood-red. It sat on the table in front of us. I knew she was being especially religious because Angela was there.

"Tell me, both of you, can you feel them?" asked Nanna.

"Who?" I said.

"The angels."

I tried to feel them. I closed my eyes. Angela

closed hers. I tried to imagine them crowded in the room with us.

"Not really," I said.

"I'm not sure," said Angela in case she got into trouble.

But Nanna didn't seem upset.

"I will tell you the truth now," she said. "After the lake Beth came to me, you know. The sliding door was working well so I didn't hear it opening. I was sleeping in this chair because it was the afternoon. Do you know what she said to me?"

Instead I wished she could have told us about when she first came to town all those years ago. When the mine hills were still red not blackened and the men's barracks were still being hammered together and everywhere makeshift houses were being built out of gidgee gum trees and canvas in haphazard streets that meandered beside the creek and gullies.

"She said at the lake she saw an angel."

Angela chewed on a fingernail. I remembered Mum rising up from the sofa.

I don't believe you, you witch.

"She said it was after she fainted. It didn't have arms or legs or a face, only lightness."

I didn't say anything because Mum said that was the way you didn't encourage her.

"Beth said, 'Do you believe me?' I said, 'Would you lie about such a thing as this?' Beth said, 'But maybe I only imagined it.' She said afterward it never seemed real, only like something she had dreamed of a long time ago. But it filled up everything with light and afterward everything was beautiful for some time. This is what she said to me."

"Then what?" I asked.

"Then she said her head ached and I gave her a teaspoon of Alka-Seltzer and she lay down on the sofa right there and slept, curled up, and when she woke she did not ever mention it again."

I opened my mouth with a question but it was only half formed.

I imagined what desert angels might look like. They'd have the wings of hawks and robes the color of spinifex after the rain.

I didn't say it. I wished we could watch television. I wished I had never come or brought the food to save her.

When I was stealing the food from the kitchen cupboards I thought it was like the time Angela and I stole the food to keep the stray kitten alive and it had worked for three weeks until I grew too bold and was pouring milk straight into a bowl in the kitchen and I was caught red-handed. And the kitten went to live at Angela's after great floods of tears and later it had a litter of deformed kittens, which caused more sorrow, and Mr. Popovitch said all that cat ever did was cause grief.

And I thought Nanna was similar and a very strange pet to try to keep alive. Instead of growing bigger she would grow crazier. And then I thought where would *she* be taken when someone found me out?

"Be honest now, Jennifer," she said quietly. "Tell me what she said to you."

I felt Angela shiver beside me. I saw the goose bumps on her arm.

"Nothing," I said.

"Nothing?"

"Nothing."

"Nothing at all?"

"Ever."

She pressed her back hump into the sofa in a dejected way. She needed miracles. All the light shining and whispered golden words floating out of mouths and rainbow-colored angel wings and heavenly voices.

"I don't believe you," Nanna said.

5 DARDANELLES COURT

WHEN EVERYTHING WAS CLEAN, WHEN SHE HAD VAC-
UUMED AND WIPED DOWN THE PLASTIC SOFA COVERS
AND DISINFECTED THE KITCHEN, FRIEDA SOMETIMES
ALLOWED HERSELF A GUILTY PLEASURE. This small
pleasure was a memory. Afterward she felt dirty just
thinking it but she told herself it was normal. It was
perfectly normal to have memories. All people had
them. The memory was of her sister, Greta, and, in
particular, Greta's skin.

She didn't know where Greta was now. She had
been living in an apartment in Munich last. Frieda
had phoned there but Greta had moved on. The man
that answered the phone had a thick accent.
Antwerp, he said. Frieda could smell the dirt on him
through the line. She sterilized the phone using
steam.

She had been ten, her sister nearly twelve. It was

sultry, a day when curtains of rain slid across the cane fields and glided over the rambling farmhouse with its peeling skin of paint and its banks of rotting wooden louvers. They lay side by side on an old daybed, downstairs beneath the house, where their mother said it was cooler. Everywhere outside it was green and dripping; raindrops quivered on the ends of leaves. This was how she remembered it: greenery, wetness, and her sister tracing a slow circle in her palm.

They could hear their mother up in the house. She was running from room to room and shrieking with laughter. Their father was chasing her round and round through the twists and turns of the old house. They listened to them run through the kitchen above them, crockery rattling and chattering, along the long hallway, in and out of bedrooms. He chased her, clattering up and down the sleepouts, down the back steps onto the wet grass, and with wild laughter back again stampeding through the house. There were no neighbors to hear.

"Now you do it to me," said Greta.

Greta lifted her own hand so Frieda could begin.

Frieda touched her fingertip to her sister's palm. She drew a circle first. Then a star. The letter G. A heart. An eye with eyelashes.

The footsteps went thundering past upstairs.

"That feels funny," said Greta.

"Can you tell what I'm drawing?"

"Only if I close my eyes."

"What's this?"

"Is it . . . a horseshoe?"

"No."

She remembered laughing. Her sister's skin, darker than her own, the type that browns to a honey color, could not read the letters she traced. The smooth firm palm was blind.

"You haven't got very clever skin," Frieda said. "Try this one."

She drew a house with her fingertip, a square with a triangle roof. A door. One window. A chimney.

Upstairs, the rumble of feet passed overhead, a long squeal of laughter.

"I can't tell," said Greta.

"Silly, it's a house."

"Let's draw at the same time on each other," said Greta.

They crossed arms at the elbow and drew circles on each other's palms.

"I can't tell which hand I'm drawing with anymore," said Frieda after a while.

"I feel like my hand is yours and your hand is mine," said Greta.

A loud crash upstairs. The footsteps stopped.

"Gus?" said their mother. "Gus?"

Frieda could not be touched after that. After her

father's funeral the mourners walked along the dirt road to their house and it seemed to her that their purpose for coming was to touch. How her skin had ached inside her sleeves. Heavy-handed women in hats and gloves demanding her to stand still before them, holding her. Oh yes, they said, oh yes, she has her father's eyes all right.

She did not like to be patted or tapped or poked or brushed or tickled or scratched. She did not like the friction of skin. For a while she thought her sister had stolen something from her with that last game. Greta let the heavy-handed ladies hold her and wipe the large glistening tears from her cheeks. This is how she remembered it: greenery, her sister's skin and tears. Later she knew, of course, that it was irrational. Nothing had been stolen from her. Part of her had simply ceased to be.

She could not be kissed.

"If you cannot kiss how will you marry?" said Greta, who later ran away from home, then her husband, then the country.

"It cannot be helped," said Frieda.

She could not bear to be handled.

The red-haired psychiatrist with the pale freckled face said Frieda had both separation and intimacy issues. He ran his hands through his hair as he talked and shut his eyes. Just being opposite him made her skin crawl.

She hurt no one by being untouchable. Was it such a bad thing? she asked Greta when they still spoke by phone. Of course not, said Greta, you are who you are. From her voice Frieda could tell Greta was thinking of something else completely; she could hear her filing her nails.

After their father's funeral the landlord said they could have five weeks in the house. He knew their mother couldn't do any work around the place, but he wouldn't kick them out just like that. But he had to make a living what with the cane crush coming. Her mother spoke softly to them then. She whispered orders: stand up tall, you must not cry, we will be all right. Their mother sat on the back steps looking out across the cane fields because she could not bear to be inside.

When they left Frieda wondered would the crashing footsteps go round and round the house forever. That wild, merry game of chase that they never mentioned and then left behind.

Years later at her mother's funeral she remembered Greta had tried to kiss her on the cheek. She had moved just in time; she was skillful at such avoidances.

"I'm sorry," Frieda said when she saw the hurt it caused.

"You're a freak," said Greta, "with a capital *F*."

Later Greta said it was only a word. It was when

she was feeling remorseful, a year later. She had left the commune she'd been living on and needed a place to stay.

"It was only a word, Frieda," she cajoled. "I could have chosen any: strange, oddball, loony tunes. All right, I shouldn't have said it, it was wrong."

But "freak" had already settled through the cracks in Frieda's skin.

When she first came to Dardanelles Court the house was brand-new and she didn't have to worry about others having left behind their dirty finger-prints and stale breath. She was in her late thirties by then. She had a good job in the technical library where she filed dead books into the compactors and mended spines and covered new acquisitions neatly and precisely.

When she spoke at work her voice, to her own ears, sounded brittle and unused. She hated the sound of it. Her face flushed each time she spoke. She preferred the silence of her small sterile home. She was considered quiet and strange but harmless.

And she felt it was too late to change.

What she missed about her touchable life was her sister, her sister's skin, that day when they had drawn on each other's open palms and for an instant be-come one another. If only she could go backward, pick over the bones, sift through things, and uncover that point, she would be changed and whole again.

But she knew that was irrational. That part of her had ceased to be.

"Do you know where I can find her in Antwerp? Did she leave a number or address?" she asked the man in Munich over the phone.

"I have no idea, lady," he replied.

And she knew that Greta was gone for good.

After she had slipped into the memory of her sister's skin and out again she sat on her plastic-covered sofa and rocked slowly. She said I only have myself to blame.

In April Dad tried to get Mum out of bed but she wouldn't budge except to go to the toilet and sometimes make herself a cup of tea. She didn't have any showers. She smelled like tears.

When I wanted to talk to her I had to kneel beside her bed.

"After RINSE do I turn it to SPIN?" I whispered.

"Yes," she said quietly, looking at me with her see-through blue eyes.

"Have you got any money for the cafeteria?" I asked.

"No," she said, and then after a while, when I was nearly at her bedroom door, "I'm a bad mother."

"No you're not," I said.

"I am."

Dr. Cavanaugh was called and appeared at our front screen door pulling up his blue walk socks.

"Here's the littlest one," he said to me even though I was nearly eleven.

Dad and Aunty Cheryl led him down the hallway into Mum's bedroom. Mum shouted at him. She said the f-word. Dad came back down the hallway and sat in his recliner shaking his head.

"Come on, Jean," said Aunty Cheryl. "Don't be like that."

Aunty Cheryl had more makeup on than usual. She'd done her hair. I saw her looking at herself in the glass doors of the buffet.

Dr. Cavanaugh stayed in the room for a while. We could hear him talking very quietly. Mum saved up some more f-words until the end of the conversation.

"I don't know what to say," said Dr. Cavanaugh when he came back into the living room. "I think we need to let nature run its course. Grief is a very powerful emotion."

Dad looked at him with his teardrop birthmark and black rings beneath his sea-green eyes.

"She's not eating," said Aunty Cheryl.

Her hand with its ringless fingers rested at her throat. She held her mascara-coated eyelashes open very wide.

"What about the children?" he asked. "Does she respond to them?"

Danielle and I were at the dining room table pretending to do our homework, only Danielle was

144

drawing a sad-faced girl and I was thinking about something bigger to break. A bike maybe or a car.

They started whispering after that.

Mum stayed in bed.

I didn't need to worry about her accidentally seeing me ride to Nanna's flat. Angela suggested we look inside the box again.

"Why?" I said.

"So we know exactly what we are looking for."

"I don't think so," I said. "Let's look for wild horses instead."

"You can't give up."

"I'm not giving up."

"You are. I can tell you are."

"Well what do you want to know?" I said.

"Tell me about the ballet shoes."

"That's boring."

"The half a broken heart then."

All through March and April Beth lied about ballet. Lying had become much easier for her. The lies didn't press on her stomach so much and make her throw up. She lied a lot. She lied boldly. Sometimes she lied like she wanted to get caught.

Her lying is a fact. It can be verified by anyone because in the end everybody was affected by her lies. For example, Aunty Cheryl saw Beth riding along the highway on a school day and stopped the car and asked her where she was going. Beth said she had two free study periods in the afternoon on Fridays and didn't need to be at school.

"Well why doesn't Kylie ever get these free periods?" said Aunty Cheryl.

"I do art, Aunty Cheryl, and Kylie does all the hard subjects," said Beth.

It slipped off her tongue easily, she smiled, and there was no stomach sickness. Aunty Cheryl puffed out her chest.

The next time Aunty Cheryl came for Sunday lunch Beth remembered what she had said and called Kylie into her room and told her that if Aunty Cheryl brought the free periods up she had to agree that it was so.

"No way," said Kylie.

"I'll tell her you know where the picture of Des is," said Beth.

Des was Kylie's father who'd left before she was born. His photo was hidden behind a baby photo of Kylie next to Aunty Cheryl's bed. Sometimes Kylie said Des was very rich and one day he'd be coming back to get her. Other times she said he was nothing but a mongrel.

When Beth blackmailed her with that Kylie started breathing in and out of her nose.

"These arty-farty subjects give the girls a lot of free time, don't they?" said Aunty Cheryl at lunch.

"I don't know," said Mum. "You don't do art, do you, Beth?"

Beth rolled her eyes.

"Of course I do art."

"I thought you had to choose between art and typing?" said Mum.

"They changed stuff around," said Beth.

"Where are you keeping all the masterpieces?" asked Uncle Paavo.

"Remember when you used to draw?" said Nanna to Uncle Paavo. "When you were just a boy."

"I never drew," said Uncle Paavo.

"You did," said Nanna. "I remember it. You drew machines. Cars and such."

Kylie eyeballed Beth from across the table. So did Danielle because she was the artist in the family.

So Aunty Cheryl was affected by the lie and Kylie and Danielle. And Mum was too, although she didn't believe for a minute the part about the free periods and threatened to find out, and Uncle Paavo, who every Sunday lunch asked to see a masterpiece, and Nanna, because it made her remember Uncle Paavo before he became very serious and old, and, in the end, even the art teacher, Miss Proust, who was among the teachers at the funeral and who introduced herself as Miss Proust the art teacher: "I never taught your daughter but I remember her well."

Beth made me lie about ballet. She said she'd tell

Mum eventually that she wasn't going to the classes anymore. All I had to do was tell Miss Elise Slater that Beth was sick. Beth said it was simple. She said it was an easy thing to do.

On ballet days I felt sick in my stomach as soon as the school bell rang. I felt like vomiting all the way home in the redback panel van. While we put on our leotards I bent over double and said I couldn't go.

"Don't be stupid," said Beth. "You just have to do it one more time."

"I'm going to go to hell," I said.

"You're already going to hell anyway," said Beth.

We left home like we were going to ride to ballet. At the end of the road Beth asked me if I remembered what I had to say. I told her to shut up. She went left so she could ride the long way around to Amiens Road. I went right so I could go to ballet. Miss Elise Slater looked sad when I said Beth wasn't coming again because of her concussion from falling over on the basketball courts. Miss Elise used it as an example to tell the class. She said our bodies were our instruments and we needed to look after them.

After ballet I had to ride to Amiens Road and wait outside the house. I didn't go into the yard but just waited on the footpath. I didn't like the house with its blank expression. All of its blinds were pulled down like closed eyes. The front fly screen gaped like an open mouth. I tried to look in but all I could see was darkness.

It seemed to take forever for Beth to come out. I rode in circles on the road. The Nana Mouskouri lady came out to talk to me.

"Here you are again," she said.

"I'm just waiting for my sister," I said.

"How old is your sister, sweetie?" she asked.

"Thirteen," I said. "I think when she's fourteen she might be going to get a tape recorder for her birthday."

"That's lovely," said the lady.

She asked what my last name was and which schools we went to. The lady seemed very interested in us until Beth came out of the house and then she stopped talking and went inside. Beth told me not to talk to her again. The boy called Marco came out onto the steps to watch her go. He didn't wave. He sat on the steps and watched her walk down the driveway toward me. She climbed onto her bike.

She smelled like Winfield Green cigarettes. Her face looked tired. She opened up her hessian bag and looked for some chewing gum. Saving Marco made her eyes so blue that you had to turn away from them. Her face glowed the way it had the day at the lake.

Miss Elise rang Mum the following week because

she was so worried about Beth's concussion. All hell broke loose again. Beth and I had to go to the studio to apologize for our dishonesty. When we walked across the wooden floor toward Miss Elise I saw she had a Kleenex in her hand.

Beth spoke very well. She looked Miss Elise right in the eyes. She told her she didn't feel like dancing anymore but she never should have lied about it. She should have told the truth. I couldn't believe my ears. When it was my turn I couldn't get my words untangled. I said it was wrong, I was sorry, she made me and I didn't mean it, all in the same sentence. Miss Elise looked at me with a cranky face while she waited for me to finish.

In the end she still loved Beth, even though it was Beth who was leaving. Even though it was Beth who organized the lying. Miss Elise put her hand out to touch Beth's face. She touched her on the cheek where the old bruise was nearly completely faded and only the slightest trace of yellow remained.

"You should still do some sort of physical activity," said Miss Elise, bringing the tissue up to her eyes. "I would hate to see your lovely physique suffer."

That night I saw Beth pack away her dancing things. She put them all in a box: her leotards, her ballet shoes, her tights, her leg warmers, her black happy shoes. I thought she should look sad but she didn't. It was just another part of herself that she gave away without looking back. She looked almost glad that it was over, that she was leaving it all behind.

"You're not going anywhere ever again until you tell me exactly where you've been going when you weren't going to ballet," said Mum.

It was a very long sentence for something she already knew.

"Is it that boy called Marco?" she shouted. "Tell me where he lives. You're not leaving this house until you tell me where he lives."

She went outside and shouted at the boys riding backward and forward past our house.

"Get lost," she said. "We're not interested. There's nothing here for you."

Mr. and Mrs. O'Malley came out onto their patio and sat down in their fold-out chairs to watch. Frieda Schmidt, at her letterbox, scuttled back inside her lonely house.

"Jean," said Dad, but quietly, under his breath.

"Do you understand?" she said to Beth when she came inside. "Never again."

New rules were going to be laid down. Thou shalt not wear makeup. Thou shalt not wear short shorts. Thou shalt not go anywhere without your cousin Kylie. Thou shalt not use your younger sisters to lie for you. Thou shalt not have a boyfriend. Thou shalt not have friends who lead you astray.

"We didn't pay all that money to Miss Elise Slater for you to go off and do whatever you want. Jim. Tell her. Did we?"

"It's a lot of dosh, sweetheart," said Dad, looking up from the horse paper. "You shouldn't have just skipped."

He winked at Beth when Mum wasn't looking.

"Great," said Mum because she could sense things even if she couldn't see them.

Beth wasn't allowed out for two weeks except to school. Mum picked her up after. Marco rang the house but Mum snatched the phone off Beth.

"Who's this?" she asked. "Why are you mumbling? How old are you? Do you know how young Elizabeth is?"

"Jesus Christ," shouted Beth.

After two weeks he left something in our letterbox. It was a tiny box. Mum found it first but let Beth open it. Inside was a silver chain with a half-a-broken-heart pendant. It meant Marco was wearing the other half and that they were in love. Her side was engraved with a *B*.

"*B*?" shouted Mum. "*B*? Doesn't he know your name?"

She made fun of Marco then. She said he couldn't spell. Beth closed her door.

"I wish you'd leave me alone," she said to Mum through the wood.

"I'm not going to leave you alone until you grow some brains," said Mum.

Beth was kept apart from Marco.

"She'll forget about him," Mum explained to Aunty Cheryl.

Aunty Cheryl puffed out a cloud of smoke and said, "I hope you're right."

Mum thought if Beth was kept away from him she would turn back into her ordinary self, back to the way she was before Marco, before Miranda, before the lake. The Beth who laughed with her eyes closed and head tilted back, the Beth who wore embroidered leotards and happy shoes and bobbles in her hair, the Beth who wasn't quite so beautiful. The simpler and not so cunning Beth.

Sometimes Marco rode into Dardanelles Court on his trail bike and did wheel stands. His bike sounded like an angry mosquito. Mum watched him from behind the venetian blinds and shook her head. Nanna stood on the front patio with her hands on her hips. She prayed to Saint Monica, who is the patron saint of disappointing children.

For the whole Easter holidays Mum kept Beth at home. Miranda phoned and when she was told to stay away she appeared at our front door. Mum, hair in curlers, spoke to her slowly and calmly.

"Miranda," she said. "Things are going to change around here."

Miranda was not allowed inside.

Beth was restless. Trapped inside the house she couldn't sit still. She stood up and sat down. She lay on her bed and got up from her bed. She started an apple, she threw it away. She sat on the back steps and smoked a cigarette. She held it in between the steps as though it was somehow hidden. Sometimes she was happy. Mostly she was sad.

In the beginning Beth filled up the whole house when Mum made her stay at home. She filled up the house with the scent of green-apple shampoo. It hung in clouds over chairs where she had sat. It stayed at the dining room table after she had been excused.

And her blond hair expanded. It grew longer and thicker. It had a life of its own. It twisted over her shoulders if she did not make a braid. It shone.

When she sat in the little living room she seemed too big for our small house. She distracted people from the television. Dad's eyes moved backward and forward between the screen and her. Mum put down a color and stared.

She moved and talked but the new quietness kept filling up her face. It rested in the wide expanse of cheekbone. In the pale freckles on her nose. It settled in her heavy-lidded blue eyes. It lay coiled in the still braid hanging over her shoulder.

She grew taller and thinner. She shed her childhood like a skin.

She could not be contained.

"What on earth will we do with you?" said Nanna.

On Easter Sunday Uncle Paavo came for lunch as usual. He came on his bike all the way from Memorial North, where mostly the streets consisted of long lines of brick flats with rows of grubby letterboxes and boardinghouses with signs outside that said SINGLE MEN'S ACCOMMODATION—AIR-CON, COLOR TV.

Uncle Paavo rode all the way along the highway in his pressed polyester trousers and his short-sleeved shirt and with his pen in his pocket and his notepad where he wrote down the prices of everything he had ever bought. He combed his pale white hair across his scalp with a wet comb and some Brylcreem and the sun dried the strands hard.

He did not look any different that day. He did not look like he needed rescuing. But I saw the way Beth looked at him, like he was somehow injured, like it was the saddest thing she'd ever seen.

Uncle Paavo's back bones creaked and popped when he took his place at the table.

"Listen to you," said Nanna. "Your bones talk more than you do."

"I am getting old as the hills," he said.

"But we love you," said Beth, sitting next to him, and she rested her pale long-fingered hand on his arm.

Her hand burned his arm. I could tell it, even though he didn't move his arm away. Tears sprang up into his eyes. No one said anything at first. An uncomfortable silence settled over the table filled up with bread and luncheon beef and Kraft cheese and tinned ham and a lettuce chopped neatly into one thousand pieces.

"Yes we do, Uncle Paavo," said Mum after a while, and she handed a bowl of potato salad to him, which was his favorite, and Beth had to remove her hand so he could take it.

"Yes," joined in Aunty Cheryl.

"Make sure you eat some of that lettuce," Nanna said to Kylie. "It will help your small bones, and you, Danielle, it will make your backbone stronger."

After that everybody talked about normal things like the price of bread and how much milk children should drink and what was the best time to shop at Kmart and everybody pretended not to notice that he was crying.

Gradually, by the end of the holidays, some of the light seemed to have faded from her. Her eyes were not so blue. Her hair was not so golden. She lay on her bed, curled, knees drawn up to her chin, facing the wall.

"What's wrong with you?" asked Mum. "Come

out of there and talk to your sisters. You've been lying on that bed all day."

"She's sad," I said.

"She is not," said Mum. "She's foxing so I let
her out."

"You can't keep me here forever," Beth said.

If I sat at the bottom of her bed and touched her
legs or tickled the underside of her feet she drew
them away from me. When she lay on her bed she
had her eyes open and her eyes moved backward and
forward as though she was watching something.
Sometimes her mouth moved around the words of in-
visible conversations.

"What are you thinking about?" I asked.

"Nothing," she said.

"Who are you talking to?"

"Nobody."

I didn't ask her if everything still felt wrong. She
didn't ask me to leave her alone. I sat beside her looking at all her rock star posters and her old ballerina
paper dolls pinned to the curtains and her Dolly
Varden lamp shade with a dusty skirt and her record
player with all her little 45s and her books in her
bookcase, which were ordinary books like *Anne of
Green Gables* and the *Nancy Drew* mysteries and
What Katy Did and *What Katy Did Next*.

I turned my Bionic Woman doll's head slowly

backward and forward to use her supersonic hearing to understand the secret conversations.

I asked her, only once, what she had done to Deidre Schelbach that day in the park. I hardly believed it anymore. We had pretended so much not to notice it that now it seemed impossible.

I asked her what had happened in a roundabout way, exactly the way that Nanna and my mother asked their questions because I had learned it from them.

"I wonder why Deidre fell down on her knees that day?" I said.

I made it sound like I was only thinking it aloud to myself and Beth didn't say anything for a very long time. She stared at the wallpaper, which was a pattern of squares and circles interlinked. Finally some words came to the surface.

"I don't know what you're talking about," she said.

Angela crossed out the half-a-broken-heart pendant and the ballet shoes. She turned to a fresh page.

"Now we're getting somewhere," she said.

"No we're not," I said.

I was checking my inner tube for punctures because I had smashed ten marbles with a hammer on the driveway and then ridden over the top of them.

Dad had taught me how to find a puncture by running the inner tube slowly through a bucket of water and watching for bubbles. Sometimes I looked for a puncture even though I knew there wasn't one. It was only a little piece of knowledge but it felt as shiny and solid as a new twenty-cent piece in my hand to know I could find the thing that was wrong.

"I'm going to ride out to the horse paddocks and steal a horse," I said to Angela when I had finished checking the inner tube.

"As if you would," said Angela.

"I would," I said. "I'm going to ride right out of town at dawn and never come back."

"They'll send out a search party like in *Little Boy Lost*."

"He couldn't ride a horse," I said. "He was a baby. They'll never find me."

"What would your mother do if you ran away?" asked Angela.

"She wouldn't notice it," I said.

Sometimes after school I climbed onto Mum's bed beside her. If she was lying on her back I put my head on her chest and listened to her heart beat. Or I put my hand inside her hand and squeezed. Sometimes she squeezed back.

"Did you have a good day?" she sometimes asked.

Sometimes I said, "Yes."

And other times she didn't say anything at all because she had no words.

"You wouldn't even know how to find water in the bush," said Angela.

"Yes, I would," I said. "Remember what Mrs. Bridges-Lamb taught us?"

We had done bush survival skills with Mrs. Bridges-Lamb. In the afternoon Mr. Starlight, who was Gavin Starlight's grandfather, had taken us down to the bush behind the oval and showed us how to find bush tucker and look for tracks. We had found the tracks of a goanna and also a dog. When he showed us he talked with a cigarette in his mouth, which moved up and down with his words. The sun scorched us. Tanya Moorhouse, who was very fair, fainted after half an hour.

Angela pretended not to be listening to me. She wrote in *The Book of Clues*.

"We have to find Deidre," she said.

The Shelleys changed their minds about Beth, slowly, piece by piece. At first they'd called her a freak whenever they saw her because of what she had done to Deidre. Deidre hadn't come back to school. She didn't go to the speedway on Friday nights. When they tried to phone her, her brother said she'd gone to stay with her aunty.

After she had been touched Deidre had gone down on her knees. All that day she had kept wiping at her head, as though there was something, some mark, which could be removed. She had cried.

No one had ever seen her cry before.

She had wept.

But then, at the end of the day, after all of the tears had passed, something had changed in her. She had wiped her eyes and looked at them and her eyes had been very clear. When they asked her to come with them to drink on the steps behind the town hall she had said no.

Simply.

Without any rage.

After Deidre was gone Rochelle became Queen of the Tough Girls. Rochelle was the size of two girls. She had pale tree-trunk legs covered in stubble. She wore her red hair short and five earrings in each ear.

She took possession over the fiefdoms of the grandstand, the laneway behind the bike rack, the cicada-filled smoking trees beside the cricket nets, the toilet blocks near the oval, all the imperial routes of travel along the highway, the court of the water tower in Memorial Park.

They called Beth a freak because they were frightened of her but when their words did no damage they stopped.

They liked that she had not told on anyone.

They liked the way she wore Marco's necklace as though she wasn't afraid.

How she went down the laneway between the science block and teased the boys from grade 10.

How she smoked a cigarette while she rode her bike to school.

There was something irresistible in the way she did not hide the bruise. She walked right past them with it showing. She let them see how they had stamped her with their sign. It was important. Bruises were badges of office. Of honor. They all wore their bruises like their black rubber-band bracelets and blue ink tattoos.

Michelle Wright was the first to change her mind. She was a girl with dark polished-wood skin. She had brown hair and amber-colored eyes. She had perfect white teeth because in her house they used charcoal from the campfire for toothpaste. She smiled at Beth, once, while all the others were scowling. Beth smiled back. A small smile. Low voltage. A dot. A dash. They Morse-coded each other with these smiles. Michelle Wright fingered one of the black rubber-band bracelets on her arm and bided her time.

I took a can of cream soda to Nanna's flat. She'd asked me to stop bringing her apples and bread. It wasn't necessary. Soon she was going to drive her Datsun Sunny to the shops. She was just waiting for her hands to stop shaking so much. Uncle Paavo was buying her bags of groceries and riding with them on his bike from town. Nanna's little fridge was half full but she was very thin, thinner than I had ever seen her. Her false teeth clacked inside her mouth when she spoke.

She was lying on her creaking bed. She had her ashtray beside her. Every movement seemed to exhaust her. When she lit her smoke it was like she was moving underwater. I hadn't told her about Angela's plan to find my voice in time for the Talent Quest. If I'd told her that I would have had to tell her I'd looked inside the box. I didn't tell her about my plans to run away.

Nanna lay on the bed smoking and not talking to me and I lay on the bed beside her. It made me remember all those weekends when Beth was growing wilder and sadder and stranger and we were sent to Nanna's so things could be sorted out. Because Beth didn't come with us anymore then, because mostly she ran away on weekends, I got to sleep on an inflatable mattress instead of next to Nanna, who smelled like dust. But secretly I had missed her. I had missed our wordless turnings and counterturnings and our secret, creaking conversations.

Back then she tried to teach me how to embroider. Nanna was a very good embroiderer. Her mother had started teaching her when she was only very small, maybe six or seven. She said because I was starting late my fingers would have already grown clumsy and I would probably never be very good at it. She said if Mum had paid a little bit more attention to our upbringing instead of letting us run wild, up and down the creek bed and out along the highway look-ing for willy-willies, things might have been different. And mostly I just ignored her when she said that.

When Mrs. Bridges-Lamb tried to teach us em-broidery on Friday afternoons, even though Massimo's father, Mr. Gentili, staged a lone protest because he said it was not a good thing to encourage in boys, she was impressed at what I could do. Nanna had taught me how to do a very neat chain stitch and I could do a small daisy easily whereas Angela's took up a large section of her sampler.

But embroidery lessons didn't last long with Mrs. Bridges-Lamb. We disappointed her greatly with our Slovenliness and our Unruliness. Sometimes we pricked each other's fingers and became blood sisters. The boys' tongues hung out of their mouths and their sweaty fingers slipped on the needles and it made her greatly upset.

She would have preferred the boys weren't involved—they didn't fit her image of embroidery class—but we disappointed her just as much, a class-room full of miners' daughters in faded blue hand-me-down uniforms and long yellow socks wilting around our ankles.

But I liked embroidering with Nanna. Apart from saying I had clumsy fingers, she was very nice. She made me sing to her or she told me stories as we went along. She told me stories of how Uncle Paavo got to be so rich by never getting married and working every day and only eating potatoes. She told me things that her mother had told her, for instance, if you are unhappy with an embroidered flower you should unstitch it. It is the same with life. If you are unhappy you must unstitch it until you find the wrong part and make it right. Everything can be fixed. Nothing is unchangeable. She told me that story when she taught me how to make a ribbon rosette.

She told me the story of the boat trip and the albatross, which she had told me one hundred times before, and how my great-grandmother was buried at sea. Sometimes she stopped in the middle of a story and said I was doing very well and maybe I wasn't going to be such a bad embroiderer after all.

Danielle always came closer when Nanna told the ship story because it was very sad and horrible and she especially liked tragic things.

"Tell us again how she was buried," she said.

"She was wrapped in a tablecloth with sunrises and bluebirds and sewn up in a calico sack and weighted down with some lead," said Nanna, "and then she was tipped into the sea."

"Where?" said Danielle. "Near land?"

"No, it was the middle of the ocean, I'm sure."

And I wondered what the longitude and the latitude were for the place of her burial and if the captain marked them in his book but I didn't say it. We kept embroidering.

"Tell me about the albatross," I said even though I had heard it a thousand times before.

"It was soon before arriving here," she said. "It flew beside the ship for days and nights, never touching the sea. It was only a week since my aiti had died and still I saw her everywhere, at the dining table, going down the stairs, the back of her turning a corner not far ahead. But this bird came then. I was standing on the deck and it was in a squall and the boat was heaving this way and that and it flew closer and closer. It flew so close that it was maybe only two arms away. So close I could see its eye. And it only hovered, like this, with its wings outstretched and it looked straight at me."

"Did it look at you like it knew you?" I asked. This was my line and it was my job to recite it.

"Yes," said Nanna. "I swear on my life that this albatross knew me. And after that I was not so filled with fear for coming to this new land and not so full of grief. Instead I was given hope."

After that story was finished we sat where we were with our needles in our hands just imagining it. Embroidering with Nanna had felt better almost than being at home, where Dad kept coming home late and bumping into the walls and Mum kept following him from room to room clicking her tongue just the way Nanna did. And where Beth seemed to take up all the space. Where she filled whole rooms with her scent and her glow and where she overwhelmed our mother's heart.

"What should I do with this?" I asked Nanna, holding up the can of cream soda.

She looked at it like she had never seen such a thing. I could tell her mind was a long way away. Slowly she came back to earth. She shivered. It was getting colder.

It was nearly six months since Beth had died. Mum still drifted from room to room, stopping off to lie on beds along the way. If Dad worked day shift he never came home afterward the way he used to. He didn't come home until late at night and I would hear him fumbling with his key in the door and then dropping things and accidentally smashing them in the kitchen while he tried to make himself tea. Nanna kept growing smaller and quieter. I had not found my singing voice.

Nanna sat up slowly on the edge of her bed.

"Now let us see if this will work," she said. "Go and get a cup from the kitchen."

I drank the cream soda from the wrong side of the cup. Some of the bubbles came out of my nose. No songs erupted from inside me but I could feel them pressing against my chest.

"Will you be coming to our house again?" I asked.

"One day I hope," said Nanna.

"I wish it was soon," I said.

Before everything happened I wished I had a double voice box like a songbird so I could sing two songs at once, the way a bird can harmonize with itself. I wanted to sing crystal clear notes. I wanted to sing them one after another in ascending order. And at the same time I wanted to let another fountain of notes descend from my heart.

Before everything happened I did not understand how the bones of a bird wing could be so similar to a human arm but end up so different. For instance, a bird has a humerus attached to its shoulder bone, just like us, and an ulna and a radius in the lower arm. In a wing most of the finger bones have been fused together to hold the primary feathers but they are still recognizable. They could still belong to us.

Before everything happened I sometimes thought Nanna's albatross story was only half true. She had taught my mother how to be the master of half-facts and she was the queen of them herself. The facts she had right were that great soaring birds, such as albatross, fly over the sea on long slim wings. They fly very high and for a long time without ever touching earth. From a distance they look like flying white crosses.

When Mum wouldn't get out of bed Nanna told me to go down on my knees and introduce myself to God. To say I am Jennifer Day. I want to help my mother. To invoke these saints in order: Saint Flora for abandoned people, Saint Gertrude for the newly departed, Saint Helena for failing marriages, Saint Genevieve for disasters, Saint Joseph for families, Saint Jude for hopeless causes, Saint Anne for all mothers. She said please tell her that I love her.

But I did not get down on my knees. I didn't invoke the saints and angels. I didn't tell Mum that Nanna loved her. Mostly I stayed away from her bedroom, which was dark as a cave and filled with crumpled sheets and her soft movements, her small flutterings, like an injured bird's.

The songs I had inside me pushed against my chest, looking for a way to escape. They writhed like snakes. I could not tell which songs they were anymore by their shape or taste. They were too badly deformed, like the strange litter of dead kittens that Angela's cat had, which Mr. Popovitch told us not to look at but we did and then afterward had to breathe into brown paper bags to calm down.

When Mum came out in May she had a shower and washed her hair and sat in Dad's recliner and turned on the television. She wrapped her yellow Japanese happy coat close to herself. She watched a whole episode of *The Wombles*. I sat beside her, kneeling on the floor, holding her hand. She tried to cook us dinner but gave up halfway through and lit a cigarette and went and sat back in front of the television. Dad tried to hold her when he came home from the pub.

"Don't you dare touch me," she said.

Mum thought she kept the new rule well but Beth still found ways to escape. She waited until Aunty Cheryl and Mum were gone together. She persuaded Kylie, who was her babysitter, with threats over the picture of Des. She told us if we loved her we would help her. She said she would do the same for us. She promised me she would go through my whole box of feathers. The whole box. Each feather. Latin name. Common name. One at a time.

She offered Danielle money for her perm jar.

The first of the winter westerlies arrived and hummed through the grandstand on the oval. The air was spiced with sulfur fumes from the stacks. She skipped school.

She left her bike in the bike racks but then doubled back along the riverbed, stepping through the remnants of creek camps, through the shadows of the bridge, along the creek beside Sandy Creek State

Primary School, where I daydreamed through the window.

At night Beth lay on her bed and waited for us to go to sleep, then she stood at the back door and looked at the night. She couldn't stay inside. She wheeled her bike across the dry grass. She opened the gate slowly so that it wouldn't squeak. She left it open for when she returned.

I heard her go.

The sky was bright with stars. It was cold but she didn't feel it. She rode along the wide empty streets. Nearly all of the houses were quiet but here and there a lone light still shone. Occasionally she heard cars prowling in the distance. The constant rumble of road trains along the highway. She rode without purpose. Up and down streets, over the river crossing, past horse paddocks, past the cemetery, the quartz graves gleaming in the dark.

A late moon rose above the ranges. She took her hands off the handlebars and weaved backward and forward across roads until she came to the park. She wheeled her bike up through the scrub to the water tower and sat on the ground among the broken glass. She watched the mine glittering over the town.

She had settled something that first time. Entering into the night was like swimming. She felt cleansed.

And part of her unraveled.

It was like shedding a skin.

Before dawn the sky behind the hills turned a deep blue. Stars still shone. The blueness slowly flooded across the sky. She lay back on the ground and watched the first of the earth-colored hawks ascend and circle above her.

I was glad to see Mrs. O'Malley outside, surveying the street like an old seagull on a rock. She went inside rocking from side to side like a skittle doll. She came back with fifty cents.

Angela and I were collecting for Mrs. Bridges-Lamb's annual spellathon. We'd been to the two Mr. Murrays' house. Marshall Murray had come down his front steps and gone through his brown trouser pockets and swayed a little in front of Angela and me.

"Tell us what you know," he said as he gave us twenty cents, which was only ten cents each.

I could have told him a lot of different things.

Even when he smiled and showed his chipped front tooth his eyes looked like he'd just seen a terribly sad thing, for instance a slag heap falling on top of a school.

Angela tugged my arm.

Mum had told us not to knock on doors because we could be kidnapped and only to talk to people if they were in their front yards. We knocked on Miss Schmidt's door mostly for the dare. Mum said there was something strange about a woman who never got married or had kids but that we shouldn't be mean to her either and call her names like Psycho Lady. We should just be wary. Little children had unfortunately been killed by strange lonely people.

"Cool. How?" said Danielle.

"Please, Danielle," said Mum.

"I only want to know so I can be wary," said Danielle.

When we knocked, Frieda Schmidt took a very long time to come to the door even though we knew she was there because her car was in the driveway. We heard her footsteps behind the door and even then she took a long time to open it as though she was preparing herself. When she opened the door she was fully clothed as though it was a weekday and she tried a smile on for size but it must have felt wrong because she stopped doing it.

I had introduced myself and explained about the spellathon and when she didn't say anything I told her I could even spell "corruption." She tried the smile on again and then motioned for us to follow her into the house. It did feel a little bit like we were Hansel and Gretel being led into the candy cane cottage only it was exactly the same company house as ours only with different furniture. And only it was exceptionally neat and there was not a thing out of place. There was a TV and a chair in front of it and a sofa with cushions arranged on it with a plastic cover over it. There was a tea set on the coffee table as though she might be expecting guests and a dining room table with six chairs.

In the kitchen there was not a dish or plate to be seen. There were no toast crumbs on the counter, not even a toaster. The oven looked brand-new. The fridge didn't have any magnets on it. And her air conditioner made a much louder noise than ours, a noise like someone saying shhhhhhhhhhh. The house smelled strange. It smelled like cleaning products and emptiness.

She gave us a one-dollar note. She held it in one corner and I took the opposite corner.

"Thank you so much, you've given the biggest donation ever in our history of spellathons," I said.

It wasn't until we were on the front steps that we realized she hadn't said a thing. And that we were taking deep breaths of the Saturday-afternoon air as though we had been inside a mausoleum.

"What on earth were you doing in there?" Mrs. O'Malley asked.

I'd proudly showed her the one-dollar note. We'd done three streets and made two dollars fifty.

"Good on you, girls," she said. "I like to see you doing such things. But here, tell me something, who are all these new girls keeping Beth company?"

She wanted to know who the Shelleys were, which side of town they came from, who their parents were and where they'd come from and how they'd arrived.

"I'm not sure," I said.

"I'm worried, you know," said Mrs. O'Malley, looking down toward the end of the street like something was coming. "There's trouble brewing on this street."

Beth grew wilder each day. She plucked her eyebrows into two thin lines. She painted kohl onto her bottom eyelids. She pierced her ears with sewing needles. She rarely smiled. The wilder she grew, the more she glowed. Her skin gleamed. Her eyes rained a soft blue light. She did not like to look at people for fear of frightening them with her beauty. The more she glowed, the wilder she grew.

Michelle Wright had broken ranks and given Beth a black rubber-band bracelet. She didn't say anything but held it on her outstretched palm. These bands were precious. They could not be bought or sold. Instead they were handed down like heirlooms. They were given by girls who left school, got married, had kids. Handed down by older sisters who remembered what it felt like to sit on the top step of the grandstand and survey a kingdom. They were hastily passed on by cousins who left town on midnight buses.

The bands provided order. They were the rules on

how a girl could gain entry to the circle. How she could leave. A girl had to have three bands before she could give one herself. The order they provided was delicate. Great reigns could be ended suddenly by the giving of bands. Plots were hatched and leaders were overthrown. Bands were removed from arms solemnly, secretly, and given to the preferred ruler. Fights erupted. Battles were fought.

"What are you looking at?" said Rochelle Peters to Beth one day after school assembly.

She came close. She rammed Beth's shoulder with her own. But the action was playful. She half smiled after she had moved away. It was her introduction. Beth would be tolerated.

Beth went with them to the top of Memorial Park, where the water tower stood. The tower was made of smooth white concrete. All around the base there were smashed beer bottles and cigarette butts. Graffiti covered the round wall. The graffiti said SHEREE LUVS MARK, SUCK MY DICK, IF YOU WANT A GOOD TIME RING MARIA S., and ROSES ARE RED AND VIOLETS ARE BLUE YOU LOOK LIKE A SLUT AND SMELL LIKE ONE TOO.

From the top of the hill the town was visible; the straight streets dissected the wide empty river, and the mine, like a giant dirty city, rose behind, billowing brown smoke into the cloudless sky.

Angela and I knew the place well. We had been to

the water tower many times before even though Mum said never to go there because it might burst and we would be drowned. She said she knew for a fact it had happened somewhere before. Perhaps in Spain.

We climbed to the water tower by a path through straggly bushland of snappy gums and spear grass. The red rock slipped beneath our feet. No matter how hot it was the tower was always cool to the touch.

Our favorite game was to lay our heads against the pipes that ran from the white concrete into the ground. Inside the pipes we could hear a ticking noise. It sounded like someone tapping a stone against the pipe. It was rhythmical as a clock. Angela said it was a water witch. When she said it we both laughed but my heart beat so hard that I had difficulty hearing.

We climbed the slipping rock path just to lay our heads against the cool pipe and listen to her tick. We were terrified and mesmerized by her. But there was also something else about the place. It was very still and quiet. When the hot wind blew, the grass made a noise like people sighing. The scrub trees whispered. It was only a few streets from home but it seemed far away. The view to Dardanelles Court was swallowed up by pale bushland.

Beth drank with her new friends at the water

tower. Miranda took rum from the caravan because it was easy and she said Kevin would get her some if she wanted because he would do everything she asked. Beth took Mum's wine from the cask without asking. She poured it into empty soft drink tins. Everyone brought something. They sat with their backs against the tower wall, waving the flies from their faces, and looked out over the town. The winter sun burned their faces.

After they drank, it was always Miranda who dared Beth to do wilder things. Beth dared Miranda back.

"I dare you to go to that house on Picardy Street," said Miranda, "where the spunky man with the motorbike lives."

"What do I have to do?" asked Beth.

"You have to knock on his door and ask him for a kiss."

"You're crazy," said Michelle Wright.

"She's a real slut," said Rochelle Peters, but in a friendly way.

"I dare you to walk out onto the highway and lift your shirt up," said Beth.

"That's nothing," said Miranda.

"You've got to take your bra off too," said Michelle Streeton.

"Yeah," said Beth. "No bra and lift your shirt when cars are passing."

"I can do that," said Miranda.

They rode all the way to the house on Picardy Street but the man wasn't home and his girlfriend answered the door. They rode to the highway and took off their bras from under their shirts by pulling the straps down through their armholes. Miranda did it first. She waited for a gap between the trucks and ran out and performed the act. Beth lifted her shirt as a road train passed. Its driver released the air horn and started to slow down. They rode as fast as they could back to the park.

They talked about climbing the water tower. The lower section of the ladder had been removed to about the height of a tall man. Miranda said they could easily bridge the difference if one stood on the other's back. They tried it once but they were laughing too much and they fell on the ground. Beth cut her arm on a piece of glass.

"Blood sisters," she said, touching some of her blood onto Miranda's finger.

"Blood sisters," said Miranda.

"Imagine the view from the top," said Beth. "I'd be able to see clearly from there."

"We'd need a man to help us," said Miranda.

"We'd need someone really tall," said Beth.

"Kevin might do it," said Miranda.

"But what would he want in return?"

Sometimes Beth allowed us up to the water tower

with them. Angela and I weren't allowed to sit close to them but we were made bold by the company. We put our heads to the pipes for longer. We tried to decipher the ticking messages. Angela said it might be Morse code. She said we needed a book about it from the library. I said witches didn't do Morse code. She said how could I be completely sure? I said I couldn't be, not completely, but fairly sure. It was before we did fractions and percentages with Mrs. Bridges-Lamb.

Beth closed her eyes when she took a mouthful of the wine. When she opened them they were bluer. Sometimes she looked disappointed that she was still where she was. She lit her Winfield Greens end to end. Always, after a while, she called out to me and told me to go home. It wouldn't even be getting dark. The shadows of clouds would be passing over the drinking girls' faces. If I argued she got angry.

"Go," she shouted.

Like there was a big rush. As though if I stayed one minute more I'd see something I shouldn't see.

"Why?"

"Because she said so," said Miranda, who tried to act like she was my sister also.

"Leave her alone," said Michelle Wright. She was the nicest of them all with her warm brown face and wide white teeth.

"You're so mean to her," she said. "You're so mean to your little sister."

Sometimes she asked me to show her my Hobbytex T-shirts. She asked me what they said like she couldn't read and I wasn't ten.

But we had to go when Beth was like that.

The tide is high but I'm moving on, I sang as we went down the hill.

I'm gonna be your number one, Angela sang back.

We sang it loudly to scare away snakes with the vibrations of our voices. We went down through whispering scrub and onto the freshly mowed grass of the park. We passed beneath the dark-headed trees and the evening sun rippled through the leaves and made moving patterns on our arms and faces.

Sometimes at the trees we could still hear their voices on the hill. The long shrieks of laughter, the wild callings. We left our patterned skins beneath the trees and went down through the turnstile gate past Aunty Cheryl and Kylie's house, where the kitchen light was already on and the smell of dinner came out through the window. And at the bottom of the hill when we turned it was impossible to tell that she was still up there with the others.

"Have you seen Beth?" asked Mum.

"No," I lied, but not because Beth had told me to.

I had lied because I didn't know what to say. I lied to protect our mother. I lied to protect Beth. I lied to protect everyone.

In the shower I tried to sing one of Nanna's Latin carols even though it wasn't Christmas and for the first time my voice took a very long time to come.

Mr. Popovitch dropped us off at the supermarket on his way to a Panel Van Club annual general meeting. The shops hadn't even opened so we sat on the seats outside and waited. Angela had *The Book of Clues* in her beaded red Indian bag with tassels.

We had our beanies pulled down over our ears and gloves on also. Whenever we spoke our words smoked and hung in the air. We had a best-of-three word-smoking competition. Angela won.

We watched all the checkout ladies arrive. We discussed interesting facts like what to do if you get stuck in quicksand, how to prepare for a nuclear war, and different ways that humans might be able to go backward in time and then we had a fight about whether it was possible to keep a fairy as a pet.

"No," I said. "It isn't."

"But we could borrow Kylie's Barbie campervan," said Angela. "It could live in that."

"It would die of sadness and starvation," I said.

"No it wouldn't. What about all those tins and saucepans?"

"They're only painted on the campervan walls. They're not real."

"Fairies are magic," she said. "It'd use its magic."

"It would die of loneliness and missing its family."

"No it wouldn't. It would survive."

We were fighting so much we nearly missed Deidre Schelbach walking along the footpath in her dirty white checkout lady dress and red parka. When we saw her we put our heads down and pretended to be in a very interesting conversation.

"Rhubarb, rhubarb, rhubarb," said Angela. "Is that her?"

"Rhubarb, yes, rhubarb," I said.

She went through the automatic doors without looking at us.

Inside we took up our positions one bench down from the cigarette counter, where Deidre was putting her bag away and opening up the register. An old man with a false leg sat beside us. I knew it was a false leg because the man said he was going to win the Saturday Morning Great Grocery Giveaway, touch wood, and he lifted up his trouser and knocked on his wooden leg with his knuckles. When we looked surprised he laughed very loudly and his belly moved up and down.

Angela smiled at him politely.

"Do you think Deidre looks any different?" she asked.

"A little bit," I said.

Deidre was serving someone. She smiled at her first customer.

"How?"

"A little bit . . . lighter," I said, but I wasn't sure.

"Not so . . . angry," said Angela, and she opened up her bag and took out *The Book of Clues*.

She chewed on the end of her pencil. She wrote

deardry

at the top of a blank page and underlined it.

"Don't do that here," I said.

"Why not?"

"She'll see us."

"No she won't."

I grabbed one end of the book and tried to take it off Angela. Angela pulled the other end. We pulled backward and forward. The man with the false leg thought it was funny.

"You're crazy," I said. "We'll get caught."

"Doing what?" asked Deidre, who had left the cigarette counter and come to stand in front of us.

Angela let go of the exercise book so that I held it in my lap. It was still opened on the page titled with Deidre's name. I closed it up. I saw Deidre looking at the writing on the cover. The picture of the girl with flowing blond hair and the toothpick eyelashes.

"What are you two up to?"

Even though she was lighter and less angry she still had a tough face. Her words were still accompanied by a bad smell.

"Hey?" she asked.

"Nothing," I said.

I turned the book over on my lap to hide the writing.

"Why's my name in there?"

"We're looking for clues," said Angela, suddenly fearless.

"Clues about what?" said Deidre. She put her hands on her hips.

"About everything," I said.

Deidre chewed on her bottom lip. She looked at me for a while. The man with the wooden leg shifted in his seat and pretended not to be listening.

"You look a bit like her, hey?" she said.

"We have the same mole."

I pointed to the mole on my cheek.

"But different as well," she said.

"Is there anything you can tell us?" said Angela.

"No," said Deidre.

"Nothing at all?" asked Angela.

Deidre laughed but then looked at the ground.

"You kids have got to stop it," she said. "Some shit you just shouldn't muck around with, you get it?"

"Like what shit?" I said.

"Like nothing," said Deidre. "Go on. Get out of here."

She waved us away with her hand.

"Go on," she said. "You've got to leave it alone."

Beth divided her time between saving Marco and the hill in Memorial Park. When she didn't come home after school like she promised, Mum sent us to find her. We walked up and down streets. We walked past the house on Amiens Road but Beth's bike wasn't there. We walked to the water tower. We walked to the caravan park.

The caravan park was like a little town. A wide main street ran down its center and the straight caravan rows ran off from either side. There were white street signs showing the row numbers. Miranda lived in row 9, the very last row, and the caravan was up against the tall chain-wire fence and the row of mango trees, which dropped their fruit in summer to rot on the ground.

We walked down the quiet main street. A group of men with long beards gazed into the open hood of a car. A stooped woman hosed out the moss-covered shower block with bleach. A crow sat on a bin overflowing with beer cans. An old black dog on a long chain watched us pass.

I secretly hoped Miranda's stepmum wouldn't be at home because sometimes she got angry. When she got angry Mrs. Bell bared her yellow teeth and her eyes turned crazy. I'd seen it before in town right outside the Blue Tongue Lounge Bar when she was fighting with another lady on the footpath. They had been fighting each other in the middle of the day but both looked like they were very tired. They had slapped at each other with weak arms, missing each other occasionally. Finally Mrs. Bell had hit the ground and lay there with her yellow teeth showing like a snarling dog that had been kicked. I was watching from the car window until my mother told me to cover my eyes and, as we drove away, to not look back.

Mrs. Bell's boyfriend, Kevin, came to the screen door. He wore a pair of jeans but no shirt. His chest was covered in thick black hair. On his shoulder he had a tattoo of a roaring tiger but his own smile was full of large white teeth like the Cheshire cat's. He was combing back his wet hair.

"They might be here or they might not," he said, grinning, like it was a very hilarious joke. "But wherever they are they'll be up to no good."

He winked at us.

I tried to see past him into the caravan but I couldn't.

"Come in and have a look if you like," he said.

"Why can't you just tell us?" said Danielle, who was (a) angry at being made to walk for kilometers looking for Beth, who she considered a troublemaker, and (b) already very annoyed at having to wear a Milwaukee back brace.

"Where would be the fun in that?" asked Kevin, and he scratched his balls.

"Pervert," said Danielle, and pulled me with her by the arm.

Mum rang Aunty Cheryl and enlisted Kylie in the search. She said Kylie was supposed to be looking out for Beth. She tried to turn it all around as if it was Kylie's fault. She yelled and shouted and threw things in the kitchen.

"I give up," she said.

Nanna came and told her it was because there was no religion in our house. She said Mum only had herself to blame. When she came she brought a bag of rags. Mum and Nanna used the rags for cleaning. Mum opened up the bag and took out a rag and I saw it was a section of an old pair of yellow shorts that had belonged to me. She started cleaning the wall telephone with it.

"I just don't know what to do," she said as she cleaned. "She won't listen to a thing I say. She is like another girl. I don't even know who she is anymore."

"She has never been the same girl since the lake," said Nanna cautiously.

"Are you still going on about that?" said Mum. "It's that Bell girl that's caused all the trouble."

"You must separate them then," said Nanna, "and you must lock her up."

"Don't be silly," said Mum. "What do you mean?"

"I mean put her in the room and turn the key.

That will learn her the lesson. Keep her here for one day. Remember I did it once with Louise."

While they planned to lock her up, Beth was in Marco's new car, an old sun-faded Holden with a dark interior and the upholstery spewing stuffing and springs. He was giving her shadow-filled kisses and pressing apart her thighs with his hips. They were at a place in the desert where men took their women. A water hole that people said was bottomless. A place where the sunlight leaped and danced on the rock walls.

"Do you sometimes feel sad?" she said, touching the pure white skin of his cheek.

"No," he said. He climbed off her, back against the door. He spat out the window. "What's that supposed to mean?"

"Nothing," she said. "Just sometimes you look sad. Inside."

He lit a cigarette and after a drag passed it to her.

"What're you going on about? Are you stoned or something?"

"I don't know. Don't worry."

He grabbed her by the legs and pulled her toward him.

"Why'd I be sad?" he said, tickling her until he made her laugh. "Hey?"

"Sorry," she said. "I don't even know why I said it."

Marco dropped her off on Memorial Drive so Mum wouldn't see him. I'd been riding up and down streets looking for her but she ignored me. She opened her bag and took out chewing gum while she watched Marco go. Marshall Murray shook his head from the patio.

"Tell me what you know," he called out to Beth.

"Nothing," she replied.

It was late. Mum had already exhausted herself. When Beth opened the door she just shook her head. From our bedroom door I saw her follow Beth down the hallway and I could tell she was thinking about locking her up. When Beth went into her bedroom Mum's hand hovered near the handle but she didn't do it.

"I'm grown up, Mum," said Beth.

"You're not," said Mum.

"Please. Why can't you understand?"

After she started drinking on the hill she was sadder. The sadness expanded inside her. She couldn't sit still for it. She lay on the sofa and got up again. She went to a window. She lay on her bed. She started a biscuit, she threw it away. She rested her head against the bathroom mirror. I saw it. The way she held her hand over her heart when she thought no one was watching. The very faint glimmer of tears in her eyes. I saw it when she chewed her nails until they bled.

"What are you staring at?" she said to me.

She sounded angry, like Miranda or a Shelley girl.

She saved a moth with the map of the world on its back. Its wings contained an inland green sea fringed in arid continents. She held it on her fingertip for a long time.

"It'll just fly into some other web," I said.

"Maybe it won't," she said.

"Moths only live a very short time," I said.

"You're such an annoying little shit," she said.

I hated her and loved her that final winter.

She saw sadness in Nanna's open-palmed Madonnas suffocating inside the glass cabinets. I saw her try to turn her face away from painful things: struggling insects; a three-legged dog; Kylie, clumsy, dropping her bag, calling out to her across the oval; a simple boy pushing supermarket trolleys; two women staggering across the highway with a carton of beer, tiny specks. On those days she felt everything suffering.

That winter the nothingness of still days slipped into her, drop by drop. Days when everything was so bright and each and every thing had a shining clear edge: the telephone lines draped across wide empty streets, the frayed edge of a white cloud, the hawks above her with trembling wings, tumbling and free-falling through the sky.

Sometimes on those days the whole world

hummed. She laid her head against it. She heard it whispering like the sea inside a shell. She heard the mine quivering and shuddering and groaning.

"What's wrong, chook?" said Dad.

He had come home from the pub and found Beth curled up on his side of the bed. He slipped his flip-flops off and lay down on Mum's side. He turned on the transistor radio.

"Hey?" he said. He patted her on the back.

"I'm going mad," she said.

"No," said Dad.

"Yes," she whispered, facing the wall.

"How mad?" said Dad. "Stark raving?"

"Yes."

"That's my girl," he said. "Come here."

She rolled over and put her head on his chest.

"As long as you're not barking mad," he said, and she closed her eyes and half smiled against his heartbeat.

She only had six months to live.

In *The Book of Clues* Angela wrote under the title "Deardry":

what does she know?

She crossed out the clue of the tough girl's black rubber-band bracelet. She sang "Total Eclipse of the Heart," incessantly, in her weak quavering voice.

"Don't," I said. "It hurts my eardrums."

"But I'm training you to sing again."

There was a terrible rumor that Anthea Long was going to borrow Tammy Hoffman's Austrian national costume for the Talent Quest and sing something from *The Sound of Music*. It would be just the kind of thing she would do.

Mr. Barnes asked me if I was going to sing because he said he'd heard I was very good. I thought, at first, that he was making fun of me. I thought it was a mean thing to make fun about but then I realized he didn't know that I couldn't sing anymore.

"Probably not," I said.

I kind of felt sorry for him because nobody was frightened of him, not the way we were frightened of Mrs. Bridges-Lamb. He wore very tight pinstriped bell-bottoms even though it was 1983. When he bent over to write on the bottom of the board the beginning of his hairy bum crack showed and everyone giggled. I called him Bum Cracker Barnsey at little lunch and that made everyone laugh.

After school in the afternoons Aunty Cheryl came to our house with Kylie and tried to train Mum how to be a mother again. She made Mum get out of her Japanese happy coat. She made her brush her hair. She made her get out the recipe book and pick something to make for dinner.

"Frankly, Cheryl," said Mum, slapping the book shut, "I just couldn't be bothered."

She poured herself a glass of Fruity Lexia from the cask and clicked the handle on Dad's recliner and put her legs up. She lit a cigarette and clicked the remote control.

"Well," said Aunty Cheryl, "what the hell's going to happen to these other two? This one here?"

She grabbed me and I became an example.

"This one spends half her days down the creek like a wild thing. Look at her feet."

She lifted my feet, which were dark brown. She pulled back my bangs to reveal my eyes. Mum looked at me, then up at the ceiling.

"Why don't you try losing one," she said quietly.

"She's gone," said Aunty Cheryl.

"Don't tell me that like I don't know," howled Mum.

Kylie, on the sofa, crossed her arms and started to cry.

Because I was finished being the example I went down the hallway and into my room, where Danielle was lying on her bed crying, and I got the hammer that I had been smashing marbles with and I got my Bionic Woman doll out of the Barbie doll box and I smashed her head in. Her head didn't smash very well because she was made of very strong plastic. It just kept bouncing back into shape and that made me even angrier.

"Stop it," said Danielle.

She covered up her face with her hands and sobbed. And for the first time I wondered why they could put Jamie Sommers back together again but not just an ordinary girl like Beth.

The worst thing about secrets is that if you let them sit for long enough they grow up and have a life of their own. If you turn your back on them you can get a very big fright when you turn back. When I didn't tell on Beth from the very beginning it became harder and harder to do it later, even when everything was going wrong. I tried to threaten her.

"I'm going to tell on you," I said when, for instance, I thought it was Marco she was sneaking out to at night.

I had spent so many afternoons in front of the house on Amiens Road. So many afternoons when I could have been collecting facts about one thousand different topics and reading volume 3 of the *Merit Students Encyclopedia,* which so far was my favorite and which began with "bat" and ended in "Cairo." I was still angry.

"Don't," she said. She grabbed me by the arm. "Please."

She had grown paler. Her hair had changed to the color of white sand. Her freckles had faded into her skin. Her eyelashes touched her cheeks when she closed her eyes against the glare. She had bright red nail polish, which was chipped. She chewed on it between drags on her cigarette on the back stairs.

"You don't even know what I'm telling on you about," I said.

She didn't care.

There are three different types of tattling. In the first type you are actually looking for something to tattle on a person for. As soon as they commit the crime, something as simple as burping and not saying excuse me, you walk casually to the nearest grown-up and tell. It usually makes you feel good afterward.

The second kind is when you know someone has done something wrong, for instance thrown a rock through the glass window of the drive-in picture theater's ticket box. You have to decide whether to tell a grown-up or not. Mostly this is because someone may have been watching and seen you in the same general area and you would like to make clear that you weren't involved.

The third is the much worse kind, when you know a terrible secret. A secret that is much worse than breaking a window or even maybe starting a small grass fire. And then being asked, begged, to keep the secret.

This is because secrets are terrible things.

Even the simplest ones.

For instance when in winter Angela whispered in my ear, "Tina Litvin wears her undies on the outside of her stockings, it's a secret, pass it on," then all day I had to think about it. The secret grew and grew inside my mind. Why did she wear her underpants on the outside of her stockings? Was it because her parents were from Estonia? Was Angela telling the truth or just spreading a very bad rumor? Had she really seen the underpants on the outside? How could I get to see Tina's underpants to verify the fact other than to ask her to do a handstand, which are banned on the playground? Was Angela telling the truth when she said Estonia wasn't really a country but a place like Disneyland where you have to pay for a ticket to enter?

Big secrets are catastrophic. However hard you try to hide them and forget them they bob to the surface and you must go over them again and again. They are taken out and touched so often they become worn smooth as a river stone. You have to carry them around inside you like a baby. The secret grows until you feel like all you are is a skin that covers it, a thin skin, easily split, ripe.

"Tell me what you are going to tell on me about then," Beth said.

I could have told on her about how she got the bruise, about the house on Amiens Road, about the drinking on the hill. That would just be for starters.

"I will tell on you," I answered.

I even did some Kylie fist clenching.

"Jenny," she said.

I knew her secret of finger crossing.

First, only with one hand, for good luck. She did that when she spoke to people. When she said hello. As though something terrible might happen. All of a sudden. And later, with two fingers crossed on both hands. That was to save the doomed. I knew it. I'd seen it. When she took her seat beside Uncle Paavo at the table she double-crossed her fingers and sat on them.

I knew the secret of her disappearing parts.

Her shedding of skins.

At night when the streets were still, emptied of all the people and all their noise, she changed. Night calmed her. She uncurled herself on the bed. She uncrossed her fingers. Each morning she emerged from the night slightly different, stiller and more serene.

When our mother went to the doctor with bad nerves because of Beth, the clinic sister suggested a nice pamphlet about puberty. The clinic sister said Beth would grow out of the difficult stage. Mum kept the pamphlet on her bedside table. It contained diagrams of girls' and boys' genitalia.

"Girls' gen-it-al-ia," read Angela, pronouncing it like it was a foreign city and then adding other exotic locations. "Lab-ia minor, lab-ia major, vulva."

"Vulva?"

"Vull-var. Boys' gen-it-al-ia. Penis."

"Don't," I said, covering my ears.

"Penis," said Angela. "Pee-niss."

The pamphlet did not mention the crossing of fingers.

The pamphlet did not mention nighttime riding.

It did not mention the unlocking of hearts.

It did not mention the sensation of doom rushing toward Beth in a wave.

It did not mention smudged mascara and several types of sorrow.

It did not mention the giving away of parts of herself.

It was a very useless pamphlet.

After the pamphlet Mum got the complete *Life Cycle Library* from the one-armed encyclopedia salesman.

She studied them carefully for clues. She read them from cover to cover. She spent a lot of time on volume 6, which was the *Parents' Answer Book on Drugs*. The girls didn't wear Alice bands or tennis skirts in volume 6. They wore bell-bottoms and ponchos. The boys had hair straight out of *Scooby-Doo*.

The volume 6 glossary contained words like blasted, black beauties, coming down, cube head, ripped, roach holder, and Texas tea. We had never heard of these words. Beth didn't use these words. It looked like Mum had been up and down the list one hundred times, underlining some words, circling others.

Angela and I didn't leave any marks when we borrowed *The Life Cycle Library*. We took one slim volume at a time, secretly. Eventually Angela grew tired of volume 1 and the diagram of the pee-niss. We graduated to volume 2, which was about having babies. We learned that it was possible after all, despite what Anthea Long, with all her expertise in yodeling, said, that a man and woman could have a baby even if they weren't married. Angela was pleased to have it in writing because she had argued it with the white-haired Anthea at big lunch.

"See, I knew it," said Angela.

All that was needed was some boy's sperm to get inside a girl's vagina.

"What if Massimo Gentili went to the toilet and some sperm came out and it flew through the air and someone was sitting on another toilet in the girls' toilets, except not me, and some of that sperm flew up into her?" I asked.

"Does sperm have wings?" said Angela.

We were more confused than ever.

"We need to get the facts straight," I said.

"We need to show this book to Anthea," said Angela.

I was filled with dread. How could we get it into my schoolbag and out of the house and back again?

Mum read all of the volumes before she approached Beth. They went into Mum's bedroom together and the door was shut. I heard Mum reading straight out of the text in a wobbling voice.

"What is a woman?" she said. "Is she tall or short, young or old? Is she warm and friendly or cold and selfish? Can she cry, does she kiss boys, is she afraid of the dark?"

It was a strange passage for her to choose because, for example, Mum didn't know that Beth went out at night into the darkness, only I knew it, and somehow when she asked it sounded almost like trick questions. Mum should have asked me the questions. I answered them in my head from the hallway. Beth was neither tall nor short but in-between. She did cry. She did kiss boys. She could be extremely cold, especially when she was bored of people, but also very friendly, which was what Mum wanted to talk to her about.

There was a long silence.

"What are you doing?" asked Beth.

"We need to talk about things," said Mum.

"No we don't," said Beth.

"We do."

"We don't. I already know about it."

"You know about it but you don't know it in the right way," said Mum.

I wished there was a hole in the wall that I could peep through. There was nothing but silence on the other side. I traced my finger over the gold pattern in the linoleum while I listened.

"If you're so clever," said Mum, "why don't you tell me how it all works?"

Nothing.

"Do you know about using a condom?"

Nothing.

"Are you going steady with this Mark boy?"

"Going steady" was in the glossary. It said going steady usually led to engagement and marriage.

Nothing.

"Because look, look here, there is a whole chapter on dating. Look, it has the pros and cons of going steady."

"Stop saying going steady."

"Are you smoking ghanja?"

"What?"

"Texas tea, grass, greefo, hay, Mary Jane, pot?"

"Texas tea?"

"Have you been getting blasted?"

"What?"

"Getting ripped?"

"Can I go now?"

"No," said Mum.

Mr. Bum Cracker Barnsey made me stay behind in the classroom after everyone left. He said he needed to discuss something with me. He wanted to know why my project on Australian prime ministers was only half finished when I handed it in and why I had drawn a mustache on Malcolm Fraser when he didn't even have one.

"I don't know," I said. "I thought he had one."

"Come on," he said. "You can't just hand things in like this. You didn't even finish your last sentence."

I had been tired. Dad had been trying to help me before he went to night shift but Aunty Cheryl kept disagreeing with everything he said.

"Don't you know anything?" she kept asking him.

Mum was watching *A Country Practice*. She couldn't help me because she had drunk too much wine but she thought the mustache was funny and then she started crying in the middle of when she was laughing and that's when I decided to go to bed.

"I got very tired and I fell asleep and then when I woke up it was morning and the project was due in," I said, because everything would be too difficult to explain.

"That's not good enough," he said. "You're over halfway through grade six, you know? Can you ask your mother to come in and see me?"

I tried to imagine it.

She would be in her yellow Japanese happy coat and her pink fluffy slippers. She would say, "Frankly, Mr. Bum Cracker, I don't give a damn."

"Yes," I said.

That afternoon I didn't tell Mum. I'd finally agreed to open the box again with Angela. She said we must have been missing something. The clue to my lost voice, the answer to everything, was somewhere inside.

We made sure Danielle wasn't around. We took the box out from its shelf and walked with it slowly through the kitchen and out the back door. We sat beneath the back steps. Angela bit her bottom lip while she waited for me to open it.

This time I was ready for the smell of fifty-cent-sized raindrops hitting dry earth. Of bicycle tires humming on hot pavement. Of bare feet running through crackling grass. Of the lake breathing against the shore.

I picked up the gladwrapped braid. I removed it from the plastic. It shone in my hands. Angela touched it timidly with just two fingers.

"This is it," she said, "isn't it?"

"You don't even know anything," I said.

"I do," she said. "It's to do with the braid. I can see it in your eyes."

"I wish you'd get rooted," I said.

"I wish you weren't such a freak of nature," she said.

She said that was it.

It was the end.

I'd never step foot in the redback panel van again.

When she was finished shouting at me she climbed out from under the steps and picked up her bike and went.

I wrapped up the braid again and put it in the box. I closed the lid. I walked up the back steps slowly and into the kitchen. Mum was standing with her back against the kitchen bench waiting for me.

"What are you doing?" she asked.

"Just looking," I said.

"Did you ask anyone if you could look?"

"No."

"I wish you would have asked me," she said.

It was the most words she had said to me for a very long time. I started crying. I didn't mean to. I cried with my mouth open and my eyes shut and with the volume turned off. I just made small noises in my throat, almost like a grasshopper clicking its wings.

"Give it to me," she said.

I gave the box to her.

I leaned against her and cried. She tried to hug me. It was hard for her. I could tell it was making her feel sick. She made the cat-with-a-fur-ball noise.

"Nanna loves you," I said.

My voice came out like a squawk.

"I don't want you to go round there anymore," said Mum.

"Why?"

"Because she's a maniac. You hear?"

She pulled her dressing gown tighter around her. She lit up a cigarette and watched me.

Angela and I did not speak for the whole weekend but mostly because she went to the Territory with her father for a panel van rally. Mr. Popovitch came second place to the silver siren panel van, which was black with a silver spiderweb all over it. It also had a lady with fangs and long blond hair with a dead straight center part. Angela said it had even won the section for soft furnishings for its shiny silver seats. She didn't mention anything about the braid or how she knew everything about everything.

I didn't mention anything about the braid either even though I could still feel it in my hands. I wanted to touch it again. I wanted to go to the box in the linen closet and open it up and touch every item. One by one. Each centimeter. Each millimeter. In the open. Without secrets.

I wanted to touch everything so I could cry again. I needed to be punctured so the tears would fall out. When I had cried something had loosened in me, a small section had peeled, and for a little while the new exposed part had throbbed. I had felt everything. After I had cried against my mother I had not felt numb. My bedspread scratched against my skin, a magpie sang outside my window and I listened to it.

I had an idea.

All we had to do was take the box and sit down at the table, Mum and Dad and Danielle and Nanna.

We needed to remember Beth. All the days, not just the last. How she ran along the footpath in her leotard and her happy shoes, dancing and laughing. How she did pirouette after pirouette in the dirt beneath the rain tree. How we lay side by side on the floor and divided up the moon.

All those days had been removed, simply and precisely, whole weeks brimming with cloudless blue skies neatly severed and discarded.

We needed Beth's name to be shouted, not whispered.

But I was too scared to tell my plan to anyone.

Instead I lay in bed at night and thought about it. I thought about the box being there closed up, forever. I thought about why Mum had chosen to keep those things that had been with Beth when she died. Why she had placed the ballet shoes among them. I thought about how long everything would last before it was nothing but dust.

My new raw part sealed over like a scab.

I tried to think about Babylon, which was once a great city. I knew that it takes thousands of years for an ancient city to vanish. Some ancient cities simply crumbled and fell apart. Some were swallowed up by desert. Some were taken over by newer cities. Some fell into the sea. I thought it would take even longer for our cities to vanish because of the stronger building materials like steel, which are virtually indestructible except in the case of a nuclear war, where everything is reduced to nothing in less than a blink of an eye.

And then I thought that in one thousand years Memorial would probably have disappeared. The plaster of Paris footprint casts we made with Mrs. Bridges-Lamb would have turned to dust. Only parts of the mine would poke out of the red sand and rock in places. All the streets scratched into the desert and all the exactly-the-same houses wouldn't be visible anymore. And if a team of archaeologists came and dug down into my room and found it exactly the way it was when everything stopped in November 1982 they would find two beds and a writing desk and a cupboard with a built-in mirror.

They would find the green and yellow geometric shapes wallpaper and they would shake their heads and exchange knowledgeable glances and say, "Circa 1977." They would be interested in the matching ballerina bedspreads but even more interested in Danielle's sketchbook with all her drawings of the end of the world.

They would throw up their hands if they found the bookshelf. They would open up drawers and find T-shirts decorated with Hobbytex artwork and neatly pressed rose-embroidered jeans and Mickey Mouse sandals. Jewelry boxes with bluebird earrings and necklaces. And on the inside of the cupboard doors they would find posters tacked: Luke Skywalker with a light saber, Olivia Newton-John, Blondie.

And they would confer before exclaiming, "An excellent and well-preserved example of the times."

But would they feel the sadness in that room?

Two girls crying into each other's hair.

Two girls holding each other tight to stop from shivering.

Nanna had a new plan for unclogging my songs. She didn't tell me straightaway, only hinted at it.

"Today we will try something new," she said.

"What?" I asked.

"Patience," she said. "Patience."

First I had to help take out all the ceramic dogs from the cabinets and dust them with a dry rag. Then Nanna wiped them over with a wet rag. It was the first time in months I had seen her do anything other than lie on her bed or sit in a chair.

"Your Aunty Margaret tells me your mother is improving, that she is getting out of bed and cooking dinner again?"

She asked it like a question for me to confirm.

"If she is feeling better I am feeling better," she said.

Then she started crying.

What I would have mostly liked to talk about was olden-day stories of the town. How everything looked when she first arrived with Uncle Paavo a long time ago. When the streets were dirt and the bridges wooden and on every corner there was a pub and people bought their groceries wrapped in newspaper and carried them in string bags.

Her two hair curtains had grown long because she still hadn't been outside the flat to get them cut. She said her nerves were shot to pieces. Her hands shook too much to drive. She'd seen a teenage girl ride down her street just yesterday, a girl with blond hair. She'd seen her out of the corner of her eye and thought it was Beth. She got a pain in her heart and down her left arm. She hadn't stopped shaking for hours.

The two hair curtains closed over her cheeks when she leaned forward and wept.

"I will not take it back," she said. "I was telling nothing but the truth."

I would like to have heard about how she always carried in her apron pocket the Saint Jude card the priest had given her on the ship after their mother had died because Saint Jude is the patron saint of the hopeless. How it was worn thin from being held. How she touched it each day in her apron pocket when she cooked for all the men in the boardinghouse with impossible names like Timmo Vitikkohuhta, Yrjo Lamminmaki, and Manu Matinpoika.

Some mornings these men went down the hole and never came back, killed by a rock fall or stepping off dark stopes by accident. Their funeral processions stretched along the dusty streets and they were buried beneath the long rows of quartz graves in the dirt cemetery. And the men at the front of the processions carried trumpets and trombones and their feet kicked up the dust as they walked so it looked like they were being carried on a cloud. The sky was impossibly large and faultlessly blue.

"Why must I say she did not see an angel?" she asked me. "What could have we done? What should have we done?"

Desert angels would have skin like moonlit ghost gums. They would have silver eyes and dirty feet. They'd ride willy-willies just for fun.

"We thought she would grow out of it," said Nanna, wiping her nose with her handkerchief.

After that we went outside.

Nanna wound down the communal Hills hoist as low as it would go. She clicked her tongue before she unpegged her neighbors' drying and put it in a basket. She turned her empty bin upside down and made me stand on top of it. She made me hang from one of the clothesline's metal arms.

"Now bring your legs up," she said. "Bring them up so you hang only from your legs."

"I can't," I said.

"What do you mean you can't? You must perform this on the monkey bars every day. Pull your body up through your arms."

"I'm not Nadia Comaneci, you know," I said.

It was a perfect still winter day and everything was very bright. When my legs were up she made me let go with my hands and hang. I looked at the large clear blue sky and desert upside down.

"Good," she said.

Then she took one end of the clothesline and started to walk fast with it and then she broke out into a little trot and then an almost run. And I spun around upside down.

"Nanna," I shouted because she was going really fast and I thought I was going to fall off or she was going to fall over.

"Yell something," she shouted.

I screamed, "Stop this thing."

Nanna stopped pushing. She stood back but she didn't stop the clothesline from going around. I kept passing her and she was smiling at me and her too-big false teeth were almost dropping out of her mouth. She was breathing hard from her running and she put her hands down on her knees.

"Go on," she said. "Yell something."

"Help me," I yelled.

"Try a song now."

"Which one?"

"Try 'Oh! Susanna,' " she said.

"Oh! Susanna," I said, "don't you cry for me."

"That's not singing," she said.

She let the clothesline wind down slowly. I couldn't stand up straight when I got down.

"It was worth a try," Nanna said, and she held out her arms for me.

I could feel her bones through her cotton dress and she smelled like dust. She hugged me for a while and after the while was up I still didn't feel like letting go. We both squinted our eyes against the sun.

"Do not tell your mother that I made you do this," she said when we moved apart.

"I won't," I said.

And for some reason it made both of us laugh.

2 DARDANELLES COURT

Philippa Irwin had exhausted the youth group's string-art supplies the day she first ever thought of running away. She opened the sliding glass door and went out into the late afternoon heat. She walked along the outside of the hall. The windows were plastered with the cellophane stained glass they had made. Her stained glass had been the star of Bethlehem. Pastor Greg had made her stand at the front of the group and explain why she had chosen it.

"I just really like stars," she had said, stuttering on the *r* in "really" and the *s* in "stars."

Once she had told her mother she was going to be an astronomer. Her mother had told her to stop being silly. She knew her mother wanted her to be like her eldest sister, Maria, who had found a nice husband. Her mother was sure her next sister, Monica, would do the same and then Philippa after that. But Philippa could still remember when Maria wanted to be a clarinetist in a real orchestra. When Maria had asked her mother about going to live in the city and playing in an orchestra her mother had been shocked. It was as though Maria had asked for a rocket ship to fly to Mars.

Philippa never told her father about wanting to be an astronomer except in her head. In her head she told him she had been accepted as the youngest child ever into astronomy school and, by the way, it was in America. No one told her father anything unless they were responses to his questions.

"Think about it before you answer me," he usually said.

Philippa rounded the corner to where the large outdoor air conditioner whirred and rattled. One of the big boys, Shane, was standing in front of it. He put his hand up in a stop sign.

"You can't go past here," he said.

"Why not?" she stammered.

"Because I said so."

Even though the air conditioner was loud she could hear the laughter from the other side. It was the breathless, high-pitched cackling of boys.

Shane grabbed her around the waist when she pushed past him. She was a lot smaller than him; she squirmed out of his arms.

"Red alert," he called. "Red alert."

Boys jumped up from behind the air-conditioner unit, five or six of them, coughing, straightening their pants, giggling, punching each other, pushing each other. Monica was sitting cross-legged on the dry grass; she was pulling her shirt down.

"What are you doing?" Philippa stammered.

"What are you doing?" Monica asked in return.

When they were all in the discussion circle Pastor Greg and Pastor John carried a wooden ark into the center.

"Give me those," said Pastor Greg to Shane.

Shane had two wooden donkeys humping one another.

After that Pastor John started asking questions about the Bible story of Noah's ark. He had his Bible pages all marked out so he had the proper biblical answers. Monica sat opposite, legs stretched out, red-cheeked, chewing her Hubba Bubba.

Philippa hoped she wouldn't get asked any questions because she would stutter and everything would go silent except for the crickets and cicadas.

That first day she ever thought about running away she didn't listen to the group discussion. Instead she imagined running away. She tried to work out how she'd do it; her first plan was to stow away on an ore train. Then she would become a famous string artist to support herself when she got to wherever she was going.

She didn't know what Monica had been doing but it was wrong, she knew that. She imagined her father's honeyed voice asking Monica about it. He would ask her to tell him why God had made Eve with breasts.

"Go away and think about it before you answer me," he would say.

He would sit down like a king in his chair and wait for her to come back, his face as calm as born-again Jesus. His disappointment with Monica would not be spoken; she would simply wither beneath his stare.

But he wouldn't find out. He wouldn't find out because she wouldn't tell. From across the circle Monica watched her. Philippa looked back into her sister's green eyes. They watched each other. It was like a thunderbolt straight out of heaven.

But the outside, the stippled desert behind the hills, the faded crumbling channel country, the Great Dividing Range, crowded in at the darkening windows of the youth group hall. Outside was as impenetrable as Noah's sea. They would never make it. They watched each other and knew that they were stuck.

Their father was the last to come. The headlights

turned into the darkened car park, wheels crunching on the gravel. Her sister beside her had an earthy smell, sweaty and wild, like one of Noah's animals. On the way home, in the silence, the black night pressing itself to the car windows, they reached for each other's hands.

"YOU'VE GOT TO GET HER OUT OF THIS TOWN," MRS. IRWIN SAID OVER THE FENCE, SWATTING A FLY FROM HER FACE. She was an expert on raising good girls.

"It's no place to raise girls unless you've got your eye on them every hour of the day," she said. "You can't turn your back on them. Send her to boarding school. Send her for the next semester. That'd be my advice. Thank the Lord my girls have never given me an ounce of trouble."

"I couldn't bear it," said Mum, wiping the sweat from her brow, shielding the sun from her eyes, "for her to be so far away."

Beth hadn't come home. She was riding up and down Amiens Road waiting for Marco. She stuck out her tongue and tasted the sulfur from the mine stacks. It caught in her throat. She rode with no hands, coughing and wiping tears from her eyes.

"Where've you been?" he said after he had slammed the car door.

"I wasn't allowed out yesterday or the day before."

"It's been days, more than two."

"I know," she said. "But I've been wearing this. I've been thinking of you."

She pulled out the pendant from under her T-shirt.

He held it in his fingers with a look almost like regret.

"Show me yours now," she said.

"I lost it," he said.

Inside he put his finger up to her mouth and then kissed her. It was no good, she thought. It was too late. She couldn't save him. She raised her arms, he slipped off her shirt.

"Did you really lose it?" she asked afterward.

"Yes," he lied.

"I don't believe you."

"You're going to get yourself in trouble," he said.

"What do you mean?"

"I dunno," he said.

She moved back on the bed. She dressed herself.

"I don't reckon you should come round here anymore," he said.

He didn't say anything for a while after that. He turned away from her. He sat on the side of the bed and lit a cigarette. She watched his profile: his lustrous black hair falling over his eye, his long eye-lashes casting shadows on his cheek, cigarette held up to his carved lips. He let the ash drop to the ashtray on the floor.

"You better not come round here anymore," he said again.

He sounded angry this time. She went to ask him why but he put his hands over his face in exasperation.

"You're too young," he said. "You shouldn't be doing shit like this. I could get in trouble, you know. Everyone's saying I could get into trouble."

"What should I be doing?" she asked.

"Maybe in a couple of years," he said, but he shook his head at the same time.

"Suit yourself," said Beth.

The Irwin girls were getting out of their car when Beth rode into Dardanelles Court.

"Don't look at her," Mrs. Irwin said to her daughters and loud enough so Beth would hear.

Mum was lying on her bed half waiting, half dreaming.

"Where have you been?" she asked. Her voice sounded sad.

"Just riding," Beth said from the doorway.

"Are you telling the truth?"

"Yes," said Beth. "I didn't do anything bad."

Beth went to the fridge and poured some wine

from the cask into a tall glass. She filled it up with orange juice, then she went outside into the garage. She opened up Dad's tool cupboard and took out the methylated spirits and added a little. Just a dash. There was something she wanted to remember but she couldn't remember it. And something she wanted to forget.

She was expelled from school after the midyear holidays, just before she turned fourteen. The principal summoned both Mum and Dad to the school to discuss the matter. Mr. Vernon, who was the principal, called in Mrs. Simpson, the deputy principal who dealt in girl matters. She sat beside Mum and took her hand.

"I don't believe you and nothing you can say can make me believe it," said Mum.

"The teacher who witnessed it has worked here for many years, Mrs. Day," said Mr. Vernon. "She would not make up such a serious allegation."

"Well, you've got it wrong," said Mum.

Dad sat very quietly. He examined Mrs. Simpson's blue-stockinged legs and the school motto on the wall: TO STRIVE FOR EXCELLENCE. It was embroidered on a banner in blue and yellow thread in fancy running writing. Dad was shocked. He scratched his head.

"Jean," he said so she would stop.

Mum wouldn't stop.

"We could go to the police over this," she shouted.

She untangled herself from Mrs. Simpson's hand and stood up.

"It's called slander, I think. Is it slander, Jim? Jim, is it slander?"

"Mrs. Day," said Mrs. Simpson, "please sit down. We need to discuss the best course of action."

"It can't be right, can it?" asked Dad.

"It's not," said Mum.

"Did you know she was sexually active?" asked Mrs. Simpson.

"She isn't," said Dad. "Is she?"

"We have no alternative but a full-term suspension," said Mr. Vernon, who had had enough, "for an act, or acts, such as this, whether you believe it or not, on school grounds. You'll need to contact the Catholic school to see if she can attend there for the second half of the year. If you want that, of course."

"Or when you have thought about it," said Mrs. Simpson, "because I know this is very shocking to you, we can sit down and discuss it further. How would that be?"

She patted Mum on the shoulder. Mum shrugged her pat away and stood up. She walked to the door.

Dad stood up and said thank you but then shook his head apologetically. Beth was waiting outside in the corridor.

"Here she is," said Mrs. Simpson quite cheerily.

Beth unfolded herself from the chair.

"The suspension will start from today," said Mr. Vernon. "Elizabeth is welcome back in the new year for grade ten as long as she can prove that she understands such behavior is completely unacceptable. Do you understand, Beth?"

Mr. Vernon talked to Beth like she was a teenager but he couldn't help but imagine it whenever he saw her. He stroked his tie slowly and then loosened it at the neck.

"Yes," she said, and she looked him right in the eyes to frighten him.

"Don't think we'll be coming back here," said Mum.

"Jean," said Dad.

"Don't," said Mum.

"Christ," said Dad.

"I mean it," said Mum.

"God," said Beth, closing her eyes.

Nothing was said in the car until Dad pulled into the drive-through liquor store and asked for a carton of beer. The liquor store attendant, Mandy, asked him for racing tips for Saturday.

"Hello, Jean," said Mandy, bending down and looking into the car.

"Hello, Mandy," said Mum, smiling her neighborhood smile.

When they drove into the sunlight again Mum brought her hand up and pinched the bridge of her nose to hold her brain in.

"Tell me it isn't true," she said.

"Jean," said Dad, almost lovingly.

Beth shifted in the backseat and looked at her chewed-down nails.

"What I don't understand," she said slowly, "is why the boys didn't get expelled for as long?"

Mum finally took Nanna's advice and tried locking Beth in her room after she got expelled. She only locked her up for two hours. She locked her up suddenly and without warning. She followed Beth down the hallway and then quickly pushed her into the room, grabbed the key from the inside of the door, and locked it from the outside. No one saw it coming. No one said anything. Mum was breathing like she had just run around the block.

"Go to your room," she said, looking at us.

Danielle and I sat on our beds opposite each other, listening over our heartbeats.

Mum said it was so Beth would learn to stay at

home, the way you lock a cat in the bathroom of a new house. Mum also said it was because Beth had done a disgraceful thing. She stood at our door and spoke to us calmly while Beth started knocking in the background.

No one had ever been locked up in our house before except for the time Kylie got stuck in the toilet and became so hysterical that Dad had to remove the sliding lock with a screwdriver. But that didn't really count. Aunty Cheryl said Kylie was so smart she sometimes forgot how to do simple things. Dad said the lock must have jammed. Beth said it was because Kylie was a retard. She got sent to her room for saying it but not locked in.

A dreadful feeling filled the house after Beth was locked up. It felt like she would never be let out. She would stay there for the rest of her life. Dad would cut a flap in the door for her meals to be pushed through.

But Beth started knocking slowly on the door, like someone truly trapped, suffocating in a small space, sending a message for help. Something in the knock was also a message to our mother. I can knock forever, it said. The knocking filled the house. Every now and again Mum told her to just keep doing it and she'd never get out.

Then she got Beth's bag and went through it in the hallway outside of the door. We heard Mum drop the contents, one by one, to the floor. The light plunk of a packet of cigarettes hitting the linoleum. Mascara and lipstick tied together with a rubber band. A fistful of loose change clattered against the wall. A dollar note drifted into our room.

"I'm going to burn this bag," shouted Mum.

Beth kept knocking.

"Let her out, for Christ's sake, Jean," said Dad.

He had to turn the volume up on the television so he could hear it over all the knocking and throwing of things.

When Mum let Beth out she *was* like a cat that had been kept in a closed space. She leaped out of the room. She fought off Mum's arms and ran down the hallway. Her face was swollen from crying. Her mascara was running down her cheeks.

Mum chased her into the kitchen.

She grabbed Beth by the braid and with her other hand opened up the Drawer of Everything and took out a pair of scissors.

"Mum," shouted Danielle, but Mum had already started cutting.

Beth and Mum got tangled in each other's arms and legs and they fell onto the floor. Mum kept cutting even when they were falling, even though you should never run or fall with scissors. The scissors were blunt. It took her a fair while to cut through Beth's braid. All the crockery shook in the cupboards.

Mum was crying very loudly as she cut. Beth had stopped struggling.

"Jesus Christ, Jean," said Dad when he came to the kitchen door.

Beth sat up with her new hair. Mum looked at her with the braid held in her hands.

After Beth had picked up her bag from the hallway floor and put back all her things inside, she banged the back screen door open and shut and wheeled her bike across the lawn. I lay on my bed and tried to sing a song. I tried to sing *The gypsy rover came over the hill*, but I only got as far as *the valley so shady* because then the song got stuck in my chest. It lodged quite close to my heart.

Mum swept up the stray blond hairs with a broom. She wrapped up the braid in gladwrap. There was nothing left in the kitchen to show what had happened there.

EVERYONE TRIED TO FORGET WHAT MUM HAD DONE
IN THE KITCHEN. Uncle Paavo was whistling as he sat
down at the table for Beth's fourteenth birthday. He
was the happiest anyone had ever seen him. He'd
even brought a small packet of barbecue-flavored
Samboys to lunch. In the pocket of his starched shirt
there was a gold pen as though he might have to suddenly write something down. His very white skin had
a bluish tinge. He had combed his thin hair down
with water and his collar was still wet.

"Good on you, Par-voh," said Dad, shaking his
hand.

"Here is the spirit of the Lutheran," said Nanna
under her breath.

Mum made everyone stand in the kitchen in front
of the radio at quarter to five. She'd put a special
message over the radio for the birthday girl. The song
they played was "Mickey." We stood at attention to

listen to it. Mum raised a warning finger at Danielle when she moved.

"Wasn't that lovely?" said Mum when it had finished. She had her hair curled and her Frostiest Taupe lipstick on.

"Do you like that song, Beth?" asked Aunty Cheryl. "We hoped you did."

"It's all right," said Beth, "I suppose."

Danielle had begged for the party without her Milwaukee back brace. Nanna turned her attention to her once the table was laid with all the food.

"Your back will never mend without this brace," she said.

"Mum," said Danielle.

"Leave her alone," said Mum.

"I will pray for your spine," said Nanna.

"How annoying," Danielle said.

"Shhhh," said Aunty Cheryl, "just let her do it and it will be over and done with."

"Our Father," she said. "On this the birthday of our beloved Elizabeth let us pray for Danielle's backbone. That if it is your will on this day it shall straighten and mend. Amen."

"Amen," said Beth.

"Why'd you say that?" said Danielle.

"I just said amen," said Beth.

"You were being a smart-arse."

"Please," said Mum.

"She was," said Kylie. "I saw it."

"No law against saying amen," said Beth.

"Amen," said Nanna.

"Elizabeth," said Dad. "Give it a rest."

He didn't look at Beth when he said it but stared at the wall. Since Beth was expelled he never looked at her. He avoided her. Even when he passed her in the hall, when he'd woken up to go to night shift, he didn't say anything. He just looked at the floor.

Beth was enrolled in Our Lady's Secondary College for the next semester, which made Nanna very happy. Our Lady's had smaller classes and very strict rules and no Miranda Bell and no boys. Nanna was so happy when she found out that she danced in our kitchen while Mum stood resting against the bench with her arms folded across her chest.

"If there was a Presbyterian school I would have sent her to that," said Mum. "I have terrible memories of that place. I would have sent her anywhere but there. A Hindu school, a Methodist school, a Lutheran school. I just want a girls' school."

"Yes," said Nanna. "Yes. I know. But here she will go into Our Lady's every day and you will see, you will see, Jean, that it will change her heart."

If Catholic girls' school didn't work Beth was going to boarding school.

"You must promise me you won't gloat," said Mum to Nanna.

"I will not be a goat," said Nanna.

"Everything is bad enough as it is."

Beth attended the party like she was a stranger. She looked bored. She yawned. The mascara was smudged around her eyes. Mum hadn't wanted any of Beth's friends to come. She had said let's just keep it simple.

It was Nanna who noticed that my voice was gone. Not when the cake came out and I could only mime "Happy Birthday," but after. Danielle had been strapped back into her brace and was crying on her bed because she didn't want to be a cripple. Beth had gone outside to lie on the trampoline. Everyone else was sitting in the living room waiting for the end of the party.

Nanna asked me to sing her a song. I said I was too busy, I had stuff to do.

"Stuff to do?" said Nanna. "Don't be silly, sing me a song."

"Sing us a song," said Uncle Paavo. "The one I like is 'Morning Has Broken.'"

"Come on, darling," said Mum.

"That's not like you, chickadee," said Dad when I stood in front of them all and shook my head slowly from side to side.

"Shut up," I finally said. "All of you."

I went out onto the front patio and sat on the steps. I didn't have the strength to break anything. I had a song inside me. It was the pointy edge of a "Gypsy Rover" pressing into my heart. I sat very still and panted.

"What is going on?" said Nanna.

She came onto the steps beside me and her light-weight tracksuit made a rustling noise when she sat down. She opened her handbag. I heard the zip. I kept my eyes screwed shut. She handed me a hand-kerchief.

"I'm not crying," I said.

"Yes you are," said Nanna.

"No, I'm not."

She took one of my unprotected hands and put it in her Hand Press.

"Where has your singing gone?" she asked.

"How would I know?"

"Is it stuck in here," she said, and one of her crooked bony fingers touched my chest.

"Yes," I said.

"My dear," she said, and she let go of my hand, and I didn't have to tell her everything if I didn't want to.

"It hurts," I said.

"I know," she said. "Do not fear. It is not forever. I know these things."

When the sun started heading down at the end of that day I went and sat beside Beth on the trampoline.

She had her fingers double-crossed and laid across her eyes.

"What are you doing?" I asked, although I'd seen her do it before when she lay on her bed.

"Listening," she said.

"Listening to what?"

"To everything."

The sun, sides bulging, squashed itself between two hills. It sent up a flare of golden light. The sky, patterned with a million tiny clouds like fish scales, was illuminated.

I lay down beside her and put my hand on her arm.

"Tell me," I said.

Inside Mum and Aunty Cheryl did the dishes. I could hear them talking and laughing together at the sink. Earlier Nanna's news that my voice was missing had barely caused a ripple because it was just the type of thing she would make up.

"She's just having a bad day," Mum said.

"Too much birthday cake," said Dad, and he poked me in the stomach. He plucked me from the ground and threw me over his shoulder and turned me around and around.

Beth, with her double-crossed fingers, didn't tell me anything. She just lay very still. The bulging sun disappeared. A cloud of cockatoos passed over toward the creek. I didn't know how she could lie so still for so long. I fidgeted beside her.

"I'm going to tell Mum," I said.

"Tell her what?" she asked. She removed her double-crossed fingers from her eyes and opened them. She looked at me.

"Something terrible is going to happen, you know," she said when I didn't answer. "I can feel it."

"To who?"

"To all of us."

"I'm really telling now," I said.

I thought the terrible thing would be everyone, a whole carful of us, careening off a high cliff into the ocean. Or all of us being in a boat like the *Titanic* and sinking. Or all of us being in a seaplane flying over the Gulf and crashing into the water to be eaten by crocodiles. All of my possible terrible things involved cars and boats and planes and accidents.

I got off the trampoline because I was sick of her and all the trouble she caused and how she always ruined everything.

I went up the back stairs and slammed the screen door open and shut.

"Beth says something terrible is going to happen to all of us," I told Aunty Cheryl and Mum.

Mum stopped washing dishes. Aunty Cheryl stood with the tea towel in one hand and a wineglass in the other. Their faces shone beneath the electric lightbulb without a shade. They still had their paper birthday hats on.

Mum opened the sliding window and called out to Beth.

"Why did you say that, Beth?" she called out. "Come inside right now."

Beth turned on her side so she was facing away from the window.

"I'm talking to you," shouted Mum.

Aunty Cheryl shook her head and turned back to the drying rack.

"You've scared Jennifer," shouted Mum. "And on your birthday too, when we've all been so nice to you."

None of my possible imagined terrible things involved anything as simple as the girl who fell.

MARCO WENT IN LATE JULY. The wild winds had come back again. They blew across the ranges and split apart the clouds into single wispy hairs. Our breath caught in our throats and ached. The place was at a bend in the road, a turn like the head of a question mark. The land fell away on either side and rose again into the fat rumps of two red hills. It was a place of curves: the rounded descent into the ditch, the series of hills like women bending over in a field, the two black tire tracks curling off into nothing.

Beth didn't say anything when she found out. She put the phone down and crossed her arms.

"What's wrong?" said Mum, and she tried to unfold Beth's arms and get her to lie down but Beth wouldn't be taken anywhere.

She did not want to close her eyes or she would see it: the car turning in the air, Marco flying upward after he was ejected in a violent arc, his back bent, the pocketful of change raining from beneath him.

Beside her, Mum's mouth moved open and shut like a fish out of water.

Marco came down in scrub among the spinifex and anthills. He landed on his head, which broke his neck. The car cartwheeled past him, threw back a wash of shattered glass that glittered in the sun.

In among the glass and spinifex and anthills he lay. Behind him the car rested on its back. Someone moaned from within its dark interior. Someone said shit. The shadow of a bird that had fallen backward through the air to study the damage slid over the red scrub floor. It cast a shadow over his face. It circled.

Among all the strange confetti—the beads of glass, the copper ones and twos, the winking twenties, Redheads matchsticks, and crumpled tinnies—a silver-plated half-a-heart pendant lay shining in the sun.

Beth refused to go to his funeral. She lay on her bed for days with the blinds pulled shut. Mum, who had never met him, never liked him, and even made fun of him, now whispered about the tragedy to Aunty Cheryl on the phone. Dad didn't know what to say. He stood at Beth's door and only shook his head. Everyone tiptoed backward and forward past the door and looked in at her sadness like it was an exhibition. A jewel inside a case.

"It won't always feel like this," said Mum, sitting at the end of her bed.

"Yes it will," Beth said.

"Do you want me to make you something to eat?"

"No," Beth said.

Nanna came.

She stood at Beth's door.

She said, "What on earth will we do with you?"

Miranda arrived, tear-swollen. Mum relented and let her in. They lay on the bed together, Beth and her, side by side, crying.

At school Mrs. Bridges-Lamb had to interrupt my bird-watching again and again.

"When the youngest Miss Day has come back to earth we will proceed with our math lesson," she said.

She had trained us already to be very quiet. Some days the only noise was the fan wobbling very slowly from the ceiling. We had learned how to open our tidy boxes very softly. We had learned how to cross our arms and wait for instruction. We had learned not to scrape our chairs. Not to chew on our pencils. Not to jump like grasshoppers when we raised our hands for answers.

But she had failed at training me not to look out the window.

I had been watching hawks wheeling over the oval from between the louvers. They weren't interesting hawks but plain hawks. Brown. Not letter wings or whistling kites. There were no wedge-tailed eagles. That was what I wanted more than anything. It would be a sign that everything would be all right. I tried not to think about Beth but she wouldn't leave my mind.

After Krakatoa exploded the sun turned green. Laika was the first dog in space. She suffocated. Millions of people were killed when the Yellow River flooded. Millions. People's shadows were frozen on walls when Hiroshima was bombed. The shadows showed people doing ordinary things like talking to a neighbor, eating breakfast, skipping rope. They sent mice into space and more dogs, monkeys too. Only some made it back safely. All the people in Pompeii probably thought there was nothing to worry about.

"Deary me," said Mrs. O'Malley. "Take a breather for a minute."

I took a long shuddering breath.

Mr. O'Malley walked past, humming softly under his breath.

"Mr. O'Malley, young Jennifer here knows all the disasters of the world," said Mrs. O'Malley.

"Does she now," said Mr. O'Malley.

Mr. and Mrs. O'Malley always had conversations without looking at each other, as though they were reading from a script, even when they were standing side by side.

"She does, Mr. O'Malley," said Mrs. O'Malley.

"I suppose she knows all the big ones," said Mr. O'Malley.

"All the biggest," said Mrs. O'Malley.

"Any of the small?" asked Mr. O'Malley.

"None of the small," whispered Mrs. O'Malley.

They looked at each other then.

A glimpse, a little piece of their story, flapping like ribbon in the wind.

"Now," she said, "young Jennifer Day. You've nothing to worry about here in the middle of nowhere. Nothing can happen to us."

Beth lasted five weeks at Our Lady's Secondary College. Each morning when she got out of the car all the girls in their checkered uniforms and brown socks moved back from her as she passed. In the corridors they held their hands over their mouths and whispered into each other's ears.

Here was the girl who gave blow jobs.

The girl with the boyfriend whose neck got snapped.

The strange blue-eyed girl.

In the small airless demountable classrooms the nuns treated her harshly because they had accepted her as a difficult case that needed to be fixed. Right from the beginning they needed to get on top of her behavior. But they had expected a lot worse.

They could only fault her on small things. For instance her daydreaming and her sliding brown socks. When she chewed her fingernails she was made to swallow the chewed pieces. That was all.

Beth made unlikely friends. At first only one or two, girls curious of the strange newcomer with her sand-colored hair and the bored, slightly disappointed expression. But then there were more. Later they flocked to her like moths to a flame.

Mostly they came with the intention of meanness.

"We know all about you," they said.

"We've heard what a slut you are," they said.

"Lucky there are no boys here," they said.

"She'll probably try to do it with Father Matthew," they said.

Beth didn't say much back. She shrugged.

"So what if I do."

They shivered in their brown socks and thin white skins.

They found her irresistible.

These were good girls, immaculately groomed, with charm bracelets and white sandshoes. They played tennis. They went to band practice. They were pretty and unattainable. They wanted to talk to her about sex. They wanted to know things. They had questions about kissing and love bites and hands on breasts. They sat on the brown grass near the cement tennis courts and listened to Beth talk about it. She liked to watch them squirm. They were both excited and revolted. Sometimes they squealed and held their hands over their ears.

They reminded Beth of porcelain dolls in cellophane wrapping with their polished skin and shiny ponytails. They were sterile and scentless.

They jostled for her attention.

Beth held her pencil to her lips like a cigarette. She was like a still-faced Saint Catherine looking skyward before being strapped to the wheel. Sometimes she looked straight through them but when she came back to earth and smiled it was like the explosion of a star shell.

Everyone wanted a piece of her.

Just to touch her checkered uniform, a part of her pale skin, to be the recipient of one of her smiles. Mostly they didn't know why. They undid their top buttons just like her. Let their socks fall down. They smoked their pencil cigarettes in class. They tried to imitate her calm disinterested features.

The Shelleys came in boyfriends' cars and parked alongside all the mothers in their brand-new station wagons waiting for the last bell to ring. They laughed at Beth's uniform and called her a cattle tick. She pulled her black rubber-band bracelet from her pocket when she stood beside the car and put it on. Miranda, sitting in the front seat, said she'd stopped going to school. She flicked her cigarette ash out the window. She stared right ahead as though she didn't care if she saw Beth or not.

"You should do something to get expelled," Miranda said. "Anything, it wouldn't take much, would it?"

"You shouldn't be talking to those girls," said Mum when she arrived to pick Beth up.

"Why not?" said Beth.

"Because they're more than half your problem."

It was the cooking sherry that she brought to school that was her undoing. And the classroom full of polished girls who smelled of it, and later the parents crying in corridors.

"But it was only a small bottle," Beth said.

She said it to Mum, who had her head in her hands in the living room. She was going through the telephone book looking for faraway boarding schools. She wanted a school with locks on the dormitory doors and occasional caning.

Beth said she wasn't going. She said she was getting a job. There was mostly a lot of screaming and crying.

"I've had enough of you," shouted Mum. "I really have. I can't get it through to you, can I? You can't just do whatever you want."

"I'll get a job," said Beth. "I really want to get a job."

"You think you loved this boy?" said Mum. "You think just because he died your whole life is over? You don't know anything about love. How long did you know him? A month, two months, do you think that's love?"

She sounded like she had been waiting a long time to say that.

Dad came home but he didn't even make it up the steps. Mum banged open the screen door against the patio railing.

"She's bloody done it again," she said.

"Dad," said Beth from behind her.

He sat down on the step and put his crib port beside him.

"What have you done now, little mate?" he said.

He looked at her properly, for the first time in months.

"She took my cooking sherry to school. She's bloody been expelled," said Mum. "I had to walk past all those wretched women crying because their daughters were plastered. She thinks she's not going to boarding school, that she's getting a job. She's just fourteen, for Christ's sake. I can't stand it. I can't stand another minute of it. Why don't you sort her out for a change? Tell your father, tell your father now what you've gone and done."

"You were fourteen when you finished," said Dad, rubbing his eyes.

"I knew it," screamed Mum. "I knew you'd do this."

She threw her arms up in the air.

Mr. and Mrs. O'Malley came out onto their front patio and pretended to look at the sky for rain clouds.

Mum slammed the screen door again when she went inside. Dad patted the space beside his crib port and Beth sat down with him on the step. He looked at her and shook his head.

"I'll try really hard," she said.

She pushed her hair behind her ears. It had grown back to just above her shoulders. She looked down at her toes. She chewed her nails.

"You give it a go," said Dad, "but it's tough. I reckon you'll only last a month or so. But that's not the point, is it? You're only young. You can go back to school later if you need to."

"I want to try it," said Beth.

"I want you to be a good girl," said Dad, putting his arm around her. "What happened to my good girl?"

"I'm trying," said Beth.

"I know you are."

Dad got Beth a job at the Mission Street Mechanics. For a little while things settled down. She didn't ride her bike at night. She stopped drinking at the water tower with Miranda and the Shelleys. A fever had broken. She had changed. It was much better. She wasn't so restless.

She opened up a bank account and saved some of her money. She could lie on the sofa without getting up again every five minutes to look at herself in a mirror, to feel her face to make sure it was still there, to pack her bag, to smoke a cigarette, to start an orange and then throw it away. Danielle asked her what she was saving for but Beth just shrugged.

She started wearing a knee-length skirt and little black pumps and she took out all the earrings from her ears, which she had pierced with sewing needles. She didn't wear any makeup. She brushed her hair and rolled it into a bun the way she did when she danced. Our mother ironed her white shirts with fake pearl buttons. When she entered the workshed she didn't look up.

Beth's office at the Mission Street Mechanics was the size of a small cupboard. Summer came early. It arrived with a blast. The temperatures soared into the hundreds. During the day the shed heated up like an oven and a small dirty fan blew hot air that smelled of grease and smoke and men. The front wall of the office faced into the workshed and was made of clear plastic. Beth was like a rare flower in a glass hothouse.

Mr. McNally, who owned the business, was short and sweaty and permanently grease-stained. He handed her piles of pink and green invoices with blackened hands. He was Scottish. He called her lass. He smiled at her whenever he could because he'd told Dad he'd look after her. Beth added up the numbers on a grimy calculator bolted to the desk.

"Mission Street Mechanics. May I help you?" said Beth when she answered the phone.

She practiced it at home in the evenings and made us laugh. Mr. McNally puffed out his chest when he heard it. Business was up for the beginning of September.

"Mr. McNally to line one, please," she said over the public-address system.

It made the mechanics and their apprentices look toward the plastic window.

Beth was very good with numbers.

"She is just like me," said Uncle Paavo.

"Only not an arse-tight," said Nanna.

Beth took the green and pink invoices and separated them. She added, multiplied, subtotaled, and totaled them again. She skewered the copy when she was done. She sorted through years of old accounts. She scrubbed the filing cabinet clean. She swept her hothouse floor. She stayed inside at lunchtime so she could answer the phone even though Mr. MrNally suggested she go across the road to one of the highway cafés.

Beth didn't go outside until the second week. She asked Mr. McNally first. It was just for a cigarette at morning and afternoon tea. Mr. McNally laughed at her choice of words.

"Are you expecting fine china, lassie?" he asked.

Beside the shed there was a gravel yard enclosed by a tire fence and behind the fence the dry riverbed lay. Beth used a jerry can to climb onto a metal drum. She smoked her Winfield Greens. Two at morning tea and two at afternoon tea. She drank from a chipped and stained cup that read REPCO 76.

Frankie was the first to join her. He reminded her of Marco with his white skin and glossy black hair. He planted his feet apart in the gravel and showed off the muscles in his arms at every opportunity he could by leaning forward to pick up a handful of gravel, by straightening a tire along the fence line, by yawning and stretching his arms above him. Because his last name was Toscani the others called him Toss.

Then came Whitey. He had faded skin and white hair. He turned the metal drum on its side and made a charade of not noticing Beth when he sat beside her and then jumping with fright when he did.

"You're a bloody dickhead, Whitey," said Toss.

Jeffrey was third, the shyest. He had the face of a cherub on the body of a giant. He built Beth an awning over her drum chair without ever having said a word to her.

"I really like it, Jeffrey," she said.

"You'd get burned, that's all," he said with his head down, pawing the dirt with his foot like a flighty horse.

Gavin came last. He was barrel-shaped with thick black hair on his forearms and sticking out from his collar like stuffing. He wore a tight fixed smile. He came under the pretense of looking for an old Sigma part that had been left in the yard. He watched her with dangerous eyes.

Beth flourished in the young men's eyes. She grew more beautiful each day. On the third Monday while she was bored she took her hair out and put it up again. Mr. McNally, noticing something different in the air, looked up from his blowtorch and found every face turned toward the plastic window. He sent Beth on an errand to the newsagent's. He stewed on it for a day before he exploded.

Toss was dancing past Beth's window. Mr. McNally grabbed him by the scruff of the neck and walked him backward toward his station.

"Keep your bloody mind on your bloody job," he shouted.

He threatened to dock Frankie's pay if he looked up from his work.

"That's ridiculous," said Frankie.

Gavin stared at her through the window. She stabbed an invoice onto her paper stake knowing her days were numbered.

Whitey's trick was to visit the cupboard office to check up on parts he had only ordered five minutes before. On the bottom of his order forms he wrote in block letters YOU ARE BEAUTIFUL, in pencil, so that she could erase them. Mr. McNally watched him closely.

"Watch it, boy," he said under his breath whenever Whitey passed.

Jeffrey drank gallons of water from the water fountain beside the office. She listened to Jeffrey guzzling while he watched her with one eye.

"Don't think I'm not onto you, laddie," said Mr. McNally.

"I'm really thirsty, Mr. McNally," said Jeffrey.

"But you're not a bloody fish."

Gavin grew louder and his grin tighter. He walked backward and forward in front of the office without looking at her but occasionally rubbing his hairy arm against the plastic the way a tomcat marks its territory.

On the last day at smoke break she took her seat and waited.

Toss struck a pose and tried some dance moves in front of her. His feet sprayed gravel and cigarette butts.

"I've already seen it," she said.

"No wait," he said. "I got more."

He patted out the borders of an imaginary window.

"She said she's seen it," said Gavin, and snapped forward like a thrown rope and pushed Toss to the ground.

He lay in the gravel with a surprised look on his face like Marcel Marceau and then Gavin was on top of him, pummeling him with his fists. She sat very still on her overturned drum with its awning. Whitey leaped onto Gavin's back and attempted to prize him off. Gavin was speechless, red-faced. Hate bled out of him.

"Stop it," she said.

She stubbed her cigarette out on the ground. She picked up her handbag. She walked inside. She bumped into Jeffrey's chest.

"Quick," he said. "I think Mr. McNally's having a heart attack."

After Mr. McNally was taken away in the ambulance she went home. She walked the whole way along the highway toward an ever-receding mirage.

The day throbbed with heat. She lay on her bed and listened to the silence. The phone call came in the evening. Mrs. McNally was very polite when she spoke to Dad. Beth would not be welcome back.

"She's a sweet girl, I know," said Mrs. McNally, "but trouble follows her everywhere she goes. Some people are just like that. We wanted to give her a go but your girl's beyond help."

Dad said thanks very much for what they tried although he couldn't see what it was in particular and especially how Mr. McNally's dicky heart had anything to do with Beth. Mum hovered in the background.

"What's going on, Jim?" she said.

"Elizabeth got the boot," he said.

"What are you talking about?"

"That was Mrs. McNally. They don't want her back."

"Why not?"

"How would I know? She was talking in riddles."

"You should have given her to me."

"She asked for me."

"I'll get to the bottom of this," said Mum, but then sat down in the living room and chewed her nails exactly the way Beth did.

Dad lit up a cigarette and pulled the recliner handle to put his legs up. They thought Beth was in her bedroom. They would collect themselves and then talk to her. On *The Sullivans* Kitty was being precious. She was arguing with her parents. Mum and Dad watched her as if it was the most interesting thing they had ever seen. When Mum finished her smoke she went down the hallway but Beth was already gone.

Mum wanted to go to the police but Dad told her not to be stupid and cause a big fuss over nothing. Aunty Cheryl said if it was her daughter she'd be jumping up and down on the spot.

"That'd help," said Dad.

Nanna came and prayed to Saint Dymphna, who is the patron saint of runaways.

"For Pete's sake," said Dad.

It was the first time Beth had run away for more than two days but she wasn't really missing. Danielle said she had seen her on her bike doubling Miranda.

"You see," said Dad. "Just wait and see. She'll realize how hard it is in the real world and she'll come home."

Beth was sleeping in the caravan with Miranda or at Michelle Wright's flat. She went with the Shelley girls into town and drank with them on the amphitheater steps behind the town hall. She was extravagant. She gave Michelle Wright money from her savings account to buy real wine in the liquor store where her boyfriend worked.

The real wine was called Lambrusco. It was red and bubbly and they drank it warm. They all said it tasted good. They drank from the bottle and it stained their lips red. Miranda got up and called out to voices she could hear down along the riverbed. The voices answered back.

"Want to have sex?" she shouted.

"Where are you?" someone shouted back.

"Just up here, baby," shouted Miranda. "Come and get it."

They ran through the streets. Past the long line at the cinema that stretched out onto the footpath. Past the hotels, doors flung open, light and shadows falling onto the footpath. Past the boys showing off their cars in front of the post office. They ran until they had no breath from running and screaming and laughing.

They went to a place called the Oasis on the highway, nearly out of town. It was a bar and a motel and a service station. The barmaid wouldn't serve them so they sat along the gutter watching the semitrailers pulling in and out.

Beth kept drinking after the others had finished. She went up to the parked cars and offered money to men to buy her drinks.

"Come home," said Michelle.

"You can't even stand up," said Miranda.

"It's only early," said Beth.

She knew there was something happening some-where. She just had to find it. She asked people coming out of the Oasis where there was a party. Some-times the men in the cars offered to take her there. But she went with the Shelleys back along the highway into town.

In town she drifted apart from them deliberately. In front of the all-night café she slipped down an al-ley. She crossed the pale stone river. She heard them calling out to her along the streets and along the riverbank, then their voices faded.

There was nothing else to drink. She threw her bottle down beside the bridge. She listened to the night like she was underwater. The muffled conversa-tions along the riverbed, campfires flickering. A car, tires squealing in the distance, accelerating, decelerat-ing, dissolving. Sprinklers chattering across parks. In the streets beneath the mine the sudden roar and hiss of copper being poured. She didn't know how many hours she walked for. She didn't count the number of darkened streets.

In the blue light of dawn, when a small chill rose from the ground, she crossed her arms and hugged herself as she walked. From the water tower she saw the earth flush first pink, then gold, all the silver rooftops illuminated. The blue highway, a ribbon tacked down with white stitching, stretching out to the ranges. She wished she could see beyond the hills.

She knocked softly on the caravan window beside Miranda's bed.

Mum went out each afternoon looking for her. We drove up and down the streets, slowly, looking for her bike. Beth was good at hiding. Miranda's caravan, Michelle Wright's flat, or any of the other addresses that she kept, the street names and phone numbers in her childish leftward-slanting hand, scrawled on scraps of paper, the bottom of chocolate milk cartons, liquor store brown paper bags, all tied together with a rubber band.

Once we saw Beth's bike at Miranda's caravan. Mum had driven straight down the main street of the caravan park. She told me to wait in the car. Miranda came to the door and scowled at Mum with her black eyes. Beth leaned against the door and chewed her nails. Mum told Beth if she didn't come home she'd call the police.

"I'm fourteen," said Beth. "I'm allowed to do whatever I want."

I sat in the car and the sweat trickled down my back and my legs stuck to the vinyl seat. Mum was silent the whole way home. When we pulled into the driveway, Mum stayed sitting in the front seat and I stayed sitting in the back. We didn't say anything.

In the end it was a policeman who brought her home but not because Mum had phoned one. It was the middle of the night. She had been trying to help a man in the street. He had stumbled out of the Imperial Hotel onto the footpath and spewed onto the road. It was beneath the harsh light, the flashing neon sign:

GIRLS GIRLS GIRLS

He was going to die. Beth was sure of it. She double-crossed her fingers so she could save him. She was so drunk she could hardly stand up. She didn't say anything, just stood near him. The inside of the bar was roaring beside them. Words were stretched and slowed. Like a tape played backward. Glasses crashed. There was a high-pitched peal of a woman's laughter. The cars flew past, leaving trails of light floating on the street. The stars blazed in the sky.

"Do you like me?" she asked.

"What?" he said.

She asked it again.

"Do you like me?"

She reached out and touched the man's checkered shirt. He grabbed her arm tight. His hand was red from holding her.

"Come with me," he said.

He led her toward the laneway beside the hotel where the kegs were stored behind a chained-up fence.

The banging on the door woke us up.

Beth's face was very small in the backseat of the police car but she was glowing.

"Get back into bed," Mum said to us.

There were no charges laid. The policeman who brought her home said it was a real shame. A young girl like her.

"Look at her," he said, as though perhaps Mum had never seen her before.

"On the streets," he said, "with a man old enough to be her father, or her grandfather more likely. Lucky I seen them going down the lane.

"What's wrong with you people?" he said to Mum, who was the only one in the room because Dad was on night shift.

After he'd gone, Mum turned on the shower.

"Clean yourself," she said to Beth. "You're disgusting."

THE BOOK OF CLUES STAYED AT ANGELA'S HOUSE. She didn't open it up again until September, the month of the Talent Quest. She hadn't written anything after:

> *the braid.*
> *jennifer's voice gone.*
> *the reason for everything.*

Anthea asked me if I was singing. I didn't even bother to answer her. She practiced her scales on the playground. Miss Hope, who taught the choir, didn't even make me come to the front of the classroom to try a note. I had to walk straight to the door to where Mrs. Bridges-Lamb was waiting to collect the choral speakers. I had never been with the choral speakers before but they'd always scared me. Choral speakers had happy voices but sad eyes.

"Hello, Miss Day," said Mrs. Bridges-Lamb.

"Hello," I said.

I looked at the ground but I could feel her studying me for a long time with her glasses on. She pushed back the bangs from my eyes.

"Is everything satisfactory under there?"

"Yes thank you," I said.

But it wasn't.

At home I had committed the crime of the century. I had broken Dad's *Easy Rider* sunglasses. His favorite glasses. The glasses he wore to the racetrack and when he wore them I could tell he wished he had a motorbike, not a green family station wagon.

"Christ oh bloody mighty, what the bloody hell happened here?" he shouted when he found them.

I had to look shocked.

"What's going on in this frigging place?" he said.

I shrugged.

Everything was going on in this frigging place.

Everything.

Bum Cracker Barnsey had asked me to stay behind when the class finished again. He wanted to know why my mum hadn't been in to see him yet. He also wanted to know why I wasn't at school last Wednesday or the Friday before because as far as he could see I never brought a note.

"Come on," he said when I didn't come up with an excuse straightaway, "I need an answer."

"I don't know," I said. My mind was blank.

"Well we'll have to give a letter to your mother and father to come for an interview," he said.

"All right," I said.

"All right what?"

"All right, Mr. Barnes?"

"Yes, thank you," he said, and I was totally confused.

I thought maybe he was trying to trick me and see if I'd call him Bum Cracker straight to his face.

When I told Angela she said, "You better stop skipping or you're going to get the cuts."

"They don't give cuts to girls," I said, but I wasn't sure.

I was back in the redback panel van. On the way home from school I showed Angela the envelope that contained the letter that Mr. Barnes had written to Mum and Dad. We lay on the red velvet bench seats and talked to each other by way of the mirrors. Mr. Popovitch drove to the high school, where we had to pick up Angela's sisters, Rolanda and Natasha. Rolanda and Natasha never ran away from home or made Angela lie. They did their homework. They didn't sneak out at night. They didn't stand on caravan steps and pretend they didn't know you.

We didn't pick up Danielle at the high school because she wouldn't come in the redback panel van. She said it was because of her Milwaukee back brace.

She couldn't bend down to get into the back. Mr. Popovitch said she could easily sit in the front but Danielle said she'd rather go on the bus. It was only so she could have tough girls call her a cripple and then write sad poems about it later.

At the high school I saw Danielle waiting at the bus stop. I sat up and saw her through the back window as we passed. I saw her seeing me but both of us didn't wave. I remembered how many times she had held my hand after everything happened and how we hardly ever talked to each other now.

Angela and I watched each other in the mirrors and then the blue sky slipping past the back window.

"We still have a chance," said Angela.

"For what?"

"For you to go in the Talent Quest and beat Anthea."

"How?"

"Number one, we talk to Miranda," said Angela. "Number two, we find the owner of the address."

My stomach sank. I crossed my arms across my chest and closed my eyes.

"I don't think that's a very good idea," I said.

At home Mum was sitting in the recliner. *Speed Buggy* was on television. I handed her my letter from Mr. Barnes and backed away. She took it but did not open it. She brought her legs down.

"Come here," she said, and when I was near her she held on to my arms with both her hands.

"Something has happened to Nanna," she said.

The hospital walls were pale green and in some places the paint was peeling. Beneath the green paint there was pale blue paint. I chipped some off with my fingernail near the old wooden elevator, which made loud clanking noises as it headed down to us.

"Stop that," said Mum when she saw what I was doing.

She'd put on proper makeup, including Autumn Plum lipstick, and a good dress because in our family everybody dressed up for disasters. She made me wear a white cheesecloth dress with embroidered flowers on the front and puffed sleeves and she pinned my bangs back with bobby pins. She didn't say a word while she did it, just breathed in and out through her mouth.

Danielle walked beside me with her arms hanging at her sides. She hadn't been allowed to not wear her Milwaukee back brace. It might have upset Nanna even more and made her have an even bigger stroke that would kill her completely. Mum said that from the front seat as Aunty Cheryl drove us to the hospital. Kylie sat between us in the back. Her faded Hobbytex T-shirt said BEAUTY QUEEN.

Nanna was propped up in a bed in an empty

ward with more peeling paint and faded black and gray tile floors. She had her head turned toward the large window that gave a view of the black mine stacks belching smoke into the dirt-colored sky. Because her head was turned I didn't see at first that her mouth hung down on one side.

When she saw us she began to cry, which was normal, but now she cried with a half-drooping mouth. Her rose-covered nightie heaved up and down. Real tears fell down her face, a long string of spit fell out of the sagging corner of her lips.

"Don't," said Mum. "Please don't."

She sat on the bed and put her arms around Nanna and we couldn't see her face anymore. Nanna started speaking but she spoke in Finn. Her Finnish words were all joined together in a line. Mum hushed her.

When Mum had finished hugging her we all had a turn. I went last. Only one of her arms worked. She wanted to hold my head between her two crinkly hands the way she always did but she only hit me in the head with one open hand instead. She didn't mean it. She pulled me in close to her face and I got some dribble on my cheek. She spoke into my ear.

"My," she said slowly. "My."

I thought she had finished but she held my head with her one hand.

"Girl," she said even more slowly, and then she let me go.

"Rest," said Mum.

But Nanna wasn't finished speaking in her strange new voice.

"I go," she said, and she beat her chest with her good hand. "I go."

"Don't," said Aunty Cheryl, and she got a tissue and wiped away some of the drool. "Have a nice sleep now."

"I go," said Nanna fiercely.

"Mummy," said Mum.

"Beth," said Nanna.

Late that evening Mum phoned the hospital again.

"I see," we heard her say. "I see."

Danielle and I lay in our beds in the dark, listening, but when Mum came to our door we both closed our eyes. Afterward I didn't know why. I wanted to know what was happening but the urge to close my eyes was stronger. It was becoming commonplace in our house: the shutting of eyes, the turning of heads, the swallowing of unsaid words.

In the middle of the night Dad came home and banged his way off the hallway walls toward his bed. I heard Mum whispering to him and then nothing.

"Is that it? Is that all you have to say?" came her voice, suddenly loud.

Dad was out of bed again. Stumbling. He was at Beth's door, trying to open it up, which was a crime.

"Get out, get out, get out," Mum screamed.

"I want to go to sleep," Dad said, and he was sobbing. "I just want to go to sleep."

He was down on his knees. I could see them in the hallway, struggling with each other. It looked like they were wrestling. Danielle got up and shut our bedroom door. After that all we heard were tears. No words. Until the tears faded into silence and all I could hear was the ticking of the Bessemer clock.

3 DARDANELLES COURT

Mrs. O'Malley talked and Mr. O'Malley sang and they avoided each other's eyes. A long time ago they had come to town to get rich quickly but ended up staying forever. Mr. O'Malley sang songs about the sea and his voice filled up the cul-de-sac beneath the flame-colored evening sky. Some people shut their windows to block out the sound of his songs and some people opened them.

When they first came Eva O'Malley didn't wear colorful nylon dresses but pencil skirts and blouses and peep-toe shoes bought from catalogs and also she had a ponytail. She talked but not in the same way that she would come to after the death of her firstborn. And Joseph O'Malley sang but usually only when he'd drunk too many, when the dances had ended and his mates cheered him up onto the stage. The way he sang later, after the baby was gone, it was difficult to describe. Even though the notes were rich and rounded and he sang in tune, for a long time it still reminded people of a man wringing his hands over and over again.

When Eva was first pregnant he sang through the skin of her belly. She lay with her legs up on the sofa and he knelt on the floor beside her and sang to the unborn child. Sometimes he made up the words and tunes and he made Eva laugh. She said Joseph, don't, you'll make me want to pee. So then he kissed her belly instead.

He often remembered being at sea. How the frigate had pitched on the gray waves and how they had walked uphill and downhill in the mess room and how men had suddenly embraced and shoved each other off again during a violent heave that sent them flying across rooms. And he remembered wondering where his life would take him. All those years in the navy, he felt he was heading somewhere, even though the ships just went in circles from port to port.

When he sang to her belly he remembered that thought and wondered if he had arrived. But he didn't think so. He would know it surely. It made him shiver, the feeling that it was all unfinished. Even after she was born, he knew it, there was some other point he would need to travel to.

He never told Eva that. She laughed when he told

her all his life he had been waiting for her. Not because she didn't believe him but because everything
back then made her laugh. She wore red lipstick and
smiled. She was hopelessly impractical. She packed
ten pairs of shoes to go out west with him.

Her mother said you'll not last one day.

But Eva refused to believe it.

She didn't feel every action in her life had been a
step toward that moment with Joseph singing
through her belly. She didn't ever think things like
that. She leafed through catalogs when she was pregnant looking for dresses she might wear again when
she was back to her normal size. She didn't give much
thought to the birth. It would all work out. She was
completely unprepared. Afterward she always remembered those days as filled with sunlight, so
bright that they were luminous. That looking back
into those rooms, those scenes, the car pulling into
the new Dardanelles Court, just painted, grassless,
the baby in the baby basket, she needed to shield her
eyes from the light.

Their baby had been named Gayle. She had been
very pretty. They were not biased. She was an incred-
ibly beautiful infant. Even the midwives who were
immune to pretty babies could not believe this baby's
sweetness. Each day when Joseph took the cage up
and the rock slid past his face he felt he was being
spewed up out of the darkness into the day. And he

took the stairs two at a time to see his daughter. He ran his hands over her legs and arms to see how much she had grown. He told her, in words, real un-sung words, how glad he was to see his littlest dar-ling, the apple of his eye. He picked her up out of her cot and examined her perfect face.

He ignored that other feeling. That there was somewhere left to go. It was easy to. He remembered asking his wife how could it be? How could it be that they had produced something as beautiful as this? And his wife, who could not find words for her con-tentedness, had been only able to smile.

The bucket that their baby drowned in was filled with water Eva was going to water her petunias with. In those days she kept a lovely garden, petunias, marigolds, white cosmos, purple salvia. The bucket was in the laundry waiting for outside. Gayle had only just begun to crawl. Both Joseph and Eva were home so not one or the other was more to blame. All they had done was turn away for half a minute. They said that in the beginning. No one was to blame. They whispered it first into each other's hair and then screamed it up and down the hallway and through slammed doors.

After the baby was gone and the bucket and the pool of water and all the frantic wet footsteps had been mopped away, the evening closed in on the house. Eva lay on the sofa with her legs up and held her belly as though she could begin it all again. There was an open cut inside her. Later, much later, she would fill it with words, when people looked at her and away from her or spoke to her about the price of groceries.

Joseph realized he had arrived at that place where he had always been heading. He was surprised to find himself suddenly there, beside the pale pink walls of her nursery, the sun setting behind the ranges, in the middle of nowhere. Evening and quietness filling up the rooms. He could not have imagined it, that it would have been this.

At some point they stopped looking into each other's eyes. Eva talked. Joseph sang. And the years poured through their fingers.

"This can't be right," Eva said, "this cheaper flour is not worth the seventy cents I spent on it. The gravy is as lumpy as ever. Mr. O'Malley, you'll have to allow me more money next week and I'll have to buy another sort. See what happens when you skimp."

Never there was such a beautiful rose, Joseph sang as he walked past her into the laundry to wash his hands in the sink.

"Are you listening to me?" she asked, and he raised his eyes so she knew he was.

It was a mistake they sometimes made. What traveled between them was immense. It washed over the table and chairs suddenly like a wave. It dashed the evening to smithereens. It blew them sideways and capsized them.

"Of course I'm listening," he said.

She began to talk immediately to lessen the pain. He sang "Abide with Me," softly, and they carefully avoided each other's eyes. Gradually they righted themselves. The night settled down around them. The ache settled. They moved apart from the table. She spoke to herself softly. Hush now, hush now, hush now, she said, even after he had gone outside to sing about the sea.

IN OCTOBER BETH GOT HER SECOND AND LAST JOB. It was at Sandy's Sports Store. Dad didn't help; she got it herself by circling an advertisement in the paper and phoning the number. Mum still wanted her to go to boarding school but Beth said it was too late.

"Let's see how long you last in this one then," said Mum.

Beth's job was to stock the already stuffed shelves that reached from ceiling to floor. It was badly lit. Rows of lures and sinkers winked inside of dusty display cabinets. It smelled of the leather of baseball gloves and the rubber of bicycle tires and years of accumulated dust. She crammed plastic bags full of tennis balls on top of boxes already filled with tennis balls. She stacked Gray-Nicolls cricket bats on top of other Gray-Nicolls cricket bats.

"If you can manage the stock," said Sandy, "you

can have a go on the register in a month or two, but first I want my girls to get a feel for the stock."

Sandy smiled at her when he said it. He had a silky blond handlebar mustache and shoulder-length strawberry-blond hair. She had tried to call him Mr. Vale but he had forbidden it.

"No one calls me that here," he said. "We're all friends here."

There was only one other girl who worked at Sandy's Sports Store and this was Sandy's daughter Moira, who was fat and combed her bangs down flat with water and every morning dragged a stool from Sandy's office and placed it in front of the register.

Beth didn't like Sandy. He smelled of desperation. He sat in his office for hours looking at his ledgers with his head in his hands. When he wasn't doing that he came to watch her stock shelves. He watched her on the stepladder.

Beth came and went from home. She packed her little canvas bag and was gone for days. Whenever she arrived back she looked tired. She ate whatever she could find and then slept for hours on her bed. Sometimes Mum followed her from room to room asking her what she thought she was doing with her life. Beth didn't answer.

"I never would have thought it'd be Beth that'd go wild," said Aunty Cheryl. "You should have got rid of that Miranda Bell straightaway."

Mum didn't say anything.

Aunty Cheryl was full of advice. She said she was glad Kylie had turned out so well. Kylie still went to Miss Elise Slater's Jazz Ballet Dance Academy. She breathed loudly through her sinuses while she danced. Aunty Cheryl said she was really starting to blossom.

Some days Sandy asked Beth to tidy up down the back. Especially the bottom shelves he said. He came and stood beside her while she was kneeling on the ground. She removed tennis rackets from their dusty jackets. While she unzipped them he watched. He stood with his arm resting on a shelf and his body facing her.

"If you can get on top of it," he said, and smiled, "I'll let you go on the registers in a month or two."

Beth worked at Sandy's Sports Store for nearly the whole of October. Mum said she was pleased with her. Beth had beaten her previous milestone without causing any incidents. Dad said she must be doing a good job. They wanted to know what Mr. Vale was like. Was he a good boss? Had she made friends with the other girls?

"Why don't you wear a nice skirt one day," said Mum. "That embroidered one, the one Nanna made."

"I'm not wearing a skirt," said Beth. "Believe me. I'm not wearing a skirt."

Nanna said it was all her praying to Saint Monica that had given Beth her second chance.

In a matter of weeks she would be gone.

A hot dusty wind arrived and bothered the town for days. It banged at windows and rolled over bins; it blew up in restless gusts. It hurt our eyes and it made us cough on our words. Mrs. Bridges-Lamb closed all the louvers and put up hessian and it felt like we were in a cave. I couldn't see any sky or birds. She said it was time to get serious. She said we were about to learn some of the most important things in our education.

While the wind banged against the louvers she told us we were going to learn about the most important civilization in history, which was the ancient Romans. They were important because of their great ideas and contributions across many fields including sanitation, building, politics, and the military. She said we would also learn how to count using roman numerals, which was very important. Mrs. Bridges-Lamb loved the ancient Romans. The other class was doing projects on the space shuttle *Columbia* but Mrs. Bridges-Lamb said that was nothing compared to what the ancient Romans had given society.

Before we got to the Romans, however, we had to learn about the ancient Greeks. Mrs. Bridges-Lamb wasn't as excited about them. She rushed us through the Acropolis. We raced past the Minotaur in his damp smelly labyrinth, barely looking back at the young maidens being slaughtered there. We flew past Zeus, the first Olympians, Marathon. We spent an afternoon with the Spartans, who seemed to stir something in her because she had to remove her glasses twice and clean the fog off them with her handkerchief. We stopped at the myth of Icarus.

The myth bothered me. For instance, Icarus's father didn't seem to care when his own son, all melting wax and feathers, fell from the sky and into the sea. Instead of stopping he just kept flying on to freedom. He did not look back once. And it was he who had thought up the stupid and impractical idea in the first place. And also, everyone in the class knew, but no one said a thing, that the sun is a lot farther away than you might expect.

After she had told us the myth Mrs. Bridges-Lamb took out a pile of butcher paper from the cupboards beneath the blackboard. She told us we were going to make our own Icarus wings. She said, in this instance, there were no rules. We had to make our wings exactly the way we imagined them.

Everyone was excited. It was the first time all year we had been without rules.

My wings were yellow. They didn't turn out the way I wanted. First I had drawn the anatomy in pencil. It had been difficult. It was hard to make both sides look the same. It was very technical and one humerus turned out longer than the other. I was only doing it from memory and I fell behind the rest of the class.

When Mrs. Bridges-Lamb said we only had five minutes left all I could do was grab a yellow felt pen and cover over the bones as best I could but the yellow felt pen started running out halfway through and everything ended up wrong. Everyone had to form a line to tack their wings to the back wall. Massimo asked if mine was an X-ray of Big Bird and that made everyone laugh. Anthea smiled at me without showing her teeth and made sure I saw her wings had individually shaded feathers.

"Shame job," she said when we went outside. "Your wings were very stupid."

"Not as stupid as you are," I said.

"Well your sister is a dirty slut," said Anthea.

"She is not," I shouted.

My cheeks were burning.

"She is," said Anthea. "My big sister said it. Everyone says it."

I pushed her. I rammed my two hands against her shoulders and she fell to the ground.

"Ouch," she said, and started to cry.

A group of girls helped her up and escorted her to the principal's office to tell on me. Angela stayed beside me.

"What's a slut?" she asked.

"Something very bad," I replied.

The day we made our Icarus wings I saw Beth on her bike and she was doubling Miranda Bell. I saw it out of the back window of the redback panel van just as we passed the football club. They were looking back at a group of boys sitting along the gutter and they were laughing. At first she didn't see me, face pressed to the rear window of the panel van, but then some of the boys raised their hands and called out because the van caused a commotion wherever it went. By the time she turned to look she was already disappearing into the distance. She waved but I couldn't tell if she was smiling. The sinking feeling was very strong.

THERE WAS ONLY ONE WEEK UNTIL THE TALENT QUEST AND ANGELA WAS FULL OF HOPE. After I told her about my nanna's stroke she said it was more important than ever. Nanna could only get better if I could sing to her. She made everything sound like it was written in a fairy tale.

We walked the long way by the riverbed to Campbell Road and the caravan park. I kept thinking up excuses. For instance, what if Miranda had left town? She was always moving. She never stayed anywhere that long. She said so herself. Or what if, instead, we just went to the top of the hill and I tried yelling or screaming and Angela could hit my back until my voice dislodged?

"Don't be silly," said Angela.

We walked to Miranda's caravan against the tall chain fence. It was very quiet.

"Go on," said Angela as though it was all my idea. "Knock."

I put one foot on the metal step and knocked quietly.

There was nothing for a while, then footsteps. Miranda stood behind the screen. She was in a man's AC/DC T-shirt. It came to her knees. Her long brown hair was unbrushed. She held her stomach.

"What are you doing here?" she whispered.

She looked behind her and opened the door slowly. She came down the steps and stood on the gravel in bare feet. She had bruises on her legs. Her skin was no longer like fine porcelain. She shivered even though it wasn't cold.

"We just wanted to ask you something," said Angela.

"About what?"

"About Beth."

"I already told the police when it happened, I don't know anything. I never saw her after the party."

She took the hand from her pregnant belly and wiped her eyes.

I couldn't believe she had tears in her eyes.

I couldn't believe her bottom lip quivered.

Real tears, two of them, ran down her cheeks.

"Do you know anything about this?" I said.

I took out *The Book of Clues* from the back of my shorts. I showed her the address.

"Normandy Street," she said aloud.

I saw a shadow, something, pass over her face.

"I don't," she said. "You kids have got to stop sticking your nose in where it doesn't fit."

"So you're saying you don't know anything," I said.

"Who is it, babe?" came a voice from inside.

"No one," said Miranda.

"What are you two little shits doing here?" said Kevin when he came to the door.

He opened his mouth into his Cheshire cat grin.

"Nothing," I said.

I closed up the book.

"Come back to bed," said Kevin.

"Bye," said Miranda.

"See you," I said.

Angela and I walked down the caravan park main street. I felt a song trying to come through. I shook my head.

"She's such a liar," I said.

That day Angela wrote in *The Book of Clues:*

> *miranda lying.*
> *visit address.*
> *the final thing.*

But we didn't go to the address. When we walked home through the park I could tell she was secretly thinking it was too late. I wasn't going to sing in the Talent Quest.

If I am to be honest it is the darkest thing I know. It happened on a night when they sat along the gutter outside of the Oasis. A man came out and asked them what their poison was. He was still dressed in his dark blue work gear. He had grime on his hands but he had cleaned up his face.

"Lambrusco," Beth said.

"Shit, you're not cheap."

"I've got money," she said. She was still in her work shirt and jeans.

"We'll buy it."

He came back with two friends and a cardboard box full of bottles.

"We'll go to the lake," he said. "Marty's driving."

"I'm not going to the lake," said Michelle Wright. "Not with people I don't know."

"Don't be a reject," said Miranda.

"I'm going," said Beth.

"I'm going," said Miranda.

"Only because you're sluts," said Rochelle Peters.

"And you're the Virgin Mary," said Miranda.

The man was John; his two mates, Peter and Martin. Marty, who drove the car, was quiet, but Peter, who sat in the back between Miranda and Beth, was loud. He laughed at his own jokes. He threw his head back. He was tall; his head nearly touched the roof of the car. He had long bangs that fell across one eye.

John rested his arm along the front seat and looked back at Miranda. Then he looked at Peter, and Beth saw the exchange with their eyes. Who belonged to who. She watched Miranda giving John the eye already, looking down at her fingers in her lap and then slyly through her long black eyelashes at him again.

They headed onto the highway and out of town. Peter opened up a bottle and handed it to Beth. She turned her head and looked at the mine lights receding into the distance.

"You're a quiet little thing, aren't you?" he said.

Beth took a swig out of the bottle and looked at him but didn't say anything. John passed a joint back.

"That should loosen you up a little bit," said Peter, and he put his hand on her knee.

Miranda wound her window right down. She undid her seat belt and climbed up and sat with the top part of her body out of the window. She let out a scream into the night.

"Hey," said Marty, "get back inside. Shit."

"She's a crazy woman," said Peter, and let out a stream of laughter.

"Just get her in," said Marty.

Miranda sat back inside the car.

"Try it," she said.

"Don't you dare," said Marty as Beth undid her seat belt.

He was slowing down the car as she sat up on the window but the wind still whipped the hair backward across her face. She held on to the inside of the car with two hands but then let go of one and used it to push the hair back from her face. It was like flying. She felt like letting go altogether. Marty slowed right down and then stopped the car. He got out and slammed his door.

"Get back in the car, all right," he shouted.

She got back in the car. He started the engine.

"Jeez, Marty," said Peter, "what's up your fucking arse tonight?"

"Shut your face, dickhead," said Marty, and he squealed his tires as he drove up the shoulder onto the highway.

At the lake it was pitch-black apart from the stars. It was difficult to see where the grass ended and the water began. Peter took Beth by the hand and led her down to one of the picnic tables. When they had finished the first bottle he opened the next.

In the darkness she could hear the water touching the shore. The lake breathed in and out against the grass and weed. The rhythm of it rocked her. She tilted her head back to look at the stars. There was no moon. Somewhere, distant, she heard Miranda laughing.

"You want a bit of this?" said Peter, and he took her hand and put it on his crotch and rubbed it up and down. She drank from the bottle for a while with her free hand.

"Are you a bit up yourself or something?" he asked.

On the ground he pulled her shirt up over her head. Her skin shone like alabaster. He made a groaning noise and then snorted as the breath caught in his throat. His long bangs hung over one side of his face. The one visible eye had a giant pupil. A single round dark hole. He tugged her jeans down over her hips. He knelt beside her face.

"Suck on it," he said.

"I don't want to," she said.

She heard the lake breathe in.

"Fucking suck on it, you little slut," he said, and he picked up her head between his hands.

He let her sit up and she spat the semen out onto the grass. She thought she was going to vomit but she didn't. Peter stood up and tilted his head back and laughed. He took a mouthful of the wine and spat it at her and laughed again.

"Hey, Marty," he called out.

There was no reply.

"Marty," he yelled.

"What?" came Marty's voice from a way off.

"You want seconds?"

When she tried to get up he punched her in the stomach so she fell back on the ground.

Afterward they drove back to town. John sat in the back between them this time. Miranda rested her head against his shoulder, her long brown hair draped across his arm. She wouldn't look at Beth. There was the smell of sex and vomit in the car. Peter turned the radio on and beat the time out from a song on his thigh. Every now and again Marty wiped his sleeve under his nose and shook his head in disbelief.

Dawn rose, gold-lighted, turning the cliff faces pink and the bush grass incandescent white. The lake disappeared between the two walls of rock like a closing eye.

They dropped Beth at the highway end of Memorial Drive. Miranda had her eyes closed, pretending to be asleep. Beth looked at Peter in the front seat but he didn't turn to face her. He stared straight ahead down the highway.

There were road trains stopped, five or six of them, parked one behind the other. She walked between two. The cattle stamped and moved. The smell of them turned her stomach. She walked along Memorial Drive past the butter-colored slice of park and then vomited into the gutter. She could hear the car accelerating along the highway. She sat for a while at the corner of Dardanelles Court with her head between her knees.

Her stomach ached. She wished she had swum in the lake. She wished they'd left her there. She would have taken off her clothes then and swum out and watched the sun rise, floating on her back. She would have been cleansed.

Everything ended where Nanna said it began.

AFTER MUM AND DAD WRESTLED AND CRIED IN THE
HALLWAY THEY DIDN'T TALK TO EACH OTHER MUCH.
Just hello and goodbye. What's for dinner? Sorry I'm
late.

Dad didn't tell us he was leaving until he left. It
was nearly a year since Beth had died. He got up one
morning and decided to leave. First he sat on the side
of the bed for a long time thinking about it. He had
his head in his hands.

"What are you doing, Jim?" asked Mum because he was supposed to be getting ready for
work.

"Nothing," he said, and let go of his head and let
it fall backward and then he stared at the ceiling that
way for a long time.

I climbed onto the bed beside him. I lay on my
stomach with my chin in my hands and watched him.

When he finished looking at the ceiling he looked at me. He smiled and shook his head.

"Oh shit," he said.

He got up and stood beside the wall and rested his head against it.

"Oh shit," he said louder. "Shit, shit, shit."

Mum came to the bedroom door. She had her hair in rollers because Aunty Cheryl said she had to start taking pride in her appearance again. She had her yellow Japanese happy coat on. She had put on her lipstick but not her eyes.

Dad stopped leaning against the wall and went down on his knees beside the bed. I didn't know what he was doing. He went down so quickly. His knees hit the floor hard. He reached under the bed and pulled out a suitcase. My mother's red lips opened into a circle.

Dad dragged the suitcase out and lifted it up and slapped it onto the bed. A cloud of dust rose up into the air. He made a noise deep in his throat. It sounded like a frog croaking.

"Get up, get up," Mum said to me.

I crawled backward off the bed. Dad went to the cupboard. He started throwing clothes from the cupboard across the room into the suitcase. A shirt with arms outstretched. A pair of trousers with legs flying. A handful of belts, buckles rattling.

Mum said, "Don't you dare."

Dad said, "Don't what?"

He stopped throwing the clothes and looked at her with arms hanging down at his sides.

"I can't," he said.

"Can't what?"

"I can't," he said. "Anymore."

Mum lay facedown on the bed and screamed. Dad dragged the suitcase down the hall. It was hard cardboard with plastic edges. It scraped along the wall. It left a scrape mark, a long gentle arc.

He picked up the phone. He phoned a taxi.

"Day," he said. "Four Dardanelles Court, yes, one, thank you."

Danielle came out of her bedroom.

"What?" she said.

Mum had stopped screaming. Dad looked at Danielle and me. It was very quiet. His hand went down to the suitcase handle.

"Where are you going?" asked Danielle.

"I can't," said Dad. "I just can't."

He shook his head from side to side. There were tears dripping off his nose. I went to go toward him but he put his hand out.

Stop.

The taxi horn beeped.

"I just can't," he said.

Mrs. Irwin noticed Beth under Frieda Schmidt's spreading poinciana tree. We had heard her yelling across the road and into Miss Schmidt's front yard because she thought that Beth was dead. We heard her from the kitchen, where we sat at the table watching Mum slowly and precisely butter the bread for our school lunches.

"What the hell is going on?" said Mum, going to the front door with the butter knife still in her hand.

"Jean," shouted Mrs. Irwin from Miss Schmidt's front yard.

When Mum crossed the road Miss Schmidt unlocked her front door and stepped gingerly onto the front porch. She was fully dressed with her stockings and blouse and lace-up shoes. Only her hair hadn't finished being done. She looked afraid of being in her own yard.

Miss Schmidt put a foot on the front lawn as though she had stepped into another country. She looked at Beth lying beneath the tree and at Mum with the butter knife. She looked at Mrs. Irwin holding her hands over her mouth like a cartoon of someone scared.

"What happened?" she whispered.

Beth was sleeping where she had fallen. Her bare feet were brown with dirt. Her hands were held together beneath her head. The first of the red flowers had fallen while she slept and adorned her hair. Her name tag was still in place on her white work shirt. It read:

Sandy's Sports Store
Elizabeth—Trainee

"Get up," said Mum.

She said it quietly, so quiet that it would never have woken Beth up. Danielle and I stood behind her.

Mum stood above Beth with the butter knife.

"Get up," shouted Mum.

All along the street screen doors and sliding windows were being opened. Mrs. O'Malley came out onto the footpath pretending to check the mail. Marshall Murray, who was watching from his patio, shook his head and closed his eyes.

"Get back inside," Mum said to Danielle and me, who had knelt beside Beth. "Go."

Beth didn't know we were there. The sun shone through the leaves onto her luminous face. A little rash of freckles ran across her nose just beneath where her long eyelashes rested. Her lips were slightly parted.

When she woke up she got a fright to see Mum standing over her with the butter knife. She sat up slowly and held her head, remembering.

Mum started yelling at her straightaway.

"You say sorry to this lady," Mum shouted.

Beth stood up and stumbled toward Miss Schmidt

and took one of her hands. Miss Schmidt didn't have time to snatch it away.

"I'm really sorry," said Beth. "I'm really, really sorry."

"It's fine," said Miss Schmidt. "It's fine."

It was because the whole of the street witnessed it that it was the final disgrace. Dad used that word.

"You're a disgrace," he said once she was inside and he had been woken up for the event. Mum and Dad thought the neighbors had no idea what was going wrong in our house.

Beth looked hurt by his words. Then she recovered herself and shrugged at him.

"Suit yourself," she said.

For some reason that made Dad laugh. He rubbed his eyes and shook his head.

"You're bloody unbelievable," he said.

When Dad said Beth was a disgrace it was his first and last harsh word to her. She was sitting on the sofa with her grown-back hair rippling over her shoulders and the black mascara smudged around her blue eyes. All the shouting had been left to our mother. She never used any *Life Cycle Library* words. She never said Passion Pop. She never said sexual intercourse. She spoke in vague terms.

It wasn't good enough. It had to stop. Things were going to change.

"All I'm hearing are bad reports about you," she shouted as though Beth had been on the news. "You know, I haven't even told your father about the police that night."

Beth was barely listening until Dad spoke.

Her foot had been tapping the floor. Her eyes had been drifting to the television as though she was bored by it all. But his words raised a reaction. For a second her eyes shone with tears. She chewed on a fingernail. It looked like she was going to say something but she didn't. Dad's words rung in her ears. She only came home once after that.

She showered and got ready for work. The sun blazed at the bathroom window. The water made her body ache. She combed her wet hair and braided it. She packed what she could fit in her little canvas bag.

She rode to work. The hills had lost their fantastical color. The mine was a black stain. The sunlight was solid, thick; she had to push her way through the day.

"You're late," said Sandy, coming out of his office, fingering his silky handlebar mustache.

"I'm sorry," she said.

"Who's had a late night then, hey?" he said when he had had a good look at her from foot to head. Her unironed shorts and shirt. The dark rings beneath her eyes. He broke out into giggles like a boy.

"Hey?" he said. "Here I am thinking you're a good girl."

She stood in front of him with her eyes on the floor.

"I think you better do bottom shelves today then, hey," said Sandy. "You'd be no good on a ladder. You'd fall off. I'd have to pay compensation. That'd be all I need."

He laughed like a maniac.

"What about doing the lures today?" he said. "That's a good job for a bad girl."

He led her down the dusty aisle to the fishing lure cabinet. He took out keys from his back pocket.

"What'll we need?" he said. "Some window cleaner, right. Some soapy water, hey. Rub-a-dub-dub, hey?"

He nudged her with his elbow.

"Fuck off," she said quietly.

"What did you say?"

"I said fuck off."

"Hey, hey," he said, putting the keys on the cupboard and smoothing down his mustache with both hands. "That's not the way to talk to your boss."

"Why'd you say rub-a-dub-dub?" she said.

"I didn't mean anything by it. Just a bit of fun, that's all. You've got up on the wrong side of the bed, haven't you, hey, no more late nights for you?"

She took her badge off her shirt. She placed it next to the keys.

"You won't get to go on the registers acting like this," he said.

"I don't want a go on the bloody registers."

She heard Moira's chair scrape backward, her surprisingly soft footfall into the cricket bat aisle.

"I quit," said Beth.

"You're fired more like it," said Sandy.

"Suit yourself," she said.

The morning Dad left I didn't go to school. I rode out of Dardanelles Court and met Angela at the end of Memorial Drive. I told her I was going climbing in the hills. I begged her to come with me. She begged me not to beg her. I said I know how to do your mum's handwriting.

"Jenny, don't," she said.

We hid our bikes at the bottom of the hill behind the roller-skating rink where we knew there were caves. We climbed with the shale and powder rock slipping beneath our feet and with the spinifex cutting our legs.

We ate our school lunches as soon as we found the first cave. I took out four Benson & Hedges cigarettes that I had stolen from a crumpled packet that Dad had left behind. We smoked one, passing it backward and forward to each other until Angela stood up and vomited into the yellow grass.

The town stretched out in front of us. Our silver-topped suburb huddled in among green trees like it was frightened. The sun inched its way slowly up the sky. Only two hours of school had passed.

We spent the day petrified, which means very scared or turned into stone. But I didn't feel like stone. My heart was beating fast. I tried another cigarette. I felt very alive. Angela cried. She said everyone would know it, everyone, her mother, her father, Mr. Barnes, the whole class. They would know she'd lied. They would know she'd skipped. I tried to calm her down but it was difficult.

She begged me to go home with her and own up to what we'd done. She said it was the only thing we could do. I told her I probably wasn't going home ever again. I was going to live up in the caves.

"Don't be stupid," she said.

"I'm telling the truth," I said.

"I wish you were the way you used to be," said Angela.

"Nothing can stay the same," I said.

"I'm telling on you," she said.

And she went down the hill away from me.

THE NURSE PUT TWO BOBBY PINS IN NANNA'S HAIR, WHICH NANNA WOULD NEVER HAVE DONE. Her hair was pinned back on either side of her face like a little girl's hair. It looked a bit like the way Mum did mine each time we visited her. We looked at each other with our pinned-back hair and sent that thought to each other. I thought I almost saw a tiny smile on the good side of her mouth.

Because she was eating proper food like mashed-up potato and mince and pumpkin and not just biscuits her face had filled out and she didn't look so tiny and crinkled. She looked younger. She had to do exercises with a ball in her bad hand, which was getting better, and she had to walk with a stick.

"Lift your leg, lift your leg," said the nurse when she made Nanna march along the hallway because sometimes she dragged it a little.

Nanna let me walk with her stick when she wasn't using it.

Mum did most of the talking. She talked more than she had talked in the whole year put together. She talked about what would happen when Nanna got out of the hospital. First she would stay in the spare room at Aunty Cheryl's house and then when she was better they'd draw up a roster and they'd look after her in the flat. We had a spare room in our house too, Beth's room, but Mum didn't offer that. That room stayed just the way it was with the door shut and when I walked past it I always tiptoed as though I might wake someone up.

Mum only talked about what was going to happen, not what had happened. She talked so there were no gaps in the one-sided conversation. Sometimes Nanna looked at her and nodded and sometimes she just stared out the window.

Mum told Nanna she'd gone to see Mr. Barnes about me. She said there had been a letter but she was going to nip the problem in the bud. Nanna took her eyes from the window and looked at me.

"I'm going to get Jenny back to ballet soon," said Mum. "And maybe, I was thinking, athletics, you'd like that, wouldn't you, Jenny? Danielle has some poems in the Talent Quest. You did a beautiful one, didn't you, look at me, Danielle, about a sad harlequin doll. Bring it next time and we'll show Nanna. We'll fix up everything that has fallen by the wayside, won't we, girls?"

It was good to hear Mum talking again but it was strange also because her voice didn't sound exactly like it used to. It reminded me of a teaspoon tapped against a teacup; it had a hollow fragile ring to it. It could break very suddenly. Danielle and I were wary of her. We stayed a safe distance away from her arms.

Dad came to the hospital once after work. He smelled very clean and he had his ducktail combed very neatly and his sea-green eyes made part of me melt inside. I couldn't let go of him at first after he asked how is my favorite chickadee? Danielle ignored him. Mum kissed him on the cheek. I saw him take in her curled hair and her good jeans and embroidered shirt with shoulder pads. Nanna made him come close to her and he looked almost frightened but she only wanted to kiss him.

"Well then," said Dad quite a few times.

He squeezed Nanna's hand-strengthening ball. I leaned against him with my back like a lizard sunning itself on a rock because it felt very good.

When it was time to go Nanna practiced holding my head in two hands.

"You must keep trying," she said.

ANTHEA LONG WON:

1. First Place Girls' Junior Vocal Character Song in Costume: "My Favorite Things" from *The Sound of Music*
2. First Place Girls' Junior Vocal Set Piece: "Perhaps Love"
3. Highly Commended Vocal Solo Open: "Do-Re-Mi" from *The Sound of Music*
4. First Place Girls' Junior Sacred Solo, Hymn, or Carol: "Gentle as Silence"
5. Everything

"Your nanna and I have been thinking," said Mum. "We know what to do about Beth."

It was the second-to-last day. Mum told me to go to the caravan park and get Beth and bring her to Nanna's flat. She said Mrs. Bell knew we were coming. She had phoned and left a message at the Blue Tongue Lounge Bar. I didn't want to go. Nanna told me to stop frowning or the wind would change. I went to Angela's first. She had a flat tire so I had to double her on my bike. She said she wasn't allowed in the caravan park but she came anyway.

When we turned into Campbell Road I had to stop doubling because the road was on a hill. Up ahead I saw Kylie pushing her bike and I looked at Angela and held a finger to my lips even though Kylie was nearly half the street away. I didn't want her to turn around and see us. Kylie has special powers, which are known as extrasensory perception or ESP, just like Uri Geller's, and she turned around straight-away and saw us.

She stopped pushing her bike and waited for us to catch up.

"Where are you going?" she asked.

"To the caravan park," I said.

"Mum says I'm not allowed to go there," said Kylie.

We got to the top of the hill, and the caravan park with its tall fence came into view.

Mrs. Bell's boyfriend, Kevin, came to the screen door.

"Hello, hello," he said. "Who've we got here?"

"Is Beth in there?" I asked. He already knew who we were. "She's got to come to our nanna's."

Kevin pretended to look around behind him at the interior of the caravan. He was being smart and I didn't like him. His glassy blue eyes glittered. Beneath his smile there was the smooth dry skin of a snake.

He opened the screen door and came down one of the steps with the smile still on his face. I looked between his legs to see if Beth's bag and flip-flops were lying on the floor.

"I haven't noticed her," he said. "But if you think I'm telling a fib you can come inside and check for yourself."

"No," I said. "Is Mrs. Bell here? She's expecting me."

"Expecting you, hey?" said Kevin. "Lar-dee-dar."

"Come on," said Kylie. "She's not here."

"She might be," said Kevin.

We stood very still. He ran his fingers through the hair on his chest. He sat down on the bottom step in front of us. He lit up a smoke.

"Mrs. Bell might be inside having a lie-down," he said. "Why don't you go inside and have a look?"

He shifted himself slightly on the bottom step, opening up a narrow passage for me to squeeze past.

"Or you," he said to Angela.

Angela was squinting her eyes against the sun. We both stood where we were.

"Come on," said Kylie under her breath.

"Well do you know where Beth might be or not?" I asked.

I started chewing on a fingernail. Kevin looked me up and down. He sighed and shook his head.

"You're a funny little thing, aren't you?" he said. "I'll tell you what. You come inside with me for a minute and I'll show you a surprise, then I'll tell you where she is."

I took a step closer to him. He opened up his mouth too crammed with teeth and smiled.

"That's right," he said. "I won't bite."

I took another step toward him but then heard the sound of feet crunching on the gravel. We turned and saw Mrs. Bell coming toward us. She had her head down and she was carrying two shopping bags.

"Shit," said Kevin.

Mrs. Bell walked straight past us and dropped the bags in front of Kevin's feet.

"This is the last week I feed you," she said. "One more week and you don't get a job and you're out on your arse."

Kevin laughed and picked up the bags and went inside.

"And you can tell your mother to keep her nose out of our business all right," she said when she turned to me. "Her slutty daughter hasn't been here for a week. She'll be at that Wright girl's place. You got that?"

"Yes," I said.

"Tell her it's not my fault her daughter spreads her legs for anyone. Are you listening?"

"Yes," I said.

"Shit," said Mrs. Bell. "Get out of here."

After that Kylie said she had to go home or her mother would be very angry. Angela said she couldn't come with me to Michelle Wright's flat because she had lied once already, a big lie about the caravan park, and she knew her mother was going to find out.

"How can she find out?" I said.

"She can just tell," said Angela. "The lies just show up in my face."

I tried to look for the lie in her face. I couldn't see anything except her shame at what had been said. Maybe that was what she thought her mother would see.

"Na-nu," she said at the end of Campbell Road.

"Na-nu, na-nu," I said in return.

Michelle Wright lived in a long row of brick flats. There was a sign on the front of the letterboxes that said PALM COURT and beside them stood one very tall palm tree. Michelle's boyfriend was lying on the sofa through the screen door of their flat. His legs spilled over the edge. His head was turned slightly toward the light of the television. When I knocked he didn't move. He called out to Michelle. Beth's bag and flip-flops were on the floor so she couldn't lie to me.

I stood among the work boots waiting while Michelle told Beth I was there. When Beth came to the door she was angry. She didn't open up the screen door but talked through it.

"What do you want?" she asked.

She had her hair in braids. She had a cigarette in her hand. She blew smoke through the mesh at me.

"You have to come to Nanna's flat because she wants to talk to you. Mum said it's nothing bad."

"Why can't you people leave me alone?" she said.

"I don't know," I said, and I felt very stupid.

She turned and put on her flip-flops and picked up her bag.

When we rode along the streets toward Nanna's flat Beth didn't talk to me. She rode ahead. I told her about haikus we had written at school and how Spartans lived in barracks and they were usually only men and what kind of weapons they used. She turned to me and looked so angry and so sad that I stopped talking and I put my head down and I pretended to check if my foot brakes were working.

Nanna opened the sliding glass door. She'd got dressed up like it was a special occasion. She wore a silk shirt and a good skirt, not her usual tracksuit. Beth put her hand across her stomach as though she had just had a sinking feeling.

Inside Mum was waiting on the sofa with her hands in her lap. The living room felt very small. There was not enough oxygen for us.

"Sit down then," said Nanna, patting the space on the sofa beside her.

She smiled. A smile on Nanna's face was very unusual. She opened her mouth up over her white false teeth. A little bit of the too-pink plastic gum showed. Her eyes wrinkled shut. She looked like she had a bad pain.

Beth tried to look unconcerned but let out a sob.

I could tell she hadn't been expecting it. It was loud.
She covered her mouth but it didn't stop another one
escaping.

"Oh God," said Mum.

Nanna held out her arms.

Beth crossed her arms and shook her head.

She started crying. It was out of the blue.

"Come," said Nanna. "Do not cry alone."

When her head rested against Nanna's breast she
cried onto her white silk shirt. Her arms hung limply
at her side. Her hair fell across her face. Nanna made
me get a handkerchief from her dressing table
drawer. She made impatient hand motions at me to
be of some use. She tried to lift up Beth's face to wipe
it but gave up because Beth was crying too much.
Tears fell down Nanna's face and Beth's face and
Mum's face. The Virgin Marys watched from the
cabinets with their bored expressions. The ceramic
dogs with their black eyes and pink noses smiled.

Gradually the big swell of tears passed. Nanna
pushed back Beth's hair from her face. She wasn't trying to look unconcerned anymore. She stayed with
her head resting against Nanna's breast. Mum reached
out and touched her arm. It was a hopeful kind of
touch. A pleading kind of touch. But Beth didn't return
the touch. I wanted her to return it. Instead it made
them both cry a little more.

"There you go," said Nanna. "It feels better to cry, doesn't it?"

Beth sat up and steeled herself for it. Nanna gave her the hankie and she wiped her eyes. Here would come all the unsaid things. An inventory of all the disappointments she had caused. A catalog of all her shameful acts. I hung my head waiting for it too.

Nanna began by pulling a cutout piece of newspaper from beneath a hand-painted bone china poodle on the coffee table.

"Many things have been going very wrong for a while now," said Nanna.

"We want to help you, darling," Mum interrupted. "We only want to help you."

"And we want," said Nanna after the interruption, "no matter what has happened, to make everything right."

"Oh yes," said Mum. "We need to start all over again. A fresh start."

"Where are the checks, Jean?" asked Nanna.

Mum took her purse off the coffee table. Nanna handed over the piece of newspaper. It was an advertisement for the School of Secretarial Studies in Townsville. Summer school commencing in November. GET A HEAD START ON TYPING, DICTATION, SHORTHAND, STENOGRAPHY. One hundred percent graduate employment guaranteed. Enrollment fee: one hundred and seventy-five dollars plus textbook expenses. Accommodation available for out-of-town students.

Mum passed over two checks. One was for one hundred and seventy-five dollars written in her own delicate hand. The other was made out by Nanna for the amount of two hundred dollars.

"For your expenses," said Mum. "What do you think?"

"Secretarial school?" said Beth.

"You will go out of this town for a while," said Nanna. "It will be good for you. You will stay with Aunty Margaret by the sea. You will come back a new girl."

"Secretarial school?" Beth said again, but quietly. She started to laugh and then stopped.

"I don't know what to say," she said.

"Just say you'll go," said Mum.

Beth said she'd come home. Everyone was to begin again. Everything was to be forgotten.

"You must not say anything about anything," Mum said to me, but I didn't know what she meant.

"Exactly that," she said. "Don't ask so many questions. You've always got a hundred questions. We want to keep the peace, that's all."

"You shouldn't say this to her," said Nanna. "Her questions are what make her. Where would our Jennifer be without her questions?"

"Curiosity killed some cats," said Mum, and then I had to feel very sad about all the cats that had been killed by falling into their own reflections in wells or by getting trapped in small holes or inside cupboards or by merely crossing the highway to explore among the anthills.

Beth was going to pick up some stuff from Michelle's flat. Then she'd come home in the morning. Mum agreed to anything. She agreed that Danielle could get her hair permed. Danielle couldn't believe her luck. She phoned to make her appointment and then jumped up and down on the spot. Her Milwaukee back brace rattled. That night she washed her hair and stood in front of the mirror for an hour brushing it goodbye.

Mum asked her if she was sure that was what she wanted. Danielle turned to her holding a long strand between her fingers.

"Of course it's what I want," she said. "It's the only thing I've ever wanted."

"You know your father loves your hair," said Mum, "and your Nanna. And I love your hair just the way it is. You don't know how lucky you are to have all that beautiful hair."

"I don't care," said Danielle.

Danielle counted out the money that she had saved by being paid to wear her Milwaukee back brace. She flicked through the pages of her perm scrapbook and found her exact perm and cut out the page carefully with a pair of scissors.

The girl in the photograph was leaning against a fence in a country field on an overcast day. She was dressed in a white handkerchief-hemmed skirt and cheesecloth peasant shirt. She had her head tilted slightly backward and her eyes closed as though she had just taken a deep breath of country air. Her luxuriant brown curls cascaded down her back. Danielle folded the picture and put it in her schoolbag for the morning.

"What are you looking at?" she said to me.

"What if it doesn't turn out the same way?"

"It will," she said.

"What if it looks stupid and it is stuck that way?"

"It won't."

"Please don't do it," I said.

"Why?" she said, interested. She was always looking for new ways to torture me.

"It will change everything."

"Everything is already changed," she said.

That night it was very hot. I turned this way and that in my bed. Mum took down the curtains in Beth's room and washed them. The washing machine groaned in the dark. Danielle told me to stop moving. We heard Mum put clean sheets on Beth's bed and smooth out the ballerina bedspread. She couldn't sit still.

I knew she was never going to stay. I didn't know it in words. With all my might I summoned up images of Beth at a typewriter and there she sat in a gray office in a bleak building. I watched her glide through ill-lit corridors carrying manila folders. I saw her take dictation dutifully. She was very still, all of her, except for her hand, which raced across the page, spewing a trail of mysterious symbols. I willed these images into existence with all my might. But I had a feeling. It was a very bad feeling. It felt like the closing of a book. The ending of things.

After I made Angela skip school and then go to the caravan park she said she was never going to lie again. That's it, she said once the Talent Quest was finished. It was too late for things.

"Come with me," I said about the address.

It was the last thing in *The Book of Clues.*

"No," she said. "You know I can't. I'm not doing that stuff anymore."

She handed me the book in her bedroom. I knew I had to go there by myself.

The address was written in Beth's hand. It was in Memorial North, a very long dismal road filled with smudged houses and flats with no grass and Hills hoists sagging with miners' clothes. The sulfur fumes hung above the street, a flat brown cloud; I breathed shallowly and covered my mouth.

I put down my bike on the dirt of number 17 Normandy Street and walked up the driveway to flat number 3. I knocked on the door. I didn't know what I would find. The tall man who answered the door had long bangs that hung over one eye. I'd woken him up from sleep. He looked at me for a while and then his mouth opened.

Beth was a swan and I am only a sparrow but we have the same mole on our cheek and some of her face is in mine.

"Did you know Beth Day?" I asked.

"No," he said.

"Did you see her on the night she fell?" I asked.

I was surprised at how brave I sounded.

"No," he said.

He looked full of regret.

He shut the door. I heard him moving around inside. The television went on. A car chase. The thud of guns.

At the end of the street there was a girl sitting on the footpath with her feet in the gutter. At first I thought it was Angela but then I saw that she was bigger, older. She had short hair. Getting closer I recognized the stripe of black roots down the middle.

"Hey," Deidre said.

I stopped my bike on the pavement with my foot.

"I seen you going in there and wanted to make sure you were all right and everything."

"I'm all right," I said.

"You're only little," she said. "You should go home."

Later, much later, she would tell me many things.

"I'm going," I said.

Deidre stood up and dusted her bum. She smiled a half smile, looking down at the road.

"You ever got any trouble you should come and see me, hey?" she said.

"All right," I said.

On the way home I rode through the hot close November air. I rode through the dog-eared streets, past the sun-faded houses, past all the families I didn't know, shut up inside with their air conditioners droning.

The highway was empty. I rode with my eyes shut. I let myself drift into the middle of the road. I could feel the desert angels everywhere. They were turning and somersaulting and soaring on open wings. The air was alive with their feathers and their breath.

A STORM CAME ON THE LAST DAY AND MY ICARUS
WINGS FLEW. It came out of the west, tentatively, like
a lady gathering up her skirts before stepping inside
a doorway. A storm lady with her bunched-up cloud
skirts revealing a deep blue petticoat of rain. The
storm lady did not move but stood behind the mine,
as though wondering whether to approach.

We slipped with sweat on our little laminate
chairs and watched her through the louvers. Down
below, shiny fat bullfrogs in the water troughs called
out with joy and in the cassias beside the bike racks
choirs of cicadas sang madly. In the scrub beyond the
oval a lone storm bird cried its warnings.

Sweat stains expanded beneath Mrs. Bridges-
Lamb's arms on her white frill-collared blouse. Her
red and white zigzag-patterned skirt stuck to her bottom when she stood up. Massimo Gentili, who was

slowly clicking down all the colors on his highly prized multicolored pen, sniggered when he saw it.

Mrs. Bridges-Lamb looked at us carefully, then she removed her glasses and listened to us. No one moved. Massimo's finger was poised above red on his multicolored pen like a kangaroo frozen in headlights. The ceiling fan, wobbling on its base, sliced through the warm, sticky silence.

The storm lady took the opportunity to step out from behind the mine and breathed the first cool breeze in through the louvers. Her breath smelled like rain clouds. Into the room she sighed the scent of raindrops hitting dry earth. The cicadas stopped singing and shivered in their shells. Every flower, every branch, every leaf, every twig opened up its heart and waited. The classroom filled with this scent of the dry earth waiting. A lost hornet hummed in through the window and hovered and then, as though realizing it was in the wrong place, left again.

Mrs. Bridges-Lamb returned her glasses to her nose. Sweat ran in rivulets from her hairline, converging into streams where her jaw met her ears, cascading down into the crinkles of her neck. The sweat washed away the topsoil of face powder, kept in a tortoiseshell compact on her desk and applied throughout the day. She looked at everyone except Massimo, who was the person she spoke to.

"Massimo," said Mrs. Bridges-Lamb, eyes settling on Tanya Moorhouse. "Do we use pen in year five?"

Massimo jumped in his seat and clicked on red involuntarily. He dropped the pen to his desk and a pained smile stretched on his face and then dissolved. He did not answer.

"Jane-Anne," she said while looking at Trevor Burton. "Do we use pen in year five?"

"No, Mrs. Bridges-Lamb," said Jane-Anne Fryar.

"Now," she said. "Whilst Massimo brings me the pen you will all open up your tidy boxes and retrieve your atlases and then wait with your arms crossed."

The opening of the tidy boxes was accompanied by the first rumble of thunder. Everyone turned their heads to the windows. Into the room came the breath of the storm again. It shimmied around the room, playing games. It touched us. Placed cool fingers on our wet necks, lifted ponytails, sent a piece of paper on Mrs. Bridges-Lamb's desk pirouetting up into the air. It raced up to Mrs. Bridges-Lamb and kissed her on the forehead just as Massimo handed over the pen. For the briefest moment she closed her eyes. She took the multicolored pen and placed it on her desk where we could all see it. That was all. She did nothing more. Clouds moved over the sun.

We had turned to our maps of Italy when the first rain fell. The sky let go of its rain suddenly in a great burst of water. We could hear nothing but the sound of it on the roof. Mrs. Bridges-Lamb's mouth moved but her voice was drowned. And then, just as suddenly, it stopped. An orchestra conductor had waved his baton at the timpanists. The roof made shocked clink-clanks and tsk-tsk sounds as it contracted. The storm bird, momentarily silenced by the downpour, started up its warning call again.

Before Mrs. Bridges-Lamb could prize back our attention from the sudden rain, a second wave came. This time it was carried on the back of a wild and unruly wind. This wind bent the cassias over and knocked down bikes in the bike racks. It rattled the louver glass. It whipped the flag around the flagpole. All along the back wall our Icarus wings whispered and rustled and struggled against the one tack that held each pair down. The wings wanted to fly.

"Front row, stand and come and sit on the floor at the front of the room," Mrs. Bridges-Lamb shouted over the wind and blasts of rain. "Quick, quick."

The second row and then the third and fourth were marshaled down to the wooden floor in front of Mrs. Bridges-Lamb. She sat on her high-back wooden chair and we huddled, legs crossed, in front of her. The rain and wind were deafening. We were cocooned by the noise. The wind pushed against the louvers. It swallowed up Mrs. Bridges-Lamb's words.

She motioned for us to squeeze closer together. Downstairs, unseen things were banging and crashing and rolling on the concrete. Above us the wind was playing the roof like a wobble board.

An explosion of thunder erupted so close it lifted our bottoms off the floor. The blackboard duster fell into the bin beside the board. A row of books toppled over dead on Mrs. Bridges-Lamb's desk. The doorknob rattled. Angela put her hand on my arm but when I looked at her I found she wasn't that scared at all. She only had the look of someone riding the Cha-Cha at sideshow alley.

And then something wonderful.

The storm took a deep breath and blew open a row of louvers at the back of the classroom. Mrs. Bridges-Lamb's mouth opened. A spray of side-on rain entered the room and fell across our maps of Italy. The wind turned the pages of our atlases quickly and shut them all with a clap and turned its attention to the back wall.

Of all the wings on the wall the wind chose mine to tear free. For a brief and beautiful moment my yellow wings were released from their pin and floated upward into the room. The whole class held its breath. They flapped three times, gained altitude on an updraft, hovered briefly, and then fell to the floor.

When we walked home the whole world had changed. Rain tiptoed on rooftops. A hawk hovered, surveying the damage. The clouds had drifted away. Water rushed out of downpipes in fountains. Everywhere raindrops sparkled.

We did not want to go home. There was too much to see. The raindrops clung single file to railings. They decorated the park fence. They illuminated spiderwebs stretched between trees. They twinkled along the edges of the slippery slide. They shone. Beneath the swing the ditch had turned into a pond. Two ant explorers had climbed on board a leaf that circled slowly on a sea.

We examined raindrops clinging to blades of grass. We opened rattlepods filled with rain. We ran our hands over the wet surfaces of everything.

"By tomorrow the river will run," said Angela at the end of Dardanelles Court.

In front of our house Nanna was pulling up in her beige Datsun Sunny.

"Quick," she said, waving her arms. "It's Danielle's perm."

Danielle was lying on her bed with hair like Leo Sayer's.

"Oh my God," I said when I saw it.

"Don't say that," said Mum.

"Dear Lord," said Nanna.

"Don't say a thing," shouted Danielle.

She turned on her side and faced the wall.

"Stop looking at me," she screamed, so we all looked at the floor.

Nanna phoned Aunty Cheryl for tips on what to do with a bad perm. Aunty Cheryl said whatever you do don't wet it. Nanna relayed the message down the hallway to Mum.

"Whatever you do don't wet it," she shouted.

"You must not wet it," said Mum to Danielle.

"Shut up," said Danielle.

She was lying on her bed with her whole life ruined. Dad was on the back steps coughing and wiping his eyes. He had been laughing soundlessly and then his laugh got caught on some cigarette smoke and he had started to cough. He had to get up and go outside, he was coughing so much. When Beth finally came home there was no one there to meet her but me. She came up the front steps and stood at the screen door like she was a visitor. I stood on the other side.

For dinner we ate meatball porcupines, which was Beth's favorite. At the table everybody tried very hard to forget what had happened. We pretended that Beth had never run away. We pretended that she hadn't fallen down drunk in Miss Schmidt's front yard.

Danielle had come to the table with her bad perm wrapped up in a scarf. She had washed her hair and tried to comb it out straight. Underneath the scarf I could see the tight curls reforming as they dried. It was as though she had a nest of snakes moving beneath the scarf.

"You really shouldn't have wet it," said Aunty Cheryl, shaking her head slowly from side to side.

"It's going to have made it a whole lot worse," said Kylie.

But Danielle wasn't listening. She eyeballed Beth from across the table. She ate her meatballs slowly, spearing them one by one, without taking her eyes off Beth, who was trying to ignore her. Mum noticed and told Danielle to stop.

"Oh great," said Danielle. "It's never her fault, is it? She's always the right one."

She said bitch under her breath as she pushed her plate away and some of the meatballs fell over the edge and onto the proper special occasion tablecloth. Her brace made a creaking noise as she got up and left.

"Christ," said Dad.

"She said bitch," I said.

"We heard her," said Mum.

"Helmet head," I called out after her.

"Stop it," said Mum.

Beth laughed. She was eating slowly and deliberately. She kept her eyes downcast. Her hair was still damp from her shower. It hung down on either side of her face in pale waves. Her face was scrubbed clean. She was the picture of an obedient daughter.

The terrible thing about meatball porcupines was that sometimes if you used your imagination the rice poking out of the meatballs could look like maggots. Angela and I once saw maggots in a dead black cat near the river crossing. We cried all the way back to Angela's house and became hysterical when Mr. Popovitch told us that nature would take its course. He had to come with an old blanket and scoop up the remains and bury them in the backyard with a small funeral service. I looked at my meatballs after Danielle left the table and decided I couldn't eat them.

"Eat your meatballs," said Mum.

"I can't," I said.

"Well try very hard," she replied.

"So what do you think of this secretary school thing?" asked Dad.

"Great," said Beth, shrugging. "It's what I've always wanted to do."

"We'll have to buy some new skirts and blouses," said Mum.

Beth nodded her head meekly. She agreed with whatever they said. Mum talked about train tickets and good 40-denier stockings that didn't run and which bag she should take. She talked about foolscap folders, new pens, and sharpened pencils.

328

"She should get a nice new haircut," said Aunty Cheryl.

Aunty Cheryl suggested something easier to manage. Something shorter.

In unison we all remembered Mum with the scissors and Beth on her knees in the kitchen.

Beth pushed her hair behind her ears and nodded without really looking at anyone. I listened and pulled my meatballs apart to remove the maggots.

"Well then," said Mum when she had finished talking.

She lit a cigarette and so did Dad and Aunty Cheryl. They stayed sitting at the table. They smoked without saying anything. Beth chewed on a fingernail. Everyone looked very sad.

After dinner Beth went out into the backyard and climbed onto the trampoline. She lay there on her back with her hands behind her head looking up into the sky. I climbed on beside her and bounced a few times.

"Don't jump, Jenny," she said. "I just want to lie here."

She lay there thinking. Her eyes moved as she thought. It looked like she was having that conversation with someone in her head, watching them pace up and down in front of her. Occasionally her lips moved around words. The way they used to in the afternoons when she lay down after school. I stopped bouncing. I rested on my stomach with my chin in my hands.

Before the rain the earth had been closed fist-tight, cringing, battered by the sun. Now it un-clenched. Curled leaves unfolded. Cowering grasses lifted their heads. Trees breathed deeply. A new wet-ness rose up from the ground. The earth opened its eyes and gazed at the star-strung sky.

"Do you know how to write a haiku?" I asked, hoping it would start a conversation.

"Yes," said Beth. "Mrs. Rigid-Ram taught us that too."

Mrs. Rigid-Ram was a horrible name that older children called Mrs. Bridges-Lamb when they were no longer in her class. They would never have dared think of a name like that if they were. Everyone knew she could read your mind if you were thinking bad things about her.

"You shouldn't call her that," I said.

Beth took her blue eyes off the sky and looked at me.

"I'm only joking," she said.

"I like her," I said.

"I know you do, Jenny," she said. "Have you done Boadicea yet?"

"What's that?"

"She's just this wild woman in England who

drove around in a chariot killing Greeks, or maybe Romans, I don't know, but Mrs. Bridges-Lamb loved her. We did her for a whole week. You wait till you do her."

She was looking back at the sky. Even while she talked I could see she was only half thinking about it. She wasn't seeing chariots or wild queens. She told me about other things that we'd learn but her sentences kept drifting off into thin air. After a while she stopped talking altogether, midsentence. She removed her hands from behind her head and crossed them on her chest as though she had reached an impasse with herself.

"Are you going to go away?" I asked.

"Probably," she said.

She lay very still. She stared straight ahead. She lay like that for a long time. The sky was ablaze with stars. The Milky Way burned a bright path above us. I listened to the clatter of Mum doing the dishes. Someone playing the organ in the Irwins' house. A car turning out onto the highway. Beth uncrossed her arms. She reached into her jeans pocket and pulled out a crumpled packet of cigarettes.

"Don't worry," she said. "Everything will be all right."

Her decision had been made. She looked at me and smiled. Already I could tell she was thinking about where she'd go. She was thinking somewhere, anywhere, there must be something happening. She sat up. She bounced up and down on her backside. She pulled a face at me. It was meant to make me laugh, so I laughed, but it was a counterfeit happiness, both hers and mine.

I forced out the laughter like a painful cough. My smile was screwed on tight. She grabbed my hand and held it hard. She hurt my fingers. I could see the sadness resting on her face like a veil. I saw it by the moonlight and the starlight.

Inside she sat in front of her duchess and brushed her hair. She brushed it in long slow strokes. The strands shone under the electric lightbulb. She put in her two blue hair combs. She painted her lips. First in delicate brushstrokes upward to the bows of her top lip, then she filled in the valley between. She painted the fullness of her bottom lip. She put mascara on her eyelashes. She drew kohl along the inside of her bottom lids. She looked at her reflection. She stared into her own eyes.

She didn't cry. She didn't say goodbye to anything. She didn't look at all the things in her room. Her old stuffed rabbit. Her record player. Her dancing sashes. Her running medals. Her tambourine with its faded pink ribbons. She put the two checks inside her bag.

"I left something at Michelle's. I'm going to get it," she said at the kitchen door.

Mum was washing the dishes. She kept her back turned to Beth. I could tell by the movement of her shoulders that she was crying. In the living room Dad and Aunty Cheryl stared ahead at the television. Beth touched Kylie on the shoulder as she passed. It was only a light touch but Kylie jumped like she had been burned by a match.

"I'll be back soon," said Beth.

The house was quiet after the front screen door banged shut. Mum went after her then. She ran barefoot across the wet front lawn.

"I told you I'll be back soon," said Beth.

"Please," Mum said, holding Beth's face, smoothing back the hair, and looking into her eyes.

All that night while I tried to go to sleep I kept feeling the words of a song trying to come through. It was a slowish song, humming along inside me. It felt like *If you miss the train I'm on, you will know that I am gone, you will hear the whistle blow, one hundred miles, one hundred miles, one hundred miles.*

ON HER LAST NIGHT ON EARTH SHE WENT TO MICHELLE WRIGHT'S FLAT. Michelle told her there was a party. It was only a few streets away. All day the road had been filling with cars. Miranda was already there. Hadn't she told her? She knew someone who knew someone.

The party was in a brand-new double-story town house. There was a crowd crammed shoulder to shoulder inside. It was filled to the brim with the smell of smoke and sweat and spilled drinks and a riot of voices, conversations rumbling and punctuated by laughter. Word spread quickly of her arrival.

She had time to put her cigarette out and her bottle down before Miranda grabbed her and they waltzed wildly around the living room. People jumped out of the way and clapped and wolf-whistled. They looked at each other while they spun and everything was forgiven. Beth's blond hair fanned out behind her. Her little canvas backpack was thrown into the corner, her black flip-flops beside it.

She drank wine coolers that weren't hers. She drank them quickly because she had no buzz. A man who played A Grade football poured her a Southern Comfort and then another. He was a big man. An eighteen-year-old built like a giant. He smiled at her while she drank. He rubbed his hand up and down her thin arm.

"I heard you give good head," he said to her.

She didn't answer but moved away from him then. She went downstairs in the cement courtyard. Cigarette butts rained like fireflies from the balcony above. Finally Miranda came and found her with her head between her knees.

"Do you want to go home?" Miranda asked.

"No," she said.

Beth wiped her nose with the back of her hand.

"Do you ever get so drunk that you forget your own name?"

"No," said Miranda.

"And then when you remember it, it's like you can't believe that's what you're called. You say my name, my name, I never knew that was my name."

She pulled herself together, sat up straighter, and tucked her hair behind her ears.

"What are you talking about?" said Miranda, laughing.

"I dunno," Beth said.

The little balcony led off from the dining room upstairs. There were a lot of people standing on it. Beth had washed her face. She moved through the crowd. She hoisted herself up onto the railing and sat there with one arm around the corner post. A wind had sprung up suddenly. It played tricks with her hair, caused the waves to twist around her face and over her shoulders like a glowing river.

It was Miranda who lit her cigarette. Beth removed her arm from the post to cup her hands around the lighter. She lost her balance and began to fall. Miranda grabbed her by the arm.

She pulled her off the rail into the crowd who had raised their arms toward her in unison. The crowd breathed deeply, together.

Someone called, "Taxi."

"You scared the shit out of me," said Miranda.

"Don't be scared," said Beth.

They brought their heads very close together.

"I didn't know what to do," Miranda whispered.

"Don't worry," said Beth.

"I was scared they'd do it to me."

"It's all finished now."

When she was leaving Miranda ran out after her.

"Where are you going?" she shouted.

Beth was standing on the edge of the long straight road with her bike beside her. A giant desert moon was rising. The wet earth sang to the sky. The stacks shouted their plumes of smoke straight up to heaven. The streetlights bowed their heads before her. She felt very calm.

"I want to see something," she said.

THERE IS SOMETHING YOU NEED TO KNOW ABOUT THE GIRL WHO FELL, SOMETHING MORE IMPORTANT THAN THE FALL ITSELF. You should forget that last and most spectacular souvenir of herself.

After the party she went down the streets looking for something. She rode past the cemetery with the quartz graves gleaming in the dark, she rode past the river that was just beginning to run, she rode past Nanna's small flat looking out into the desert.

She turned into Dardanelles Court, where all the poincianas reached out to each other across the cul-de-sac and the moon watched her through the leaves.

Marshall Murray saw her from the bedroom window. He was rolling Arthur on his side so he wouldn't choke on his own vomit. He saw her go past on her bike. He thought, for a moment, the air around her was surrounded by light. Frieda Schmidt saw her too. It took her breath away. The girl was trailing cigarette smoke and a glow. She put a hand to her heart, which ached.

The O'Malley house was all in darkness but inside, in the silence, lying side by side, Eva and Joseph heard the wind pick up and the sound of bicycle tires on pavement. Philippa Irwin woke from a dream where she was speaking in slow steady sentences without stammering. She opened the window. She smelled the rain and heard the singing night and smelled green-apple shampoo.

Beth rode past our house.

I was sleeping.

I did not see her go.

I WAS AT SCHOOL WHEN THE POLICEMEN CAME TO THE
HOUSE. It was ten o'clock in the morning. I was sitting
in my chair with my arms crossed waiting for Mrs.
Bridges-Lamb to speak. She surveyed us with her
glasses on and then she tried it with her glasses off.

"I want you to listen very carefully to what I have
to say," she said.

She turned her back to us and wrote in large neat
letters FRACTIONS.

"Fractions," she said, "are a very important part
of life."

She put one of the ends of her glasses into her
mouth and watched us.

"I believe that in the last few weeks none of you,
yes, not one of you, has been taking fractions seriously at all."

The policemen were opening the gate and walking up the front steps onto the patio and knocking on

the metal border of the screen door while Mrs. Bridges-Lamb drew the large cake again. She was dividing the cake up into pieces.

It was Mum who came to the door because Dad was on night shift and was asleep. When she came to the door and saw the two policemen she let out a small cry.

"What's wrong?" she asked.

"Is it Mrs. Day?" said one of the officers, who was very thin, holding his hat in shaking hands. The other, who was stockier, stood silently chewing on his bottom lip.

Mrs. Bridges-Lamb asked me what fraction of the cake I would have eaten if it was divided into six and I ate two pieces.

"Two-sixths," I said.

"And what if you ate three pieces?"

"Three-sixths."

"And what does three-sixths equal?"

I looked at her blankly. She put her glasses on and sighed.

"Yes," said Mum. She was Mrs. Day.

"Can we come in, Mrs. Day?"

"Yes," she whispered.

She had been vacuuming in the living room. The two officers stepped over the vacuum cleaner. They stood looking at Mum with their hats in their hands. Mum held her hand over her mouth.

"Is your husband here, Mrs. Day?" asked the thin officer.

"Yes," said Mum. "He's asleep."

"I think you should wake him up," said the other.

"What's happened?" shouted Mum. It was a three-quarter shout, one-quarter wail.

"I think you should wake Mr. Day," said the thin officer.

His hat shook violently in his hands but his voice stayed calm. He looked very young.

"Jim," screamed Mum down the hallway. She staggered toward the bedroom door.

Dad came out with only his undies on. They were red. His beer belly hung over them. When he saw the policemen at the end of the hallway he said sweet Jesus and went back into the bedroom and pulled on his shorts.

"What's going on?" he shouted.

Mum stood at the door with her hand over her mouth and didn't answer him.

"I'm very sorry," said the thin officer when Mum and Dad stood opposite them in the living room. The stockier officer motioned them to sit but they kept standing.

"There has been an accident and your daughter has died."

"What?" said Dad.

He had never heard anything so improbable.

"Which daughter?" screamed Mum.

"I'm sorry," said the thin officer, and he held out Beth's school ID. "Elizabeth Jane Day."

"No," said Mum.

She collapsed against Dad, who half dragged, half carried her to the sofa.

"How?" said Dad. "What do you mean?"

"Mr. Day," said the thin officer, "it appears she has fallen."

After little lunch we had to sit very quietly and think about taking fractions seriously. How would we ever understand percentages if we couldn't do simple fractions? How would we function in society if we didn't know a half from a quarter? How could we even begin to think that we could move to grade 6 if we didn't know the difference between a numerator and a denominator?

In the silence I started off with the numerator and denominator. The numerator sat on top of the denominator, didn't it? Like a monkey on a man's back? Or was it the other way round?

"I hope you are all thinking about fractions," said Mrs. Bridges-Lamb in a menacing voice from her desk.

In the silence I heard footsteps coming from a long way away. They started somewhere near the headmaster's office and echoed on the wooden floorboards of the veranda. As they drew closer the classroom louvers began to rattle. It sounded like an army marching toward us.

"What's going on?" said Mrs. Bridges-Lamb to herself and to us in a warning voice. "Keep thinking."

The footsteps turned the bend onto our grade 5 veranda. I looked up from my thinking and saw first the headmaster, Mr. Kilburn, flanked by a thin policeman and then my father and Danielle.

Dad looked in through the louvers at me. I had never seen the type of expression he wore on his face before. It looked like a mixture of sadness and pain but then when I had been summoned from my seat to the door and I was standing in front of him he broke out into laughter. It was a terrible laughter, it lasted only a few seconds, three loud hiccuping guffaws that cascaded into sobs. Dad grabbed me by the top of my arms and shook me without saying a word. Then he placed me beside Danielle and commenced the march back down the veranda. As I passed the louvers to my class I looked inside and saw thirty faces, white, slack-mouthed, sweaty, staring back at me.

Halfway down the veranda Danielle took my hand.

It was a lady named Mrs. Lee, who collected bottles for recycling and lived in a half-falling-down house, who found her. Our mother had talked about Mrs. Lee before because she used her as an example of how lucky we were. She said what if you had to live in a house like Mrs. Lee's house and I was your mother but I had to collect bottles to find money to feed you? Children still starve, you know, she said. She didn't know then that Mrs. Lee would find Beth in among the broken glass and cigarette butts at the base of the water tower.

She was lying on her back. Arms stretched behind her head. There was nothing in the day to suggest such a deviation from the norm. The sky was pale blue with clouds streaming like a running lady's hair. The wind rolled the yellow grass over all along the sides of the hill. The sound of trucks spilled off the highway and into the streets. The ticking witch ticked slowly in her pipe. Mrs. Lee dropped her bags and a hundred glass bottles rolled away, in a fountain, down the hill.

Mrs. O'Malley was on her patio when our car turned into Dardanelles Court. When I turned to face her she only nodded at me. The cicadas were singing and singing and singing, one-noted, one-worded, the double drummers drumming and the green whizzers hissing. The one word sounded like "please." The whole world was falling down.

I unstitched all of my embroidered daisies. The ones from school and the ones I had made with Nanna. I unstitched them until my fingers bled.

345

Our mother screamed and screamed and screamed. She screamed in circles, finishing where she began. She screamed long panting screams as though she were giving birth. Aunty Cheryl pulled us away from the bedroom door.

Nanna bashed the Bible against her forehead until a red mark appeared and then the beginning of a bruise and when Dad tried to take the book from her hands she spoke in her other language like a banshee. The phone rang and rang and rang.

When night came I could not stop shaking. Every part of me shook. My teeth shook in my gums. My hair shook on my head. My fingers shook against the cup.

I shook in my bed when Danielle placed me under the sheets. She tried to hold my arms down to stop me. We didn't say a word to each other at all. We talked to each other with our eyes like wild animals.

Danielle took the bedspread off her bed and put it on top of me. She put my dressing gown over the blanket and then her dressing gown. She climbed in beside me and put her arms around me. She held on to me tight to stop the shaking.

I shook violently, thrashing under the blankets, but Danielle kept holding me. It seemed like hours before I stopped shaking. I cried tears onto her hand, which was beneath my head. She cried tears into my hair.

In the house there was a feeling like a trapped bird beating its wings against a cage that remained until the shaking subsided and the cool outflowing of tears began. Then the feeling of the trapped bird disappeared. I may have slept. Danielle moved apart from me. There was no noise in the house.

In Dardanelles Court the wind breathed against the windows and rattled the doors. In the blue night fat-bellied clouds rolled across the sky. The moon rose and gazed down on the town. A willy-willy danced along the street.

There was no thunder. No lightning. The sky held in its storm belly with a moon-shaped buckle.

Marshall Murray woke.

Lord, he said.

He sat up with his old bones sawing against each other. He staggered to Arthur's door but his bed was empty. He found him in the living room, with the bottle beside him on its side. The TV hissed. The wind tapped and whispered at the windows.

He turned on his bedroom light and drew an old suitcase out of his cupboard. He threw in some clothes. He pulled on his best jeans and a good shirt, reached into the dark of the kitchen for his hat on the wall, the keys on the bench. The car sprang to life beneath him, one turn of the key. He did not check the oil or water; there was no time.

Joseph O'Malley woke with the wind. Eva opened her eyes at the very same time. He felt for her hand. The night shivered against the house.

They turned to each other.

He looked at her eyes. She looked at his eyes.

He touched her cheek. She touched his cheek in return.

"It was not our fault," she said.

"It was not our fault," he said.

"Do you know how much I loved her?" she wept.

"We loved her, we loved her," he wept in return.

The house rattled and jittered and creaked. The roof threatened to go.

Frieda Schmidt held apart the blinds with two fingers. Her heart ached. Her skin ached. She re-arranged the knives in the knife block, blew away imaginary crumbs from their tips. How would she go on? She dressed herself.

She glimpsed herself naked in the mirror.

She was pale-stone-colored. She moved stiffly. She went to lace up her shoes but instead carried them to the front door, where she threw them into the night. The power had gone off. From the emergency drawer she took a candle and lit it. She wanted to light them everywhere. She wanted to torch the house. Make one giant candle. She left the house shoeless without combing her hair.

She passed the place where the girl had fallen and

slept beneath the tree, candle flame flickering in her hand.

She banged on the door until Mrs. O'Malley came stumbling in her nightgown.

"I'm so lonely," Frieda Schmidt said.

It was ferocious, her sorrow. She held her hand to her mouth, apologized.

But Mrs. O'Malley stretched out her hand.

"Come in," she said. "Come in, come in. Don't stand outside."

Monica Irwin woke to the sound. She found her sister sitting on the edge of her bed.

"What is it, Pippa?" she asked.

"Something's happened."

In the dimness they could hear their parents breathing side by side in the next room; they hadn't woken. Their father, with all the answers, hadn't heard a thing. Philippa slid the window open quietly and wave after wave of storm-wet air entered the room. Monica watched her sister's hair lifting with each gust.

"It won't be forever," Monica said.

"Promise it won't be forever," said Philippa.

"We won't be here forever," said Monica.

"Don't leave without me."

"I promise I won't leave without you."

The river came down. It swallowed up all the crossings. It dismantled fences and took them away on its brown rolling back. It wiped away river camps, it uprooted and took away gum trees, speared them over the crossings and jammed them into spillways so that giant fountains erupted into the air.

It roared at its own might until it broke its banks.

By the time dawn came Marshall Murray was a long way out of town heading inland.

The storm without rain had broken up into a thousand little pieces. The new sun illuminated the broken clouds pink, the grasses golden, the hills in the distance a glistening gray. He stopped on the side of the road. He wound down his window. He heard the earth talking again.

BEFORE EVERYTHING HAPPENED I WISHED I COULD
SING LIKE A NIGHTINGALE, A BIRD WITH THE MOST
BEAUTIFUL SONG IN THE ANIMAL KINGDOM. Night-
ingales aren't found here. The *Merit Students
Encyclopedia* says they are found in Europe, mostly
in forests and groves, and their song is heard most
clearly in the still of night. Throughout history the
nightingale has been captured and carried to all four
corners of the world even though the world is round.
They have been expected to sing inside of golden
cages for kings and queens and princes and prin-
cesses. And even though they have been prisoners
they have sung like they are free. Their voices are so
beautiful that sometimes fingers have reached for
keys and gilt doors have been accidentally left open
because nothing that heavenly should be contained.

But afterward people have wept when the
nightingale has flown. They have lamented when

they tried to remember her song. They have wanted her back. They have wept in the dead of night in quiet still gardens over the absence of her. It has driven them mad.

We took *The Book of Clues* and walked to the dry river. We went to the place by the sand track.

"We've done everything we can to get your singing voice back," said Angela.

We didn't bring a shovel but used our hands and a tin can to dig a shallow grave at the foot of the tallest of the white-hearted trees. Angela watched while I covered the book with dirt and placed a rock on top.

It felt right. A good and final ending. When it was buried we scratched our initials into the trunk with Mr. Popovitch's penknife.

I knew it would wither. The pages would turn in on themselves. Our childish words would fade with each season's rain until they vanished altogether.

"Maybe now," said Angela.

But after everything that had happened I never expected to get my voice back.

When Nanna came home from the hospital she said she most definitely did not need to stay with Aunty Cheryl in a spare room on an uncomfortable bed. She went home to her little flat. The sliding door and all the sliding windows were opened up to let out the smell of the dusty Blessed Virgins and Craven

"A" cigarettes and some jamming fruit that she had left on the shelf. Uncle Paavo and his new lady friend, who we weren't allowed to stare at, came and dug up all the dead gerberas and the roses on their last legs and planted purple vincas, which Nanna whispered were really weeds, because they wouldn't need as much work.

On weekends I was allowed to stay with her to help. She held my face in her crinkled hands and kissed me on the forehead each time. I got to put the camp stretcher beside her bed and we creaked backward and forward to each other all night. Sometimes she lay on the bed with her hand across her heart and I watched her chest carefully to make sure she was breathing. In the dark I could see tears shining in a pool on the surface of her eyes. When the pool overflowed one would slide in a well-worn path down into her hair. I recited the Litany of the Saints to her like a poem to make her feel better. She still did not come back to our house.

She gave some of her Virgin Mary statuettes to Mum, her favorite ones, because one day Mum had opened up her jewelry box and put her necklace with the cross back on. She started doing Hobbytex again. The T-shirts didn't have words on them anymore. They were just pictures like a yellow star or green hills with a road leading somewhere or a giant rainbow. The pictures were stiff with color; she used whole tubes and they scratched our skin when we wore them. Some nights there was no sound in the house except a Hobbytex nib filling up a yellow ray of sunlight.

Mum's voice remained hollow and fragile like a china teacup but we got used to it and knew that her old voice was never coming back. She packed up Beth's room. All the posters were taken down from the walls and all the running medals and dancing sashes. The tambourine bells tinkled as they were lowered into the box. The ballerina bedspread was folded up. All her brown-paper-covered exercise books were stacked in a pile. Danielle and I took the record player and all the records into our room. All that was left was the bed stripped bare and the empty desk and the geometric-print wallpaper. The door stayed open.

Sometimes I went and sat on the bed and closed my eyes. I tried to communicate with her. I tried to think of interesting questions about heaven. But I never heard or felt anything in return. All I could hear was Mrs. Irwin watering the yard or a lawn mower or an Ansett jet crossing over, bringing people back into the heart of nowhere.

Dad picked us up for lunch on Sundays. He called me chickadee and piggybacked me all the way from the car. Afterward we got small tins of Coke and packets of chips while he went into the public bar. Sometimes he let us walk the short distance to the highway to watch the trucks coming and going and the willy-willies spinning madly along the shoulder. Once a week he came to pick Mum up for dances. He combed his hair back into a very neat ducktail. Mum curled her hair.

Danielle drew me a picture of a girl without sad eyes. Her perm was almost gone. All that was left was beautiful oak-colored waves cascading over her shoulders. They almost hid her Milwaukee back brace. Kylie's face filled out so she was not so spindly. Her hair grew thicker. Her skin grew clearer. She didn't have rages so often. She decided she wanted to be a marine biologist. Aunty Cheryl said she was blossoming and even Mum had to agree.

My voice came back on grade 6 breakup day.

It was after I had spread a very bad rumor about Mrs. Bridges-Lamb and I had been summoned to her classroom. The rumor was that every year before the end of grade 5 Mrs. Bridges-Lamb started fattening up one child by giving them extra treats from the good behavior lolly jar. On breakup day that child went missing. I said this had been happening for as long as anyone could remember. I don't know why I even made the story up. It scared a girl called Clarissa, who must have never read *Hansel and*

Gretel or not been able to tell the difference between fact and fiction. She started to cry and told Mr. Barnes.

Mrs. Bridges-Lamb said she couldn't let me finish grade 6 without first talking to me.

"I know you have always been very good at making up stories," she said, "but this one was particularly hurtful."

She said she didn't want me to go to grade 7 still doing such hurtful things as well as skipping school and throwing rocks and hanging around down the creek looking for wild horses and pretending to live in caves.

"Grief is a terrible, terrible thing," she said.

I just shrugged.

"But I probably don't need to tell you that, do I?" she said.

"You are such a clever little thing," she said. "I want you to look after yourself. You could be anything you wanted. What do you think you'd like to be?"

"Nothing," I said. "I want to be nothing."

"I remember when you wanted to be an ornithologist," she said. "And you did excellent morning talks on *Elanus scriptus.*"

That made me feel sad. It made me think of all those hot still days when I watched the hawks through the louvers and tried to understand their behaviors while everything, everything was falling apart.

"That was a long time ago," I said, and it felt like years had passed.

She wiped my nose with her hankie.

"It feels like only yesterday," she said.

"Sorry for saying you eat small children," I said.

"That's all right, my dear," she said.

When I was leaving the classroom I noticed all the Icarus wings up along the back wall, only these were new wings, made by new children, and I remembered the day when mine had flown.

At the doorway Mrs. Bridges-Lamb rubbed her hands together.

"Grade-five breakup this afternoon and I'm feeling a little hungry," she said.

That really made me laugh and for the first time in a very long time I felt something loosen inside me but it had been so long I didn't know what it was.

It was when I was walking home with Angela through the park that it happened. She was telling me about a book in the library that was about how to be a witch. She said she was going to get it out and start doing spells and stuff. There was one spell that made you highly beautiful and another that made you know who you were going to marry. She said I couldn't get married until I got underarm hairs. I was just listening and looking at the sky when I noticed something very small far in the distance.

The small thing was flying very high. It was flying only as high as an eagle would fly. At first I didn't believe it. I thought it may have only been a whistling kite. I needed it to fly lower so I could see. I didn't want to get my hopes up because I was only just beginning to feel better.

And as if it could sense my thoughts the tiny bird in the distance let itself roll over backward the way wedge-tailed eagles do. It fell down, freely, through the blue sky.

"Are you listening to me?" said Angela.

I stopped walking and just stood still. The bird fell down, down, down through the sky until it evened out and unfolded its wings and I saw the open finger-shaped edges. I saw its diamond-shaped tail.

It soared in a large circle above me. I swear it on my whole life. It circled above me three times. It came closer each time. It came so close I could see its eye. Just the way that albatross looked at Nanna all of those years before. And then it beat its wings, one, two, three, and I could feel the wind of it on my face.

Away it went. Over the trees in the park. Over the water tower. Over the mine. Over the lake. Over the desert. Over everything. Away from us.

And I was not so filled with fear.

Inside me something loosened further and before

I even realized it a song was coming through. Standing right there in the park I sang a sudden song. I sang "Gloria in Excelsis." I sang it so strong and clear the words hung in the air above us. Angela dropped her bag and jumped up and down.

"You're singing, you're singing," she screamed.

All the way home I sang.

Through the scrub side of Memorial Park I sang *Good King Wenceslas went out on the feast of Stephen, all the snow lay round about deep and crisp and even.* The rain trees crowded over us and shook their rattles with joy. All the way down the hill I sang *By the rivers of Babylon, where we lay down.* Through the turnstile gate I sang *I got a girl called Boney Maroney, she's as skinny as a stick of macaroni.* Angela put in some requests but all I could do was shake my head because the songs just kept coming.

In Dardanelles Court I sang *Swing low, sweet chariot, coming for to carry me home.* Mr. and Mrs. O'Malley came rushing to their patio and clapped and cheered.

My voice was clear. Clear as a ringing bell.

Frieda Schmidt stood in her front yard and smiled. I saw Philippa Irwin at her window. I sang her *Hosanna, heysanna, sanna sanna ho.* She waved at me. We were running, Angela and I, and Angela was ahead of me shouting through the front gate.

"Mrs. Day, Mrs. Day, her voice is back."

I stopped at the front gate and I sang *Hallelujah, hallelujah, hallelujah.* I sang them slowly, ascending and descending, perfectly, like a bird with a double voice box.

I saw Nanna's Datsun Sunny in the driveway and she came quickly to the front door. I was very glad to see her. And behind her was Mum with her arms held out for me.

ACKNOWLEDGMENTS

I would like to acknowledge the Queensland government for their ongoing commitment to and support of writers through the annual Premier's Literary Awards. I would like to thank Madonna Duffy and Rob Cullinan at the University of Queensland Press, Catherine Drayton at InkWell Management, and Erin Clarke at Knopf Books for Young Readers for their belief in this story. And of course more thanks than can be mentioned to my family, especially my mother, who often fed and watered me while I wrote, and my partner, Chris, who carefully prized me away from the computer from time to time.